THE

BOOTLEGGER'S
DAUGHTER

OTHER TITLES BY NADINE NETTMANN

Decanting a Murder
Uncorking a Lie
Pairing a Deception

PRAISE FOR
THE BOOTLEGGER'S DAUGHTER

"*The Bootlegger's Daughter* is a tremendously entertaining journey back to Prohibition-era Los Angeles. The two main characters, Letty and Forman, are strikingly fresh and appealing, and they drive a story that never fails to surprise and satisfy. Highly recommended."
—Lou Berney, Edgar Award–winning author of *Dark Ride*

THE

BOOTLEGGER'S DAUGHTER

A NOVEL

NADINE NETTMANN

LAKE UNION
PUBLISHING

Published by Lake Union, Seattle

www.apub.com

Amazon, the Amazon logo, and Lake Union are trademarks of Amazon.com, Inc., or its affiliates.

ISBN-13: 9781662515583 (paperback)
ISBN-13: 9781662515576 (digital)

Cover design by Caroline Teagle Johnson

Cover image: © Collaboration JS / ArcAngel; © bluehill75, © igor170806 / Getty Images; © ssboyd / Shutterstock

Printed in the United States of America

For anyone who has secretly wanted to be strong or stronger, not realizing they already were. And for my mom, Gillian, and my husband, Matthew, with so much love.

CHAPTER ONE

LETTY

This is the first time we've had intruders, though I've been waiting for them for years. It's not the sputter of a Ford's engine or a barn owl looking for its mate that stirs me out of my sleep but, rather, a sound I hear daily at the winery. Except this time, it's not me making it.

On nights like this, the warm desert wind blows across the valley, kicking up the dry soil and rattling the branches of the eucalyptus, but this noise isn't triggered by the weather.

This is the squeak of the barn doors as they're pulled slowly and deliberately open. The hinges I refuse to oil for just this reason. The doors I always keep locked, even if I step away for only a minute, as the last barrier between strangers and our wine.

I'm already out of bed, my steps silent as I move into the living room, a thin layer of silt on the wood floor from the crack in the windowsill. The house is quiet, my mother still asleep.

Swirling rumors, confirmed by the occasional article in the *Los Angeles Times*, warn they've hit the city's wineries, emptying the supplies of the few that still remain after the last eight years. But we're out in the San Fernando Valley, far away from city lights, where the land goes for miles without a building in sight and the Pacific Electric Red Car Line doesn't quite reach.

And yet, they've come tonight.

I'm at the window, pulling my wool jacket onto my shoulders, the thick fabric weighing heavy. Even in the darkness, the figures are noticeable, their silhouettes moving alongside the two-story barn I helped build to keep people like this away. The *locked* barn.

They already have a barrel out the door, their movements awkward as they try to maneuver it through the dirt.

I grab my father's rifle from above the fireplace, where it's been for as long as I can remember.

The gun is cold yet familiar in my hands as I step outside, my foot catching the screen door behind me with perfected ease from years of preventing the sound of it slamming. I don't want them to know I'm coming.

Not yet.

The October moon provides a glimmer of light as I move barefoot, better to quiet my steps, the only sound the slow churn of the soil from the barrel they're rolling upright in the dirt.

There are two of them, one a little taller. They're not used to dealing with wine. I can see that by the awkward way they try to roll the barrel, moving it on its end.

I raise the rifle as I get closer, focusing on the taller one as he growls hushed commands to the shorter one.

"No, like this. You're rolling it too fast."

"If I lay it down, the wine will spill out."

"It's plugged." He moves the barrel, full of this year's harvest and ready to be bottled for the church, onto its side.

They move faster.

As do I.

Preoccupied, they don't notice my approach.

My finger slips around the latch of the rifle as I come to a halt, aiming at the midsection of the taller one. "First rule of winemaking is always lock the doors," I say, my voice firm and steady.

The smaller culprit nearly falls over at the sound of my voice.

"The second one is always have a gun."

The taller one freezes, like one of the deer that come down from the hills, pausing in the headlights of my truck, not a muscle twitching even as danger approaches.

I take another step. "And the third one," I say, the barrel of the gun still focused on my target, knowing that the bullet won't miss, "is to shoot anyone who tries to steal our livelihood."

"Billy . . ." The smaller one's voice is thick with unmistakable fear, the kind that is hard to mask and even harder to swallow.

"Shh . . . ," Billy admonishes, smacking his accomplice on the arm.

"We were just walking by your property," the smaller offers. He can't be more than fifteen, his voice still breaking. "We found this barrel out here. We were going to put it back for you."

"Shut up," Billy says, and hits him again as he looks at me as if choosing his words. "It's better if you go back inside. This doesn't concern you."

"I disagree," I say, taking two more steps forward, the hard dirt steady under my feet, the rifle unmoving in my hands.

"Don't get any closer. I'll shoot you," Billy warns.

"Not if I shoot first." My voice is as steady as my aim. They don't have a gun, or if they do, it's not out yet, and I'm one tiny flex of my finger from putting a bullet in Billy's chest.

Billy doesn't move, his arms failing to reach for a gun, his feet not shifting to leave. The two of them are like the coyotes I've seen around here, meek and skittish unless they're hunting prey.

And I'm not prey.

"My wine is not leaving this property tonight. So you have two options: leave the barrel where it is or end up in one." I slide my foot forward, and the shorter boy moves back.

Even with the lack of light, I can make out their faces. One is young, but Billy is closer to my age, in his early twenties; the overalls, baggy shirt, and build tell me he likely works on one of the farms in the valley. There's a wave of familiarity, and his name sticks in my head. "You Carter's boys?"

Carter, foreman at the dairy plant, lives about a mile down the road. I've only seen his family once, when my mother went to ask about milk a few years ago, but I'm confident it's them. They probably walked here.

"Boys? I'm old as you," says Billy as he shifts. I can't remember the name of his brother, but it doesn't matter at this point.

"We should go, Billy," says his brother.

"Lawrence," I say as the name comes to me.

"Ignore her," Billy barks. "I told you it was just women at this place. Weak, and no man to protect them."

I move closer, a rock piercing the arch of my foot, but the pain is no match for the adrenaline pumping through my veins.

Lawrence glances at Billy, who shifts to the right.

I follow him with the gun, and it's not lost on him, his eyes focused on the rifle.

"I'm going to say this one more time. If you don't leave the wine where it is, tuck your tails between your legs, and scamper away, I'll make sure you never get to scamper again."

Billy's face is a mixture of surprise and indignation. "What would you do? Call the cops? They won't get here in time," he says with a laugh, though I detect a note of fear in it.

"You've underestimated a lot tonight. The cops do what they like in this town. Most farmers would just put a bullet in the both of you, bury you out back. No one would ever know. Me? Since we're clearly neighbors, I'm going to let you go and pretend this didn't happen. But either of you come back here, you step one foot on my property, and I promise you'll never be heard of again. I'll bury you so deep, not even the rains will bring you up," I warn. "You have one minute to decide."

"Ignore her," says Billy. "She won't do nothing." He turns, puts his hand back on the barrel, and starts to push it, the wood grinding into the dirt below.

I track his movements with the rifle. "Roll that one more time and you're taking one to the chest."

"Billy . . . ," his brother pleads.

Billy stands back up, his hands on his hips. "Don't listen—she's bluffing."

I shift the gun to the left, the movement so slight it's noticeable only to me. Like the times I used to purposely miss while shooting cans off the fence with my friend Charles when we were young. Just enough that he would think I wasn't a good shot. Then I'd place a bet on hitting it next time. And I always did.

I pull the trigger.

The sound echoes in the night, the bullet flying right past Billy's arm, followed immediately by a muted thud as it hits the wood wall of the barn. The recoil pushes my shoulder back slightly, but it's nothing like the first time I fired when I was twelve.

Lawrence is off, scurrying to the road like a squirrel avoiding a train car as it throttles down the tracks. But Billy doesn't move, either in shock by the near miss or still holding strong.

I cock the rifle again and take my aim. "Next one goes right in your chest. Do we have an understanding?"

He stares at me, waiting to see if I'm going to move. I don't.

But I also know I'm out of bullets. I had only one, and I just used it as a warning.

CHAPTER TWO

LETTY

The night is silent. Even the crickets have quieted, the gunfire disrupting the peace of this chilly fall evening.

But Billy breaks it.

"You missed," he says, his voice piercing the air. It's different now, void of the confidence it held a minute ago.

"On the contrary. I felt generous enough to give you a warning." My palms are sweaty, but my aim is steady on his chest. If only I had another bullet.

I step forward, the gun resting against my shoulder. "Your minute is almost up. I'd say you have about ten seconds left." I'm three feet away now. Even the worst gunner couldn't miss at this distance. But even the best gunner can't fire without a bullet.

I have to think fast, especially if he decides to charge or grab the gun. "Stay here and die or leave and live. Either way, you never touch my wine again." I raise the rifle toward his head. "You have five seconds."

He looks at me, his eyes unmoving.

"Five. Four. Three."

He leans back. "I'll remember you."

"That makes two of us. And you have no idea what I'm capable of. Two. One."

He moves slowly to the side, his eyes fixed on me, trying to retain his cool, but it vanishes within seconds as he takes off to catch up to his brother, who is probably half a mile away by now.

I wait until he's off the property to lower the rifle, finally exhaling, my lungs as empty as the chamber of the gun. My hands are shaking, their steadiness having dissolved as soon as Billy was gone.

I sling the gun onto my back and roll the wine barrel into the barn with ease, pleased to see that they didn't think to grab any of the bottles ready for the church delivery. They could have been off the property before I caught them.

"Small rewards, Letty," my father scolded when I first helped him with the harvest ten years ago. I had picked as many grapes as I could carry, nearly all of them falling to the ground before I reached the basket. "You do too much, you lose it all."

The lock on the barn doors is broken, the latch hanging to one side, so I fix it as best I can for tonight. Doesn't matter. I won't sleep much more anyway.

I retreat to the house, returning to the same undisturbed quiet as when I left, the door closing silently behind me.

"Who was it?" My mother's voice startles me. She sits on the sofa in the front room, her white nightgown the same as in my youth. It ages along with her.

"You're awake."

"It's hard to sleep when there's gunshots."

"A few visitors after the wine. I didn't want to wake you. And *gunshot*. I only fired once."

She leans back into the couch and nods, but her attention is still fixed out the window.

I remove the glass from the lamp on the side table and light the wick, the soft glow soon bouncing on her face, her brown-and-gray hair pulled into a low ponytail. People say I look like her, the same nose and brown eyes. But she has the years of life on her, especially the last few, and they've transformed her face into one marked with sadness.

"How did they get in?" Her voice is soft now, the weary tone I've grown used to over the last few years.

"They broke the lock. And you know I locked it."

"I know you did." She's familiar with the routine, the aspects of safety we take to ensure our product, our livelihood, remains intact. "Where are they, the visitors?"

"They're gone," I say as I place the rifle back above the fireplace.

"But you fired the gun."

"I didn't hit them. It was a warning."

"It was dangerous."

I glance at her, the creases around her eyes deeper since my father left. They almost eased when his body was found in the river a year later. Almost. "I was careful. And if they took the wine, we wouldn't have enough money to eat. Besides, I wouldn't shoot them. You know I wouldn't."

"You might."

I smile. "Not tonight. Check the gun."

She pauses, unsure of my motives, but finally stands up and moves over to the hearth. The gun is foreign in her hands, her only experience being the few times I've shown her how to use it in case intruders come while I'm away. But she knows enough to open the chamber.

"There's no bullets." She looks at me, perplexed. "What if they didn't leave?"

"Sometimes a warning is all you need."

"I don't like that, Letty."

"They came; I handled it. It was Carter's boys from down the road."

"From the dairy plant?" She purses her lips together, the same familiar gesture she makes when she's thinking about her next step. "I'll talk to their mother."

"Don't. I took care of it."

A small smile appears at the corners of her mouth. While other parts of her life didn't work out—including a dying farm and a dead husband—she wanted to raise a strong daughter, and she did. "What made them come now? They've known about us for years. We've never had a problem out here, away from the city."

"I don't know," I reply.

"They'll be back," she warns. "You know they will."

I place my hand on her arm. "Maybe, maybe not. I'll be waiting if they do." And I know she's right. People always want what they can't have. And no one has been able to get wine for the past seven years—not legally, anyway, since that January day in 1920 when the entire country went dry. "Then I really will shoot them."

But I know I won't. I couldn't even shoot the birds when my dad was teaching me. I preferred the cans, my aim becoming sharp and steady, but when we shifted to the birds, I couldn't do it.

"It's because they're moving," said my father. "They're harder, that's why."

But I knew the real reason. You don't kill living things.

He soon lost interest in teaching me how to shoot. A daughter who couldn't follow in his footsteps. Didn't have the strength to do as he did. Maybe that's why he left his gun when he chose his new family.

I learned more about shooting without him. When you're the one left to defend your family, you pick up on survival skills pretty quick.

"Will you be able to sleep more?" I ask my mother. "It's still early." My eyes flick to the space where the clock used to sit, but we sold it ages ago. Its shadow is outlined on the wallpaper from years of sun.

"I'll try." She moves slowly to the middle of the room. "What about you?"

I shake my head. "I'll wait for daylight and then fix the barn doors. Keep us safe."

"You're a good girl, Letty Hart."

"I know."

But I can see from her face that there are words she refuses to say. That she didn't want this for either of us. That life is supposed to be easier than this.

She retreats to her bedroom, and I take her place on the sofa, keeping my view on the mountains, where the glow of the new day will dawn soon enough, and on the barn that holds our wine. The wine we need to keep afloat. The wine we can barely hang on to as it is, with or without intruders.

When my father was here, he always said there were three main things to remember about sacramental wine: make it simple, don't label the bottles, and don't drink the product. I follow two of them. He didn't follow any.

CHAPTER THREE

FORMAN

Officer Annabel Forman leans against the wall of the station as she smooths her skirt, the blue fabric as close a match as she could find to the uniform the male officers wear. The Los Angeles Police Department doesn't issue uniforms to women, but she made sure she matched, even if it is a skirt instead of trousers. Her hair is tied back neatly under her cap in a bun, and her shoes are polished as well as the men's, even better than some. And yet, a few of the men still won't stand near her at the morning meetings, as if being associated with her will somehow diminish their own stature.

The captain, Earl Warrenson, looks around the room of officers who have gathered for the check-in. "We have a special announcement this morning." He meets the eye of every officer, even Annabel, though they don't call her that. While they sometimes refer to each other by their first names, they only ever call her Forman, as if Annabel is too much of a reminder that she is female. It began the moment she started two years ago, and they've never strayed once.

"We have an officer among us," continues Warrenson, the left side of his lip pulled up in a semipermanent snarl, "who has gone above and beyond their duty. And perhaps due to aspects about who they are, might not have been given appropriate credit during their time here at the station." His eyes land on Forman, and she pulls away from the wall, standing at attention.

"It's tough being in their situation, but they've come through, time and again, and it's about time they are rewarded for this perseverance."

Forman keeps her lips pressed tightly together to hide her growing smile. When she joined the LAPD, one of the first female officers after Alice Stebbins Wells opened the door in 1910, she told Warrenson she wanted to be a detective. That she was going to work hard and get there. Even though the LAPD didn't have any female detectives, he said she would need at least two years on the force and a big arrest to make it happen. It was only last week that she'd interviewed numerous young women, gathering their witness accounts, which finally led to the capture of William Booth, a notorious criminal wanted for a variety of crimes from peeping to assault and robbery.

"I've known for a long time that this officer has wanted to be a detective. Wanted to solve crimes in this beautiful city of ours, and I'm proud to say that today is that day."

Forman pulls her shoulders back and her chin up.

"Congratulations to our newest detective . . ."

Her heart races.

"Officer Wallace."

The men in the station clap as the youngest member of the force, Daniel Wallace, looks around sheepishly, a grin on his face. Forman forces herself to clap along with the rest, but the world is spinning, her eyes having trouble focusing. Daniel has only been on the force for one year, his father a senior officer here, and as far as Forman knows, he hasn't solved a single crime. He even bungled a robbery pursuit last month, allowing the suspects to get away as he fumbled with the patrol car keys.

"What a surprise!" exclaims Daniel as he takes his place next to the captain.

"You earned it, Daniel. You won't let us down, will you?"

"No, sir. I'll make you proud."

Warrenson puts his hand on Daniel's shoulder. "Welcome, Detective Wallace. Now let's go clean up this city."

Several officers shake his hand and congratulate him, mentioning celebratory drinks after the shifts are over.

But Forman stays back. She's not interested in the accolades. She waits for most of the group to clear until Warrenson is free.

"Congratulations to Wallace," she says, meeting the eyes of Warrenson, his bony frame towering nearly a foot above her, even though she's taller than a lot of women. "He *earned* it, you say?"

"What's this about, Forman?" Her surname sounds different this time. She's never really minded them calling her by her last name. In fact, it made her feel like she fit in more. But something about the tone of his voice doesn't sit well with her.

"I've been here two years, and last week I was an integral part of solving the William Booth case. I've met all the requirements you laid out for me when I was hired. I want to fix this city. I want to make detective."

He doesn't respond. She imagines him silently listing the reasons why it's never going to happen. "Well, that's a little tough," he finally says, his breath a mixture of coffee and an early-morning cigarette.

"Why? I want to hear you say it."

He smiles, a familiar snarl on his lip. "Because we already have a new one. Detective Wallace. There's not room for two. Check back next year."

"You know I deserve that promotion. You know he's only being promoted because of his father."

Warrenson points his finger at her. "You'd be careful to watch your words, Forman. Talk like that could get you thrown out of here. You know the only thing worse than being a disrespected officer? A disrespected ex-officer."

Forman pauses, but she's not ready for this conversation to be over. "I want to be a detective."

"You can't."

"Why not?"

He laughs, showing the gap on the right side of his mouth from where a suspect punched him years ago, knocking out his tooth. "We don't have female detectives here. Stick to what you know. To what you're capable of."

Forman steadies her stance, crossing her arms and staring him straight in the eye. "I'm capable of more."

"Get on your way, Forman. Your shift started fourteen minutes ago. Keep to your penny arcades and dance halls."

But Forman isn't done. Not today. Not ever. "You know I'm worth it and can do the work of ten men. Give me a chance to prove it."

"Work of ten men, huh?" He snickers, and some of the remaining officers in the room join in, without the slightest effort to hide their eavesdropping.

"Eh, give her a chance, Captain," says Beaucamp, one of the more seasoned members of the force. "At least she'll stop bothering you, then."

"You think she can do this?" Warrenson says, challenging Detective Beaucamp.

Forman hasn't had much interaction with Beaucamp over the past few years. She keeps to her own business and the men keep to theirs.

"I didn't say that," continues Beaucamp. "But I figure if she tries and fails, you don't have to deal with her bothering you anymore." He laughs, and the two men near him follow suit.

Forman ignores them, her focus only on Warrenson. "One case. Give me one case to prove it to you." She flicks her hand at the group, so slightly they may not even notice. "And to everyone else that I can do this."

"One case, huh?" Warrenson replies as he sits down at his desk and folds his hands in his lap.

Forman refuses to break eye contact. "One."

Warrenson finally nods. "OK. I'll give you a case."

Forman's shoulders relax as she exhales. "Thank you. I won't let you down."

"We'll see."

Recent cases cycle through her mind: the robbery suspects that Wallace let get away, the unidentified body found behind the bank. As far as she knows, they haven't been assigned yet, or if they have, they're not being actively investigated. "How about—"

"Oh, you don't get to choose, Forman. I'm giving you a case—you're not taking one." He opens the drawer behind him and flips through the files. Officers Miller and Jacobs lean over to see what file he's looking at. They nudge each other, grins on their faces.

Warrenson pulls out a folder and tosses it onto his desk in front of Forman. "If you can solve this, I'll promote you to detective. Heck, I'll even have my wife bake a cake to celebrate the occasion."

Forman doesn't move; a sudden feeling of unease threatens her resolve from a moment ago. Everything she's wanted is now in a folder only a foot away, but there's a reason the officers are laughing.

He picks it up and holds it out for Forman to take. "This case and only this case. *If* you solve it."

"I will." She tries to take the file, but he's still holding on to the edge.

"You have two days."

"That's not—"

"Two days," he repeats as he releases his grip.

"Two days," says Forman with a nod, the unopened file in her hand. She doesn't have a desk—only the senior officers do—but she carries it back to an empty one and sits down, feeling the eyes of the rest of the officers on her.

The pale folder is in front of her, holding whatever it is that can take her to the next level.

Blocking out the surrounding noise and her own doubts, she opens the file.

CHAPTER FOUR

LETTY

The lock on the barn is intact, but the bracket on the left door, where the bolt slides in, has been smashed away, the effects of a strong attack I didn't hear in my sleep.

Broken but fixable. Immediately. Never leave things incomplete or unfinished—that was my father's advice. Or rule, rather.

When we were building the barn, I had hammered in several boards at the top, the nails in one line, with an idea to finish the bottom row later. Except I forgot. It was only when my father was doing a final check that it came up. He pointed to the row, his strong arm tapping each space I missed. "This is not your best work."

"I was going to do it," I replied.

"You do it as you go. Don't leave anything unfinished." He might never have seen the missing nails, but that changed when someone pointed them out to him.

I grab the tools and brackets to get started. This time, I'm putting two brackets on the door.

The sound of my mother canning peaches echoes across the dirt lot while I work. She's canned the last few years, her attempt to gather some extra income in between grape harvests. We've had peach trees here for as long as I can remember, the orchard on the south side of the house, opposite the vineyard. There was a plan several years ago to expand the grove from the original fifteen, adding five more trees every year. It remains at fifteen.

But still she continues, cutting the fruit we have and making the syrup to fill the tins she sells to neighbors and the local markets. And yet we never eat them, as if the peaches are for everyone else. Just like the wine.

I work on the door, the weathered barrels inside stacked high against the walls of the barn I helped my father put up nine years ago. Only a year before the government hammer of Prohibition came down with the Eighteenth Amendment and changed a successful winery into one just getting by. But unlike our neighbors—their abandoned wineries the relics of a livelihood torn from their grasp—we're the only ones still left in the valley. The only ones who were able to secure a deal with the local church to provide altar wine and keep our business going. Barely.

I stepped in when my father left, taking what I learned from him and teaching myself as much as I could after that. A few mistakes here and there, but now it's been three years, and everything is routine. Even though I no longer have the help of the four workers who left a few weeks after he did, worried that we might no longer be able to pay them—not even giving us a chance to try.

I hammer the last iron spike in, the metal flush with the wood. This time the brackets are strong and unyielding.

I close the door and lock it, the nails on the right side uneven, the sign of an apprentice hand. My hand.

My father made the other door, the nails in a perfect line. I leave that one closed. Perfect in his woodworking, imperfect in his life.

The lack of uniformity between the two doors used to bother me, a mistake I wished I could correct. But even though the nails aren't evenly arranged, they're doing their job. And they're a reminder that *I* built some of this.

Now to clean up the remaining evidence from last night's disruption. The bullet.

When I was ten, my father picked up the wooden slingshot after I broke the kitchen window. "Don't leave signs of mischief," he'd said. "That's the first thing that will attract more."

He wasn't even scolding me for misbehaving. It was the fact that things weren't in order, that the proof was still there. And even though he left us years later, the shame that I'd disappointed him stays with me even now. Some rules you can't shake, even if the judge is no longer around to enforce them.

I move along the outside of the barn, searching for the bullet's entrance wound in the wood. I know it hit. I heard the soft thud of the metal entering the sidewall, like a misguided bird running into one of the windows.

But the area is intact.

If I can't find it, maybe no one else will, either. But my father's words ring in my head, and trouble is the last thing we need.

I'm near the end of the building now, where stray plants fill the dirt, the ones that grow whether we want them to or not, protected from footsteps and truck tires.

I push the weeds down as I cover the last few feet. And there it is, between two scraggly California sagebrush plants: a splintered hole on a plank near the bottom of the barn.

The soft dirt would have been better, but the only thing I was aiming for last night was an inch to the left of Billy. In that sense, I hit my mark.

There's no metal to be seen, the bullet deep and hidden, my fingers useless in their effort to pry it out. But I have something that will help.

I reach into my back pocket and pull out my Remington, unfolding it open, the handle smooth from years of use and constant carrying, the blade slightly rusted and dull. Time in a vineyard—and being the only one who prunes the vines—has taught me that a knife is useful at all times.

The blade slides easily into the hole, and I work the wood until I can feel the knife on the side of the bullet.

Perspiration forms under my cap, a well-worn beige newsboy with a wide front brim, as the soft morning sun is replaced by the stronger light, the fall breeze providing no relief, only additional gusts of warmth.

The bullet finally pops out, landing in the dirt. I slip it into my pocket and trace with my fingertips the hole it left in the wood, the last vestige of the night's mischief.

I start to stand, but notice there's a line through the wooden boards on this side, a slim opening, the line not following any grain of wood. While I helped my father build the barn, I have no memory of this. But I was frequently sent away to pick up supplies or deliver the wine to the markets when we were still able to sell it there.

I thread the knife blade through the space, running it along the line as I push the plants away. I follow the gap for three feet and then down on each side, like a small door.

I glance back at my mother. I can hear the sounds as she's still working at her canning station inside the carriage house, where I no longer park my truck. It doesn't need protection from the harsh California sun as much as my mother does.

My mother slams the lever down to seal each tin, the amount of time between each one methodical and measured, reflecting a seasoned hand in practice. She usually does about twenty cans on Saturdays, and she has to be halfway through by now.

I turn back to the barn and this odd little door and move the dirt aside. In the center is a branded image of an owl. A routine visitor at the farm, the animal who watches from the dark, observing, waiting to strike.

I *definitely* haven't seen this before. Below the owl is a small metal handle.

I pull, a shallow breath escaping as I do. The wood resists, a heavy weight to it as it pushes the dirt, then swings up from the top, the rest of the soil lifting as it does.

It's a panel, already sliding into the space above the gap to hide it, as if the door never existed at all and the large square gap was the only thing ever here.

"Mother!" There's no reply, no movement from her. "Virginia!" But she's too far away, the noise of her efforts apparently dwarfing my voice.

I look back at the opening, a square of darkness. I pause, deciding whether I should get a torch, but I'm too curious to take the time. I step inside, my foot dangling for a moment until I feel the ground a few feet below, dirt falling in as I do.

The space forms a tunnel, the sun providing a brief glimpse of a wooden passageway. It turns into a stairway as I descend. After a few more steps, I can finally stand upright. Keeping one hand in front of me and one to the side, touching the wall for balance, all the remaining daylight from the opening now long gone, I press forward, the only sound a slight creak on each wooden stair as my feet hit them.

I reach a dirt floor, the soil moving around with my shoes. I must be under the middle of the barn now, probably dug before construction, back when I was still helping in the old winery on the far edge of the property. Before the threat of Prohibition made us want to build a new one close to the house, where we could keep an eye on it.

I reach out as I move around the room, my fingers grazing the round tops of barrels in the darkness.

But I don't need light to know what's inside. The scent is a familiar one from my childhood. From before Prohibition. Before he left. It's a memory I've tried to push out of my mind the last few years, as all of them are tainted with his abandonment, but this one comes with family evenings, my father turning the pages of a book as his left hand holds a glass of amber liquid. Or sometimes sitting with a family friend in the living room, both of them toasting with their glasses. The same spicy aroma is here, layered in its aging with wood from the barrels.

Brandy.

CHAPTER FIVE

FORMAN

Forman throws the file down on the captain's desk, the papers spilling out as it lands. "This is a joke, right?"

"Do you see me laughing?" he says, but a smile forms on his face, and he does a slow blink. "You said to give you any case. So I did."

Forman points to the file in front of him. "This is not a case. This is a fool's errand."

Warrenson leans back in his chair and folds his hands in his lap as if he's ready for an argument that will have no impact on his decision. "Why not, Forman?"

"I said a *case*. You gave me an inquiry into the theft of an item that wasn't even stolen. Mrs. Michaels? You have to be kidding."

Miller and Jacobs, who clearly must know what case Warrenson pulled, snicker to each other, failing, or not caring, to hide it.

"I don't know, Forman," replies Warrenson. "Burglary is a serious issue. It's a crime. But if you can't handle it . . ." He shrugs.

Forman doesn't break eye contact, her fists tightening as she holds her ground. "There have been seven of these over the past year. *Seven* from Mrs. Michaels. It's a well-known joke around here. She loses things and finds them months later. This isn't a real case."

"Ah, but it *is* a case," he says. "You did say you would solve *any* case I gave you."

Her fists are tight, but she forces them open. She takes a seat and grabs the file from his desk, flipping through the pages with increasing rhythm. "A car that she didn't realize her husband lent to a friend. A dress that was in her closet the whole time. A ring that she put on her bookshelf and found a month later. A music box that was at the repair place and she only remembered when they phoned her to pick it up." Forman looks up from the file. "And now a necklace missing at her house. This is nothing. It's another object she's misplaced. I deserve something more than this."

Warrenson pushes his chair back and stands. "You said you wanted a case, any case, but if you feel this is beneath you, then that's another issue."

"Give this to Wallace and give me something else. You wouldn't even investigate this." The file loosens in her hand as she realizes that's the point. "There's nothing to solve here."

"This is all you're getting. If something is lost, then you better find it. A real detective, or one who thinks they can be, would solve it."

Miller and Jacobs chuckle in the background. Forman glances at them, but they're not worth her time. Besides, making a comment to them will only fuel the fire.

She turns her attention back to the captain. "What about the body outside the bank? Let me solve that one."

"That's not your case." He taps the file. "*This* is."

Forman stares at Warrenson, her eyes narrowing. "Wallace didn't have to solve anything like this before his promotion."

He points his finger at Forman, his knobby knuckle close to her cheek. "You are not Wallace. Don't forget it."

"No," she says. "I'm not. I'm Annabel Forman, and I deserve a real chance." She stands but doesn't move away from the desk.

The air is heavy between them, neither wanting to back down, but Forman knows Warrenson has the upper hand. There's nothing she can do if he doesn't give in. She waits for his response, blocking his exit if he were to try to move around her. But he doesn't. He just stares right back at her.

"Well." He puts his hands on his hips. "This is your case. Some might say it's a chance. It's up to you if you squander it."

She glares at Warrenson and then at Miller and Jacobs. This is it. There will be no other case. No other opportunity. A case no one can solve because there's nothing to solve. But this is it.

"OK," she says.

"OK?" Warrenson's eyes go wide, his eyebrows high on his forehead.

She holds up the file, the papers bending in her grasp. "If I find this necklace, we have a deal? Even if it's just at her house. I solve this, I'm promoted, correct?" She motions to the officers. "There are witnesses here to hold you to it."

A sly smile appears on his face, his eyes cold and calculating. "Sure. If you can find it, you'll get promoted."

Forman turns on her heels.

"But," Warrenson reminds her, "you only have two days."

She turns back to him to meet his eyes. "That's impossible. Mrs. Michaels won't figure out where she put it for at least a month."

"Two days. Detectives have to move fast. Besides, if it's not something to be solved, it should be easy, then. Right? And I promise you'll get promoted. I'm a man of my word, Forman, and I'll make it happen."

"What's this?" asks Detective August Raymond as he enters the station room, his steps broad, as if he wants to take up as much space as possible to make up for the fact that he's a few inches smaller than everyone on the force, including Forman. "Another promotion? Two in one day?"

"Possibly," says Warrenson. "Forman wants to be a detective, but she needs to prove her worth first."

Raymond removes his dark-gray trilby, which is marked by a flat bow on the left side of the black band. The hat is an obvious attempt to give him more inches. The effort reveals his cropped brown hair, but he quickly puts the hat back on, as if the change in height was too much.

"She'll do it," replies Raymond, his eyes focused on her through the round glasses he wears on his diamond-shaped face, the familiar scar on his chin looking like a barber's close shave went wrong.

His seriousness is nothing new, but his encouragement surprises Forman. One of the more admirable officers on the force, he's always been nice to her, though he's kept his distance. He's been an officer for twelve years and earned everyone's respect the first year, when he returned to work the day after he was shot in the arm during a traffic stop.

"You're back early," says Warrenson.

"Three restaurant workers thought it was a good idea to set up a still in the backyard. Owens is processing them now."

"More?" says the captain. "You always seem to find them."

"I'm good at my job. I clean up the city." He looks at Forman. "You will, too. What's the case?"

"A burglary at Mrs. Michaels's," she replies in a neutral voice.

Raymond puts his hand to his mouth to hide his smile but quickly regains his stoic demeanor. "The lady who loses everything? Cap, you couldn't have given her an easy one?"

"On the contrary, Raymond. It is easy. A simple lost and found. If Forman figures it out, well, then, things are going to change around here."

Raymond lowers his head with a nod of approval. "Good luck."

"I'll be just fine," she replies in her same calm tone. "I don't suppose you want to lend me a car to visit Mrs. Michaels or pair me up with another officer who has a vehicle?" she asks Warrenson.

"Now," says the captain with a smile, "that would be cheating, wouldn't it?"

CHAPTER SIX

LETTY

When I emerge from the side of the barn, Father O'Leary's old Model T is in the driveway. A charitable parishioner gifted it to the church so the good father could visit those who are unable to leave their homes. It's often filled with fruit and vegetables, donations to help those residents. But today it is empty. My mother is already near the car; Father O'Leary and Charles, his assistant, stand next to it as they greet her. Father O'Leary is in his robes, and Charles has his usual outfit on, including suspenders to hold up his brown pants and a wide-brimmed hat, as if he's going to spend the day in the garden.

I scramble to close the opening in the side of the barn before they can notice, though thick clumps of dirt stick to my pants. I don't want anyone to see the space, especially not the priest. We can't do anything to risk losing our contract.

Before my father left, he always said that church was his saving grace. As long as he had church, everything would be fine. It's funny to think that now it's also ours, but not in the same way.

Father O'Leary is this side of seventy, with thinning hair and a round face always sporting a tight-lipped smile. My mother adores him, but part of me thinks it's because he buys our wine. I appreciate what he does for my family but don't like the helping of guilt that always comes along with it.

"Haven't seen you at church recently," he says to me as I approach.

I'm still trying to wipe away the dirt and dust from the pants I've worn since I started helping with the winery—the heavy fabric stands up to the vines, the truck, and the updates that the buildings, including the roofs, require from time to time.

"It was harvest, but I'll be back soon," I promise.

"I hope you will."

"It's a surprise to see you here, Father," I say, hoping to get him on another topic.

My mother nods, but her face seems different, as if she's just been given some bad news.

"Would you like to come in? I can make some tea," I offer.

"No, no, Charles and I simply wanted to stop by to talk with you both. It won't take a minute."

I glance at Charles, but he's not meeting my eyes today, his focus on the ground in front of him, as if wishing it would swallow him whole. We've known each other since we were kids, having grown up within a few miles of each other, and he's always gone out of his way to help people. He started working for the church right after we graduated high school, and I know he'll never stop. His face is the type that should be on the silver screen—chiseled in just the right sections, soft in others—yet he wants nothing to do with Hollywood.

He's usually so eager, so excited to see me. Not now. Something is wrong.

"The new delivery is ready. I was going to drop it off this afternoon." I motion toward the locked barn doors, but it's a small effort for the trouble I already know is coming, the one I can feel between the four of us, the words they haven't yet said heavy in the air.

"That's what we're here to talk about. The archdiocese has made some, let's say, adjustments," Father O'Leary says, looking first at me and then my mother. "All wine for Mass will be sourced from one winery in order to keep a better handle on the distribution. Apparently, there's been concern about unaccounted-for wine, so they're tightening up the process, canceling all of the small winery contracts and pulling from a larger one downtown."

"No," says my mother, her head shaking. "Father, you promised. Years ago. Even after Richard left, you promised you would keep this contract." Her voice is strong, but I can detect the waver that happens when tears are about to fall.

"I'm sorry." Father O'Leary clasps her hands, his eyes searching her face. "I wish there was something we could do, but it's not up to us. I tried to fight it. I did."

"We can't survive if you do this." I wait for him to look at me. "This is our livelihood."

He turns, his eyes meeting mine. "My child, it's not up to me. But the church will be here to help you."

"We're still going to take what you have for us now," mutters Charles. His focus remains on the ground, the guilty expression on his face the same as when he tattled on me for standing on the Red Car tracks as a streetcar approached when I was nine.

"Yes, yes, as Charles said," continues Father O'Leary. "I'm afraid I delivered the bad news first, silly me." He smiles and wipes his brow, but I know the sequence of the news was deliberate. Give the bad news and then reward with the good, ending on a sweet note, a gift of false hope. Except it doesn't always work. Like right now.

"We're going to purchase this recent harvest," Charles continues. "But there will be no more after this season."

This season. That's all we have left. "So we have a year?" I'm trying to gauge how long we can pay the bills before the money runs out and creditors come for the farm. A year will be tough, but there might be enough time to figure out another way to create revenue.

"Six months," says Charles.

"More like three," replies O'Leary, a sympathetic smile on his face.

"I tried to convince them." Charles looks up, his eyes finally meeting mine, their usual bright blue dimmed by the guilt I can see he feels. "I told them we wanted to still work with you, but it was an overall decision. A streamline to stop . . . in case wine goes missing."

The heels of my boots sink deeper into the dirt as his words hang in the air. "You know it hasn't."

Charles nods, but he looks to the ground again. While sacramental wine is exempted in the Volstead Act, allowing churches to still serve wine during each Mass, we've never let a barrel out of our sight. And he knows it.

"Well." Father O'Leary claps his hands together. "Now that that's out of the way, shall we take some of the bottles with us? It will save you a delivery later."

"It was hard enough getting permission to let us keep you for more deliveries," says Charles. "But we made it work. For you."

"Well, that, and we didn't want to encourage any, um . . ." O'Leary looks around, a nervous laugh escaping from his lips. "Illegal activities."

"Bootlegging?" My mother's hand is on her chest. "We would never. I hope you know that. Even when Richard was here, the three of us were strictly against that."

Father O'Leary's nod is genuine, the one I've seen over the years when he knows it's a difficult situation. He trusts us, which means there's still a chance.

"I beg you to reconsider." I move closer to him. "You can keep it going. Tell them again you want to work with us."

"It's not my decision. Feel free to take it up with the archdiocese, but this was a clear directive. They're not going to move on it." Father O'Leary glances toward the barn. "But shall we?"

I unlock the newly repaired doors, and for the first time ever, a feeling of dread settles over me as I enter the barn. The large space, lined with barrels and bottles gathered in the back, usually so full of hope and celebratory memories, is now a ticking clock, signifying the end of the farm and the land my grandfather bought sixty years ago. The land my father so casually discarded when he left. The land that I managed to save. The land that is our home, my mother's and mine.

I loop my hands through two of the jugs, their larger size created specifically for the church, and walk past Charles. He's thin and lanky, without much muscle, and he moves slower than I do, so I usually carry the wine when I make a delivery. He tried to carry them all for me in the early days, but I moved faster and ended up getting more done. I think it hurt his pride at first, but he hasn't commented on it since. In the time it has taken me to carry three jugs to Father O'Leary's car, he's only taken one.

"I hope you'll be OK," says Charles as he picks up another jug.

"We've been through worse." My tone isn't as friendly as it should be, but the news has shaken me.

I place two more jugs in the back of the car.

"Can I say I'm almost relieved?" Charles puts one jug on the floor of the front.

"Relieved?"

"Winemaking is dangerous," he says as he walks back to the barn.

"Relieved that we're now out of work? Charles, we're going to lose everything."

"That's not what I meant. I didn't like the thought of you both out here alone, when people with guns can come and steal your wine. It's not safe." He's back to looking anywhere but at my eyes again.

"Did you have something to do with this? Was this you trying to help?"

"No, of course not." He reaches out to touch my arm but hesitates. "I'm sorry. I care for you, that's all. I want you to be safe."

"We will be," I say flatly as I grab more jugs and carry them outside.

Father O'Leary stands next to my mother, watching as Charles and I do all of the work.

"I know this isn't good news," he says. "But we hope this doesn't end your relationship with the church. There are a lot of youths that could be a big help." He glances at the house. "Help you work on the place, perhaps help you harvest the peaches. The whole diocese is reaching out to girls on the streets, encouraging them to seek alternative employment arrangements."

"We can't pay anyone," my mother says curtly, pulling her arms close around her, as if her knitted cardigan will suddenly provide more warmth. "We can barely cover expenses ourselves as it is."

"I know. I'm sorry. But the church is here for you both. I'm sorry it came to this."

"We are, too," I interject, but my voice is not soft. "This choice will destroy us."

"We all make tough choices in our lives, Letty." His mouth forms into another sympathetic smile. "Life is a series of decisions, and we have to deal with the consequences of those decisions."

"I agree." I pick up the last jug, fourteen in all, and make a decision. One I know I will have no thoughts about changing.

CHAPTER SEVEN

LETTY

Father O'Leary's vehicle kicks up dust and dirt as it leaves the property, the car driving faster than usual.

"This isn't good, Letty. This isn't good at all." My mother's eyes shift to me, already filled with worry and sadness. "At least we have the peaches."

"Come here, I want to show you something. But first let me grab a torch."

I lead her into the secret tunnel, the light illuminating everything I couldn't see before.

There are three vats on the far side of the room, similar to our wooden wine vats but smaller—these only reach my height. On the right are six barrels lining the wall, the ones I felt on my earlier visit, and additional ones on the other side.

My mother stands near the entrance to the room, her eyes on the barrels. "What is it?"

I touch my nose. "Can't you smell it?" I cup my hand and hold it near the first vat as I turn the tap. A golden-brown liquid flows into my palm as if it's been waiting years for its release. And it has.

There's enough in my hand for a sip, and I hold it out to my mother. "It's brandy."

She shakes her head and leans back, as if she has just encountered a skunk that's both rabid and aggressive. "No. Not these lips."

The brandy is still pooled in my palm, though some has dripped through my fingers and down my sleeve, the scent sure to follow me for the rest of the day.

I glance at my mother, hesitate for a moment, and then drink it. The spicy liquid coats my tongue with caramel and oak, and then burns all the way down my throat. It tastes the same as the sip my father let me have from his glass as he spoke with a neighbor about the upcoming changes with the new laws.

Although my palate has been limited to wine these last eight years, this brandy matches that first taste. My father was proud to drink only high-quality brandy. It was something he mentioned every time he poured it for a friend.

I look at my mother as I wipe my hands together, the moisture spreading to both of them. "It's good."

Her shoulders move slightly. "Your father had good taste in things, at least at the beginning."

"Did you know he had this here?"

"I remember when he built it, but I thought it was never used. He said the room was to store wine at a cooler temperature."

"Did you know he had the brandy here?"

She shakes her head. "You're not the only one your father kept secrets from."

The memory sweeps in, the sound of the screen door slamming in my head, my father walking past us, a large canvas bag on his back. "I can't live two lives anymore. It's not fair to you and it's not fair to me."

"Why are you choosing *them*?" my mother cried. "You have a family here. A daughter."

He shifted his attention to me, a glimpse of emotion in his eyes I've never been able to define. "I know." He adjusted the bag, hoisting it higher on his shoulder, and walked down the driveway, with enough decency to leave his faded green truck behind.

I stood on the front porch with my mother, my pinkie hooked around hers, watching him stand near the edge of the property as a car pulled up and drove him away.

The anger briefly turned to grief a year later when his body was found in the river, the final realization that he would never return.

"Close it up." My mother's voice stirs me back to now, her words nearly echoing in the secret room around us. "He left it behind like he left us behind. Hammer it shut. It doesn't exist, like he doesn't exist."

But the news from the church is still heavy on my mind. "It's worth a lot, and we need money."

"If they find it here, we'll be arrested."

"How would they find it?"

"They find things. They're always looking, Letty. It's not the only thing we'll lose." My mother has her hand on her neck, her fingers tracing the line of the locket containing photos of her parents. "We'll lose the church."

"We've lost that already. You heard them. They're not continuing the contract."

"We'll lose each other."

"That won't happen."

My mother shakes her head. "Let's leave this here. It's his. We'll have nothing to do with it." She releases the locket, the silver metal resting still, as if it had never been held. Her hands return to a folded position, as they do when she's trying to hold on to a situation she no longer controls. Like the day he left.

"We have the canning. That will get us through. We'll be fine." She smiles, but her eyes don't. I know she's trying her best to hold it together, and I don't have the heart to tell her the few cans a month she sells won't stave off the creditors the moment they smell a struggle. That we're barely covering the bills as it is. That when the sacramental wine stops in three months, we'll lose the land her father bought when he came out to California.

"You're right," I reply, the lie tasting foreign and dry, the residue remaining on my tongue long after the words are gone. "The canning will get us through."

But I'm already thinking of my next step.

One barrel only. One barrel to get us through until we can figure out how to make ends meet. One, and my mother will never have to know.

I already know where to go. A family friend from long ago, before they moved to the city. A friend who knows the seedier parts of the City of Angels. The darker side of life.

CHAPTER EIGHT

FORMAN

The walk up the hill from the Red Car Line has Forman out of breath, and though several vehicles passed her on Beachwood Drive, the road to the Hollywoodland sign, no one offered her a ride. She's finally reached the open gates of the sprawling Michaels estate and sees she still has a driveway to climb.

Mrs. Michaels's house is bigger and grander than Forman's distant view of it had led her to believe. Seeing it alone on the hill, without other houses to compare it to, she had pegged it as smaller, but now the expansive footprint of the foundation is clear, as is the height of the two stories that tower above the driveway in their mock Tudor style.

Forman's calves burn as she makes it to the top, pausing to fill her lungs as she looks around. There's a small building next door, with barn doors and stalls, as well as a garage near the back of the house and probably many more buildings on the estate behind. This is quite a different beat from her usual one that takes her by the picture shows, skating rinks, and dance halls of the city to interview girls who might be subject to prostitution. The class of people who live in this part of Los Angeles, and especially on estates like this, likely could never imagine the type of worries the girls she usually encounters have on a daily basis.

Forman knocks on the large oak door, the sound muted by the thick wood, the moment unanswered. Maybe the necklace has already been found. The report was taken a few days ago. It could be all fine now, and by chance, Forman could even take the credit. Then she could solve real cases.

Forman removes her notebook from her bag, pushing aside the other contents, including a police call-box key to report crimes, a rule guide, and a first-aid book.

The door opens to a woman with dark eye shadow like Clara Bow's, rouge on her cheeks, and curled brown hair swept up with the ease of a Hollywood starlet, yet her face isn't familiar.

"Good afternoon. I'm looking for Mrs. Michaels."

"I'm she." Her left eyebrow rises as her eyes drift to the badge on Forman's coat.

"I'm Officer Annabel Forman."

The eyebrow remains arched. "I was unaware they had female officers."

Forman's attention shifts to the gems around Mrs. Michaels's neck: large diamonds with smaller ones in between. If the missing necklace is anything like this one, she thinks to herself, it's not just a sentimental loss.

"They do, and I'm here to investigate a lost item."

"Incorrect."

"Sorry?" Forman's grasp on her notebook loosens.

"Your information is incorrect." Her eyebrow finally drops, and she raises her chin. "It was not lost. It was stolen. You're here to investigate a theft."

Forman presses her lips together, her perfected police demeanor falling back into place. "Yes, a burglary."

Mrs. Michaels opens the door wider. "It's about time you boys or"—she pauses—"*people* took my claim seriously. I swear I detected a bit of laughter when I called to report it."

"We take everything seriously," Forman tries to assure her as she steps inside, her heels echoing on the black-and-white tile floors, every inch polished, a spiral staircase up ahead. Dark wood side tables are topped by vases bursting with flower arrangements, the containers from far-off lands, and candles sit in ornate holders throughout the room. It's like a scene out of *The Great Gatsby*, which Forman read last year. There is probably a pool around, too, where guests are treated to lavish parties without a care for the cost.

"Well," says Mrs. Michaels, her brown eyes narrowing. "How do we begin?"

Forman looks at the notebook in her hands and flips to an open page. If this case is anything like the other ones tied to Mrs. Michaels, the necklace is likely here somewhere. "Where were you when you last had it?"

"Last had it? No, I didn't have it. It was in my room."

"Let's look there, then." Forman glances toward the stairs. A house of this stature would have the bedrooms on the second level.

But Mrs. Michaels isn't moving. "It's not here. I told you it was stolen. This doesn't bode well if you're doubting me already."

"I'm simply eliminating factors, Mrs. Michaels," replies Forman. She has to admit that every detail of this woman's makeup and hair is exquisite, and nothing seems to be out of place on her or in the house. "I should see the scene of the crime. It's the best way to get to the heart of the matter, don't you agree?"

"If you must." Mrs. Michaels moves toward the stairs, where a tapered red runner covers each step to the second floor.

"It says in the report your husband is a businessman. What does he do?"

Mrs. Michaels pauses midclimb, looks back at Forman, and says, "Business," before continuing her ascent.

The second level matches the opulence of the first but with decidedly less decor, as if visitors don't come up here often. Or at all.

A young maid dressed in a starched black-and-white uniform steps back against the wall as Mrs. Michaels passes.

"What about the staff? Have you questioned them?"

"Don't be silly. They know better than to steal from me." Mrs. Michaels pushes open a door to a room with a large canopy bed and nightstands, a window with a sweeping view in front of us. "This way. Don't step on the rug."

Forman carefully steps around the pristine white mohair rug and follows Mrs. Michaels into the dressing room. The closets are lined with fur coats that are too warm for most of the California year and silk dresses too far out of Forman's price range to even think about.

"I keep my jewelry box in the safe." She points to the metal door behind her. "But I went to a party Wednesday night and was tired when I got home. I left the necklace here." She taps the center dresser, an island in the middle of the closet. "As you can see, it's gone. Now, what are you going to do about it?"

The dresser, pink to match the rest of the closet, is empty, with no jewels in sight. Still, this is just the beginning.

"What does the necklace look like?"

"Now that's the kind of question I expected. Diamonds with lace threading and three very large emeralds."

Forman makes a note in her book and looks around the dresser. She opens one of the drawers to find it filled with stockings, each one folded over in perfect unison with the one next to it.

"No need to open those. It's not in there. It was stolen."

Stolen like the car, the ring, the dress, and the music box before it. Forman glances around, debating where to go next. "May I look in the jewelry box?"

Mrs. Michaels clucks her tongue. "You don't believe me."

"I'm being thorough. Surely you want someone investigating who is thorough, Mrs. Michaels. A stolen necklace is a serious matter." Forman's voice is stern, the promotion weighing heavy on her mind.

Mrs. Michaels lifts her head, her chin sticking out. "Yes." She waves her hand in a circle. "Turn around."

"Sorry?"

"I have to open my safe. I don't open it in front of anyone, let alone a stranger I've only just met."

Forman faces the door to the bedroom and listens to the sound of the clicking. This is a fool's errand; she can feel it.

"Finished. You may look now." Mrs. Michaels is holding a pink satin box, the safe behind her already closed. "This is where I always keep it, but as I said, I left the necklace on the dresser that night." She places the box on the island.

Although the box is small, the number of jewels in it is not. Necklaces, rings, bracelets—all adorned with multicolored gems of red, green, blue, and, of course, white, the sparkle of diamonds. It's a wonder Mrs. Michaels even knew the necklace was missing with the amount of jewelry in here.

Forman picks through the box, her stomach tightening as she searches for the diamond necklace with lace threading and three large emeralds, the finding of which will give her everything she's been working toward.

And there it is.

In the bottom of the box, on the right-hand side, the jewels pushed together in a tangled knot, as if it were thrown in haphazardly, unlike the rest of the necklaces, which are neatly curled in the velvet.

Forman lifts it up as relief floods through her like the Los Angeles River during a storm. She doesn't bother to hide her smile. "I've found it. It was in here all along."

Mrs. Michaels sneers, as if told she was unwelcome at her own party. "That's not it."

Forman looks at the lace diamonds and three emeralds. "It's what you described."

"That's the sister one to it and simply goes around the neck. The one I lost is three times that size and covers much more." She motions a few inches down her chest.

"All right," says Forman with a nod as the feeling of victory fades. "Let's keep looking."

"I told you it was stolen. Why are we looking in my house?"

"Covering all of our tracks."

"Well, it's silly." Mrs. Michaels moves toward the bedroom door. "It's not here, and I feel like you're not giving this the proper attention."

"I promise you, I am." Forman flips to a new page in her notebook, resigned to treating this like the robbery that Mrs. Michaels is insisting it is. "Was there anyone here the next day, Thursday, who might have seen it? Perhaps one of the staff? I'd like to talk to them."

Her face changes. "Thomas," Mrs. Michaels says in a whisper, as if to herself.

Forman waits for more, but Mrs. Michaels stares at the wallpaper as if seeing its lilac flowers for the first time.

"Thomas," repeats Mrs. Michaels a little angrily.

"Who is Thomas? Is that your husband?"

Mrs. Michaels whips her head around so fast, Forman's worried she might injure herself. "Don't be silly. I would never . . . Thomas is, well, Thomas. But he was here that day." She strikes her palm into her fist, her movements out of character based on Forman's experience with her so far. "That snively Thomas. I leave him alone for ten minutes and this is what he does."

Forman writes his name in her book. "What does Thomas do? Is he staff?"

"Oh no. I would never have him on staff. He only delivers."

"What does he deliver?" Forman waits to write the answer, her pen hovering above the paper.

"I'm not comfortable with you writing this down."

"Every detail is important." Forman looks up at her. "What did he deliver?"

Mrs. Michaels looks away, breaking eye contact. "Supplies . . . Disregard. It wasn't him."

But Forman doesn't let it go. "Where can I reach Thomas?"

"No." Mrs. Michaels's eyes move rapidly back and forth. "My mind has changed. I want this to stop. The necklace is gone, and it no longer matters."

"Mrs. Michaels, you reported the theft. We're going to follow through."

"No. Not anymore." She looks at Forman. "You need to leave. Now."

CHAPTER NINE

LETTY

When I pull away from our house in my truck, my mother watches me, standing in the driveway like she always does, as if I'm going to do exactly what my father did. But I'll never leave her.

She thinks I'm delivering some of her peaches in the city. Making a little more money from her canning efforts this morning. And in a way I am.

The constant wheeze of the truck's engine when it's competing with other cars is absent as I pass the area where we fill the truck bed with baskets of grapes from our vines. It always seems to run better when the tires are on the familiar dirt roads of home, though it's not the home I remember. The valley has changed, even in my twenty-four years. Movie theaters, land development, and the dams they're building in the hills to hold the new reservoirs needed to quench the thirst of a growing city.

The trees cast shadows on the road as I head south, the Santa Monica Mountains reaching toward the sky. The farms are first, the orchards still brimming with life, their citrus and avocado trees in perfect lines. Then there's the Hooper place. They kept producing wine even after the Volstead Act passed, creating a clock that ticked down for a few months until Prohibition was enacted. The Hoopers got away with it for a couple of years, but like everything in life, it eventually caught up to them. My father watched from the road as agents slammed axes into the barrels, the wine flooding into the dirt in front of their house. The red river of San Fernando, they called it in the newspaper.

When my father left, we thought the same might happen to us, but my mother went to the church and begged Father O'Leary to keep the deal going. And he promised right then that as long as we produced wine, he would buy from us.

Until today.

I curve through the Cahuenga Pass, the chaparral-covered hills my familiar transition from country life into the bustling world of Hollywood. The rail line to the side is empty, the trolley cars between schedules, as I descend to where the farmlands and dirt roads have been replaced by boulevards and buildings that get taller every year.

The city is a different world from the valley where I grew up, the only similarity the Pacific Electric Red Car tracks that thread into the valley, but the streets here have more cars, weaving in and out, on a race to get somewhere more important than where they've been.

A new movie director seems to come to Los Angeles every month, the lure of Hollywood and the amiable climate tempting those with money to film here. They arrive in the city already on their way to the top, while those of us born here are still trying to climb a ladder that wasn't provided for us.

I stop on Hollywood Boulevard. The Hollywood Hotel is to my right—where Rudolph Valentino used to live—and a mile or so down, the heart of Hollywood is buzzing with crowds around the theaters, including the one where Douglas Fairbanks put his feet in the cement a few months ago. But I'm turning left. To Sal's Barbershop. It's also on the boulevard but not part of the swanky celebrity scene, though I hear stars sometimes rent apartments in the building next to Sal's. The boulevard is quieter here, with jewelry stores, cafés, and music shops.

I arrive at Sal's, the shop less busy than usual, with four of the five chairs vacant as I enter, but it's never been fully empty any of the times I've been in here, mostly with my father.

Sal's giving a shave at the last chair, both men silent as he works. The client holds today's newspaper, the top of it moving as the ceiling fans do their best to keep the fall heat away, but all they do is circulate the hot air.

Sal's gray hair forms a ring at the bottom of his head, the bald top shiny as it reflects the overhead lamps while he tends to the man. His blade carves away the foam and whiskers with a seasoned flick of the hand, a routine he's been doing for decades.

He glances at me, winks as if he sees me every single day instead of once a year, and returns to his work. I've known Sal, a soft-spoken man of few words, my whole life. He lived with his daughter a few farms down from us until they moved away to the city when I was about ten. The age where you really know true friends, before school, boys, and life get in the way.

"Appreciate it, Sal," says the man in the chair as he gets up and peels a bill from his money clip. "Great job." He looks at me as he passes and puts his hand on my shoulder. "Sorry, babe, I don't think they do broads here."

"Well, I guess I'm out of luck, then," I say as I glare unflinchingly at him in the mirror instead of meeting his actual gaze. "Maybe I just want to feel the coldness of a blade across my skin."

The man leans back as he stares at me and then shakes his head. Still shaking his head as the door slams behind him.

"Scaring the customers, Letty," says Sal as he wipes his hands on a towel.

"Only the ones that have already paid." I smile. "I didn't like his tone."

"I'm sure he didn't like yours, either, but to each their own." He nods. Still the man I grew up with, always even keeled, seeing every side. When my father left for his new family, Sal didn't choose sides but also never spoke of him again. It's like a tear in the wallpaper, better left unnoticed and unspoken about until one day you don't even see it at all. It just blends into the design. "Margaret is over at the dress shop if you're looking for her."

"Actually, it was you I wanted to see."

Sal's face doesn't change.

"People talk to you. They come in here and share their secrets."

"They might." His voice is slow and cautious. He tosses the towel on the stand.

The door opens behind me, and I turn to see Margaret. Her brown hair is bobbed like the film stars, her red lipstick is in a Cupid's-bow shape, and she's wearing one of the latest dress fashions from Mrs. Wilson's Dress Shop, where she works. She wants to be an actress and still hasn't made it, but at least she sells dresses to them, if that's any consolation.

"Letty! Let me guess—you've come to the city to finally buy a new dress, and you just stopped here to say hi to my pop before crossing the street to me." She puts her hand on her hip. "I've been telling you for years, dresses will look like the cat's meow on you."

"You've been telling me for years I need to spend more time in the city."

"And I'm not wrong." She flashes a mischievous smile. Everyone else thinks she's sweet and innocent, with her large brown eyes and unassuming baby face, but I know better. We broke more than a few rules back in the day when we were kids, Charles always telling on us. "So what really brings you here?" she asks.

"I had a question for your dad." I turn back to Sal, but the atmosphere has changed, and an awkward tension fills the air. Sal seems to know I'm about to ask a question I shouldn't. "Have any of your clients ever mentioned what someone could do with a barrel of brandy?"

Sal doesn't react, but I remember a comment before the start of Prohibition, how he was gathering a stockpile of alcohol. Apparently, my father was, too, but I wasn't privy to that conversation, only the evidence I found today.

"If someone had a large amount of alcohol," I continue, "not wine, and wanted to do a quick sale for some fast cash, how would that work?"

Sal moves his chin back and forth as he waits to reply, his hands in the pockets of his white apron. "Why do you ask me?"

"Because you know everything about this city. People talk in here."

"She's not wrong, Pop."

His eyes flash to Margaret and back to me.

"You know people around here—"

"No, I don't," he interrupts. "You'd be smart to stay away from that." The calm demeanor I've known all my life is gone, replaced by a mask of fiery emotion. "Stay away from everything in that world. If your dad knew . . . he wouldn't approve."

"My dad made his choice that day he left us. He didn't get a say in our lives after that, and he certainly doesn't now that he's dead." I can feel the heat rising in my chest.

"That world will only lead to danger. I don't know where this brandy is, but dump it out and forget you ever found it." He tosses his combs and then his scissors in the drawers, slamming each of them shut.

"The church canceled the contract today. We have about three months, if that. I need to do this."

He shakes his head but keeps his attention on his station. "Dump it out," he repeats in a slow drawl before looking at me. "You need a job? Go with Margaret. But stay away from the life you're alluding to."

"Yes," says Margaret, her tone softer than I've heard it before. "Come work with me."

I exhale, my shoulders falling as I do, and turn for the door, leaving them both inside. The sun is setting near the ocean, casting shadows on the tall buildings that dwarf me, making me feel boxed in, claustrophobic.

The door opens behind me and Margaret steps out.

"I'm not working at the dress shop," I say before she has a chance to convince me otherwise. "Not that it's bad. But it won't be enough to keep the winery. And look at me. I haven't worn a dress in years. I surely can't sell them."

"I understand." Margaret motions to the side of the building, where there are no windows. "Follow me."

We walk over, and she reaches under her dress, pulling out a small metal flask strapped to her leg. "Here, I bet you could use a swig of this."

"No, thanks." I glance around. "Too many people can see."

"Are you sure that's the only thing stopping you?" Margaret asks with a shrug as she opens the top of the flask and takes a drink.

"You play with fire, my friend."

She grins. "Fire is fun." She tucks the flask back under her dress. "Were you serious? About the barrel of brandy?"

She's stoic all of a sudden, and I am taken aback. I can't remember seeing Margaret like this in all our years together. She's a few months younger than I am, but she suddenly seems years older.

"Yes."

"How much do you want for it?" She wiggles her eyebrows but still doesn't smile.

"I don't know. I have to find out how much it's worth."

"Don't tell my pop," she says, keeping her focus on the cars passing in the street. "But I know a place we can go if you really want to sell it. A secret place."

I think of the few months we have left until we can't pay our bills, the history of our house built by my grandfather, and the land I've spent the last few years cultivating, making my own. "I do," I reply.

She nods. "I thought you didn't like this side of the business. What changed?"

"Everything."

Her lips form into a smile that says she's ready to break all the rules. I saw the same smile on her when we were about eight and she stole eggs from the neighbor's chickens. "OK, then." She glances at me. "You're not dressed like the others will be."

I look down at my winery clothes, the faded duck-cloth pants, my beat-up boots, and the long-sleeve blouse I wear to keep the sun off my arms as I harvest grapes or tend to the vines. "Does it matter?"

"Not at all." She grins. "Follow me."

CHAPTER TEN

FORMAN

The sound of the slamming door still echoes in Forman's ears as she stands on the front porch, knocking again. Mrs. Michaels practically pushed her down the stairs, her hands on her back as if even the sight of Forman for one more moment was too much. Her parting instructions were to forget everything she heard today and to forget she had even been there.

But Forman isn't going to do that. She needs to find out about Thomas, the current suspect in this case, but the refusal of Mrs. Michaels to come back to the door is yet another obstacle.

She knocks one more time, to no avail. With no other option at the moment, she makes her way down the driveway, every step away taking her further from solving this case. What is so secret about Thomas's deliveries that Mrs. Michaels no longer wants to pursue the theft? Forman wonders. And if Thomas *did* steal the necklace, why would he take that risk, robbing one of his wealthy customers right under her nose?

The guardhouse on the other side of the gate has a matching exterior to the mansion on the hill. The gates were open when Forman walked in, so she didn't bother to stop at the guardhouse, but she walks determinedly toward it now.

Mrs. Michaels may have told her to forget about the missing necklace, but Forman has a case to solve and a promotion to earn. All she has to go on is that there was a deliveryman named Thomas. But there are other people here who might know more.

The older man inside looks up as she reaches his post, stepping out to greet her. His white hair is slicked back, and he has a toothpick in his mouth. His uniform, like the staff's in the house, is properly fitted, the olive-green suit buttoned up to his neck and down past his waist, where his arms hang, holding a clipboard.

"You here to see Mr. Michaels?"

"No. Mrs. Michaels."

The guard shakes his head, his weathered mouth remaining tight lipped. "You were here already."

So she *was* seen when she arrived. "Yes. I'm investigating some missing jewelry."

The guard rocks back on his heels. "I don't trust you police types. You're always asking the wrong questions."

"I'm not like other police."

He stares at her. "'Cause you a woman?"

"No. Because I take every case seriously, including this one." Forman removes her notebook from her bag. "What's your name?"

The old man looks at her warily.

"It's only a name."

"Harry," he says slowly.

"Harry, I'm Annabel Forman." She extends her hand, but he doesn't take it. "I'm looking for Thomas. Do you know where I can find him?"

"Thomas?" He adjusts the toothpick in his mouth and then rolls it to the other side with his tongue. "I don't know about that."

"Thomas. He's a deliveryman."

"I know who he is. I just don't know if I'm supposed to tell you. The Michaelses are private people."

Forman presses her lips together. He's not going to tell her anything he doesn't want to. "I agree. But I'm looking into it for Mrs. Michaels . . ."

"Then let her tell you." He steps back inside the guardhouse, but Forman follows him into the small room, the open door doing little to clear the stuffy air inside.

"You don't have to say a single word about them. I only want to know where I can find Thomas. Not anyone else. Only Thomas."

The guard sits down, the chair squeaking as he does.

"When is his next delivery?"

"Never." He looks up at her. "He won't be here no more."

"Why not?"

He stares at Forman, his eyes narrowing as his forehead creases. "You're the fuzz. I'm not telling you nothing." His last word is muffled as he coughs, his whole body shaking, his face turning red.

Forman steps forward to help, but it's clear this is routine for Harry, whatever ailments have happened in his life now catching up to him.

The coughing fit continues, and Forman shifts, not sure if she should step away. It reminds her of her aunt, who had a cough that lingered for a while. Only hot lemon tea seemed to do the trick, and unfortunately, Forman doesn't have that handy. But she does have something.

She removes a butterscotch candy from her bag and holds it out to him. "I carry them around in case I want something sweet during the day, but it will help with a cough."

He nods and takes the candy, his trembling fingers unwrapping the paper.

Forman waits until the butterscotch is in his mouth and the coughing has receded to try again. "Why won't he be coming here anymore?"

Harry looks up at her, his eyes softer than before. "It was his last delivery. Michaels found someone new."

And that's why he stole the jewels. Not for the money but perhaps out of spite. "Did you see him often?"

He pulls the toothpick from his mouth, stands up, and spits just outside the door, immediately placing the toothpick back in his lips on the other side from the candy. "Oh, he'd bring a supply every week, sometimes more if there was a party."

"Is there anyone else who was here last Thursday? Outside of the staff?"

He shakes his head and rolls the sweet over his tongue. "He's the only one who came here that day."

"For a delivery."

He nods.

"And he was delivering . . . ?"

"You're a cop—you figure it out."

Forman looks up at the large house, the facts ticking through her mind. He came once a week, more if there was a party. A mansion where opulent parties are thrown. And it becomes clear. "Alcohol?"

Harry doesn't react, but his eyes glisten, and she knows she's hit the mark. "I don't think we need to talk about that. They mind their business, and you mind yours."

"Of course. But do you know where I can find him? What part of the city?" Forman is hoping for something specific like an address, but even a general area will help.

Harry tilts his head and removes the toothpick, the wood wet and shiny. "I ain't helping nobody with that. Or anything else." He puts the toothpick back in his mouth, sits down, crosses his arms, and focuses his attention down the street.

CHAPTER ELEVEN

LETTY

Margaret walks at a fast clip as I follow alongside her down Hollywood Boulevard, dodging businessmen leaving their offices, eager to get home.

"Don't you have to get back to the dress shop?"

"No, I closed up for the day. I was coming by to chat with Pop, and there you were. And before you go thinking that I'm doing you a big favor, I was coming here anyway." She smiles, her pace increasing. "Only a little bit farther."

"Good," I reply, though I can feel my stomach tighten with nerves.

We turn down the next street and then down a dim alley between two tall buildings, their height blocking a great deal of the remaining daylight. A newspaper ruffles in the breeze, dancing along the asphalt, but other than that, the area is swept clean.

And we are alone.

There's only one reason to go down an alley. "A speakeasy," I venture.

Margaret glances at me. "Look at you, country girl, you already know."

"I'm wiser than you realize, Margie. You moved away a long time ago."

"It's only Margaret now." She grins and starts counting as she walks, stopping when she reaches twenty. There's a nondescript door, like the others in the alley, without even a handle, but I can see the outline in the wall.

"You have the password?"

"Of course. But they change it all the time."

"And how does one find out the new password?"

"I have my ways." Margaret knocks twice in quick succession, pauses, then gives a single knock.

A small peephole, the size of a pair of glasses, opens in the door.

"The president," whispers Margaret.

The peephole closes.

Nothing happens.

A cold breeze funnels through the alley, and I rub my arms as we wait for the door to open.

"Strange," says Margaret. "A customer today told me the new password was 'the president.'"

She repeats the pattern with two knocks, a pause, then a single one. The hole reopens.

"The president," she repeats.

It closes.

I look over my shoulder to see if anyone else is coming down the alley so that we can hear them say the password, but we're alone. We stand in silence as I go over the words in my mind. And then it clicks. "Let me try."

"You're an expert suddenly?"

"Maybe." I move past her and repeat the knock rhythm.

The slit opens again.

"Calvin Coolidge."

It closes, followed by the sound of a sliding bolt.

"Well done, Letty. You're smart. You know, you should come to the city more. We could hang out more often."

I laugh. "Maybe we will," I say nervously as I step into a dark hallway, past a man sitting guard who shuts the door behind us. A thin line glows ahead, the outline of another door.

"Always dark before the light, my old friend," adds Margaret, as if she can read my thoughts.

We move down the hallway, my boots and her heels echoing on the tile. We reach the door, the muffled sound of music coming through it.

It opens to a large room with a low ceiling, the space filled with people dancing in dresses that sparkle and high-class tailored suits, while others stand with a cocktail in one hand, a cigarette in the other. Only one woman, seated at a round table, glances at us as we enter, a lace headband across her forehead.

Curved booths line the right side of the room beneath polished wood paneling interspersed with patterned burgundy-and-gold wallpaper. Chandeliers with jewels looped from them are every few feet, casting a glow on the smoke that hangs in the room as girls swirl around the dance floor. On the left, a band with a bass player, trombonist, saxophonist, and drummer sits on a small stage surrounded by red velvet curtains, a vacant piano nearby. The four musicians are in the middle of a jazzy tune, one that has most of the crowd dancing. A girl in a purple-and-silver dress near the front is doing the shimmy, a number often banned in dance halls, her movements causing the fringe from her dress to flap back and forth.

This is not a small speakeasy or one of the ad hoc setups I've heard about. Margaret has clearly taken me to one of the best. A hidden realm, shut off from the rest of the city, where music and alcohol meet without a care for the outside world.

"Welcome to fun, Letty!" Margaret shouts above the roar of the band. "It's about time you let loose." She loops her arm in mine, and we move through the crowd.

A few faces look familiar, as if I've seen them on the screen when my mother and I have been to the movies, but I'm not sure. Everything is new.

The music slows, and couples pair up to dance. We weave around them, dodging the small round tables in this part of the room as we make our way to the bar at the far end of the club. A man stands at the polished wood counter that reflects the lights, a large selection of bottles behind him. There's a wooden overhang, but it's missing the detail found in the rest of the room, the edge of it flat and abrupt.

Then I notice that the wood above it matches the paneling on the other walls. It's a fake front that will come down in case of a raid. Clever.

"Did you miss me?" Margaret taps on the counter and grins at the man behind the bar, his curly brown hair and full beard framing a tanned smile.

"Glad to see you're back. You brought a friend." He puts out his hand. "Otto."

"Letty." I shake it, his grip strong but his palm slightly sweaty.

"It's Letty's first time in a speakeasy," Margaret says with a giggle. "She might have some questions for you."

"Uh-oh. Another one converted. Well, welcome to what we call the Nine." He fans his hands out at the bar in front of him, the bottles behind him, and then around at the dancers.

"The Nine?"

"It's because we figure we have nine lives, like a cat, before we're shut down." His eyes glisten as he grabs two glasses from the counter and puts them in front of us. "So, what can I get you on your first day on the other side of dry?"

"Oh, she isn't dry," says Margaret. "She makes wine. Legitimately, church and everything," she adds with a note of pride, even though everything has changed.

"Made wine," I correct.

"Ah, one of those. So why your first time?" He shifts his attention to Margaret. "You trying to keep us secret from paying customers?" he says with a smile. "Saving the fun all for yourself?"

"Otto, you know that's not true."

He smiles, wipes the bar with a white cloth, and looks at both of us. "Well, what will it be tonight?"

"Something swell," Margaret replies. "Your choice."

"And you?" He looks at me. "I'd offer you wine, but you can have that anytime. I'd recommend something different, like jag juice."

"You have wine here, too?"

"We have everything. Pick your poison."

I don't normally drink. Not even my own wine. I only taste it to make sure it's developing well. But a lot has happened today, given the cancellation of the church contract and the discovery of my father's secret supply. Today has changed everything. "Your choice," I say.

"Look at you, Letty Hart." Margaret puts her hands up to her eyes like glasses. "I'm not sure I even recognize you."

"It's been a long day."

Otto flips the glass in his hand and winks, reaching for the bottles behind him.

"Nice shoes there," says a man in his midthirties, his blond hair slicked back. His suit is expensive, I can see, and he wears a smirk along with it.

"Thanks," I reply as I glance down at my well-worn boots from the winery. "They do the job."

"And what job is that?" He leans on the bar. "I haven't seen you here before."

"Then you haven't been looking."

He laughs, clearly amused. "Can you dance in those?"

I've barely danced in my life, but I might be able to mimic the couples on the floor. "Maybe the next song."

He looks at Margaret. "What about you? Or are you not a dancer like Bootsy here?"

The comment makes me laugh. I've never had a real nickname before. Letty, short for Loretta, is as close as I've gotten. But I like the sound of Bootsy.

"I'm game," says Margaret. "But I have to pay for our drinks first."

He tosses a few bills on the bar. "Your giggle juice is taken care of. Dance?"

She takes his arm, and they strut to the dance floor.

Otto is pouring a few different drinks, his hands quick and seasoned. I look at the bottles lined up behind the bar. Whiskey, gin, brandy, and wine. "You have a lot of choices there."

"Have to keep the customers happy." Otto pours a glass of wine and hands it to a fellow who hasn't even ordered but nods when he receives it and puts money on the counter.

"You know their orders already."

"The regulars, yes. Unless they want to change things up." He fills a silver container with alcohol from different bottles and shakes it, almost to the beat of the music. He pours the golden liquid into two small glasses and pushes one toward me, then puts one where Margaret had been standing. "Welcome to the real heart of the city, Letty. It's a wild ride."

I stare at the drink in front of me. "What is it?"

"A sidecar. Brandy, triple sec, lemon juice."

"Brandy? You don't say." I smile and pick up the glass.

Couples dance back and forth alongside Margaret and her new friend, their movements lively and fast, and I find myself bobbing to the music as I watch them, the illegal cocktail in my hand. So this is what the city has been doing at night while I've been trying to scrape by.

I bring the glass to my lips and take a sip. It's tart, the lemon threatening to overpower the brandy. The second taste is smoother, but I pause after that, not wanting to impair my judgment in this world I've only just entered.

There's a continual flow of customers coming to the bar to order drinks, handing over more money than I've seen all year.

"I never realized how much money is made from . . . what did you call it? Jag juice?"

"People want what they want, and they're willing to pay for it."

A man orders two sidecars, and Otto makes them with ease. The couple toast each other before retreating to a table in the corner.

"Aren't you worried about being arrested?"

"Again, the nine lives. But all those guys are paid off anyway."

I swallow hard and decide it's now or never. "If I had, say, a barrel of brandy I needed to get rid of, would you be a person that could make that happen?"

Otto's eyes flash with recognition, but then he turns away and wipes down the pristine counter again. "We don't talk about that in here."

Just then, Margaret comes off the dance floor, a delicate line of perspiration on her forehead. "Letty, how come you're not dancing?" she asks.

"I was hoping to find, um, someone."

A wide-eyed smile appears on Margaret's face. "You can find people and still have fun." She glances at Otto. "OK, so here's the deal. Letty needs a little help. Someone to make some deals. I know you can make that happen, point her in the right direction."

Otto shakes his head and continues wiping the bar.

"Otto, you can tell us. You know me, and Letty here is like a vault. I told her this would be a great place to, well, move some product."

"We can't buy it; you know we can't."

She moves forward and taps her gloved finger on the bar. "I know you can't, but you know someone who can."

Otto locks eyes with me, as if he's debating whether he can trust what he sees.

"Just one barrel," I say. "A quick deal."

Otto waits to respond until another couple has moved away from the bar. "Shorty Paulson."

"Shorty," I repeat, but Otto puts his finger to his lips. "He's the bootlegger in the booth over there, the black hat with the white band. He's the supplier here."

I turn to get a look, but my attention falls not on the booth but on a familiar face walking toward me through the swirls of cigarette smoke. A face I never thought I would see in a speakeasy. Charles.

CHAPTER TWELVE

LETTY

I step forward to get his attention, and it takes a moment for him to recognize me. "Letty?" His face lights up, and he approaches. "I didn't expect to see you here."

"The surprise is mutual. Father O'Leary know you're here?"

He shakes his head. "I have nights off. Besides, I'm allowed to go out."

"To illegal places?"

"In case you've forgotten, I don't work for the police."

I nod, but as I look around, I realize they're probably in here, too.

Charles leans forward. "Letty, what are you really doing here? Your father wouldn't approve."

"My father doesn't get an opinion anymore—"

"I leave you alone for one minute," interrupts Margaret as she sidles up to us, "and you've already snagged a beau."

"Not exactly. Do you remember Charles? He grew up near us."

Margaret looks at him, and her eyes go wide. "Charlie One Shoe!"

Charles turns a shade of red, and my hand is already over my mouth to hide a giggle. Poor Charles lost his shoe one day at school and the nickname stuck.

"You grew up well," she says.

"I work for the church now." He stands up straighter and shifts his shoulders, as if trying to shake off the shoe memory.

The music changes, and the band launches into the upbeat "Charleston."

"Mind if I take Charlie for a spin?" asks Margaret as she glances at me.

Charles shifts awkwardly. "Oh, I wouldn't want to do that to Letty."

"No, it's fine," I reply. "You two go ahead."

"Come on, Charlie. It's been an age." They move to the dance floor, and I step back to the bar, but I catch Charles glancing over at me, like he feels bad that I'm standing here alone.

"Bartender," says a lady in a flapper's dress, the yellow color evoking the wild daffodils in the valley and matching the feather sticking out of her headband, "I want wine."

An older gentleman in a pressed suit puts his arms around her. "What's this, my darling?"

"I want to order wine," she repeats, tapping on the bar to get Otto's attention.

"Sir, the lady has a request."

"Coming up," Otto mutters.

The gentleman nuzzles his face into her neck. "You like the wine here, darling?"

"It's the bee's knees. Best in the city." She looks at me. "I've tried a lot."

Otto pours her a glass of red wine, and the two of them move to one of the nearby tables.

I push my drink onto the bar, barely any of it gone. "Wine is popular tonight."

"Everything is popular," replies Otto. "The people here drink everything you've heard of and many things you haven't. But the regulars, they're like the waves on the ocean, always the same. It's part of their routine, and they don't know any different."

Margaret is kicking up her heels with Charles, her movements fluid, while his are awkward and out of step, as if he's never danced before.

"Margaret comes here a lot, doesn't she?"

"Not as much as others, but more than some. She brings a fun energy when she does, though."

"What about him?" I motion to Charles.

"Can't say I've seen him before, but there are always new faces."

They keep dancing, but the tune won't last forever, and while Margaret has Charles distracted, it's time to meet Shorty.

"So," I say to Otto. "Mr. Paulson, first booth?"

"Yep."

I look over at the booth. "Bootleggers are pretty dangerous, aren't they?"

"You could say that. Worried?"

"Never." I leave the bar, grabbing my drink before I do, and move toward the booth in the corner. It's darker than the others, as if someone has purposefully dimmed the light above it. It has the best view of the entire room, though, I notice.

Shorty Paulson wears a fedora slanted to the right and a fitted white vest beneath his black suit, and he holds a cigar between two fingers in his left hand. A woman in a pale-green dress sits at his side, and a large man, nearly too big for his coat, stands near the table. His hands are crossed in front of him, ready to punch someone if they get too close or look at Shorty the wrong way, I imagine.

But I don't let that deter me.

Shorty has a glass near him on the table, the amber-colored ice the only remnant of his drink.

"It's a good evening for a party," I say, approaching the booth.

He turns to look at me. "Agreed." He looks me up and down for a beat, and then says, "I don't believe we've met."

"Letty Hart." I extend my hand and he shakes it.

"Shorty Paulson." He looks back out at the crowd and takes a long puff of his cigar. "I don't think I've seen you here before." His top lip barely moves as he speaks.

"I came with a friend."

"Which one?"

"In a room full of your friends, clearly one of yours." I raise my glass a little to him.

He looks me over again. "You know, you don't dress like a woman."

"You don't dress like a bootlegger."

His guard, standing nearby, laughs. "Shorty, she knows who you are."

Shorty ignores him, keeping his attention on me. "I dress how I want."

"So do I."

A smile appears on his lips, revealing a gap between his two front teeth. "OK then." He whispers to the lady next to him, and she stares up at me as she slides out of the booth. "And what do you do, Letty Hart, that brings you to this speakeasy?"

I survey the room, too: the couples chatting with each other, the large group dancing, and Otto behind the bar. "I'm a winemaker," I say, taking a sip of the cocktail in my hand, the lemon still puckering my lips.

"I'm not looking for a wine supplier," responds Shorty, his eyes on the dance floor.

"I didn't offer."

He nods approvingly. "I was wrong. You do belong here. What kind of wine?"

"Sacramental, out in the valley."

"Letty . . ." He pauses. "I've heard of you."

"Possibly. But that's not why I'm here." I take another drink. "I'm looking for some advice."

"Nothing is free."

"Nothing ever is."

He waves his hand at the room. "You're here, so at least I know where you stand."

66

"My presence tonight doesn't prove anything, and also, I'd like to sit."

Shorty smiles, his mouth closed this time. "You're a funny one. That will serve you well." He motions to the seat next to him. I slide into the booth. Charles and Margaret have moved to this side of the dance floor, and Charles is watching me, his movements slowing as he does.

"I have something that might interest you. A barrel of high-quality brandy." Instead of avoiding eye contact with Shorty, as I'm sure he would prefer, I stare him straight in the eye.

He perks up. "Brandy, you say? Where?"

"That's for me to know. Are you interested?"

The bootlegger picks up his glass and tries to pour whatever has melted off the ice into his mouth. He's in no hurry, but he's not the only one who can wait. I take another sip of my drink.

He places his glass back on the table, takes a deep breath, and says, "You want to sell me this brandy?"

"Possibly. I need to sell it to someone. You're my first choice."

"I'm honored."

"Don't be. You happened to be in the first place I looked."

Shorty grins again. "We'll get along well. I tell you what, there's a garage at the corner of Selma and Vine. Bring some of your brandy there tomorrow morning, say, at ten, and we'll see if we can make a deal."

"Why don't we make a deal right now?"

He laughs. "You think that's how this works? I have to taste the product first, doll. It needs to be quality for me to buy it. Tomorrow morning. Come alone. Don't show? I'll come to your place, and believe me, you don't want that."

The large man standing to the side chuckles.

Shorty taps the table twice, and I know it's my cue to leave.

I stand and move toward the bar.

"And Letty?"

I turn around.

"Don't be late."

CHAPTER THIRTEEN

RAYMOND

August Raymond pulls a drag from his cigarette, the smoke swirling in the air around him. It's freshly rolled, not one of the Lucky Strikes his friends buy, persuaded by the advertisements. The creasing of the paper, the sprinkling of the tobacco—it's what he always does at moments like this. A routine familiar solely to him, those few minutes before the task at hand, when he's alone with the information and his cigarette. The only time he ever smokes.

The night air is cold, a dampness brought by the fog that crept in overhead from the ocean. It's quiet here, a nearby cricket producing a solemn chirp every so often, and in between drags of his cigarette, Raymond catches the sweet scent of whiskey rye floating in the air. This is definitely the right place.

Raymond tosses the stub to the ground, his uniform-issued shoe grinding the tobacco into the dirt, what's left of the paper now soiled and ready to fly away with the next breeze.

It's time.

He unbuttons his coat as he walks toward the door, the wooden building almost slanted in its construction, unable to keep out the rare California rain but capable of hiding the contents inside. Until tonight.

Raymond's gun feels warm as he takes it out, the handle heated by his torso and insulated by his coat.

He raises his hand to knock and almost smiles as the thought of breaking from his routine briefly crosses his mind. He lowers his hand. Business as usual.

One swift kick and the door flies open.

"Time's up, boys. Police," he says as he moves inside, his gun poised and ready for the group.

But there aren't many.

There aren't even a few.

Only one. A scrawny man in his forties with dark curly hair, dirt smudged on his face, and his clothes long past a wash. He scrambles back to the wall, moving loose straw with him as he does, but there's nowhere else to go. Raymond is at the only door, as if he planned it, but in reality, the lack of a second entrance or exit is a bonus point in his favor.

The scent of whiskey is thicker in here, and Raymond keeps the gun pointed at its maker, enjoying the moment of an animal caught in a trap, the only sound the still as it drips the amber liquid into a large barrel.

Drip.

Drip.

Drip.

The man puts his hands up and looks away, a grimace on his face, as if he's waiting for the bullet.

Laughter roars from Raymond. "Relax, I'm one of you." He puts his gun back in his holster and walks over to the still, a homemade copper contraption that is large and solid. "How many gallons do you get out of this?"

There's no reply. He glances at the bootlegger, whose face is marked with fear, his eyes wide and no movement in his chest, as if all breath has escaped him.

Raymond adjusts his glasses and presses on one of the tubes. "It's sturdy. You probably make good stuff. You have a good setup."

The man doesn't move. Eventually, he nods warily. "What did you mean when you said you're one of us?" His gravelly voice is marked with years of alcohol and hard living.

"Ah, I work for Blue. Perhaps you've heard of him?" says Raymond, who continues to inspect the tools in the workshop. "He's one of the biggest bootleggers in Los Angeles. I take care of business for him." He picks up a metal ladle, the side dented, the handle awkward. The formerly round cup is still slick with the sweet residue of fresh whiskey. He sniffs it, taking it in.

"But you're a dry," says the bootlegger.

Raymond lets out a one-note laugh, the scent of tobacco accompanying it. "You think he got to where he is on his own? We all need a little help. Even if it crosses our other duties."

The bootlegger stands, keeping his palms against the wall. He's taller than Raymond but spindly.

"What's your name?"

"Collins," he replies. "Walter Collins."

"Well, Collins, I'm August Raymond."

"Federal Agent August Raymond?"

"No, not one of those. Not even an officer tonight." Raymond picks up a bottle of whiskey from the four that line the edge of the wall near the still. "Mind if I?"

Collins, still uneasy, shakes his head.

Raymond opens it and waves it in front of his nose. "Yes, I was right. Blue, too. This is the real deal." He takes a swig, the taste of burnt wood and malt flowing into his mouth, chased immediately by the ever-pleasant burn of satisfaction. "That is excellent. You make this?"

Collins steps away from the wall, his hands sliding into his pockets as his shoulders get higher. "Yup."

"All by yourself?"

"Don't need anyone else but me."

"Good. It's easier that way." Raymond lowers himself onto a bale of straw, the bottle still in his hand. This is his second favorite moment, after the cigarette. The discussion. "Blue's always on the lookout for talented booze-makers. Men who know how to pull a real whiskey. It takes a solid hand, and I sort them out for him." He takes another swig from the bottle and puts it down, the cap barely resting on the rim. "I'm here to make you an offer." He waves his hand around. "To start, it would get you out of here."

"What if I don't want out of here?"

Raymond shrugs and crosses his leg across the other knee, the gun shifting on his hip as he does. "Blue is powerful. Can really take a guy places." He holds up the bottle. "You make stuff like this, he's definitely interested. Money, fame, power. It's all there, waiting for you."

Collins steps forward, the stench of sweat radiating from him.

Raymond stands up, but he's not worried. Collins is not a threat. "You only make whiskey, or you have more? The more, the better."

"I have more. I can show you."

"Great. Lead the way." Raymond motions to the door.

Collins grins, his crooked teeth framed by sunburnt lips. "Blue, huh? Who'd have thought it?"

"You're right," says Raymond. "Who'd have thought it?"

Collins walks out of the barn, Raymond only a step behind. The night air is just as still as it was when Raymond first arrived.

"I keep it over in my shed," says Collins.

"You don't say." Raymond puts his hand on the bootlegger's shoulder. "I'm so glad we met tonight, Collins. That it worked out for me to be here."

This is his third favorite moment.

Collins chuckles, his shoulder moving under Raymond's hand.

Raymond waits until Collins gets one more step in front of him before he swivels his palm at the back of Collins's neck and slams his other hand around the front. It's a swift motion as Raymond squeezes, the rough stubble digging into his hand, the breath draining from Collins before he even grasps what is happening. The struggle is fast at first, as limbs flail, but slows quickly.

Collins crumples to the ground.

Raymond glances around, stretching his neck from side to side before pulling his arms together, the release of a job well done.

He grabs the dead bootlegger's collar and drags his lifeless body toward his car.

CHAPTER FOURTEEN

LETTY

My mother prepares a Sunday roast in the kitchen, a soft hum as she works to prep for the day ahead. Even though it's just the two of us now, she always cooks a full Sunday dinner.

While she's preoccupied, I cross the property and climb into the secret room beneath the barn. The barrels are in front of me, all brimming with liquid money, but I can't take a whole barrel to Shorty's garage. Nor do I want to. Don't reveal all of the product. Besides, I only need some for him to taste.

I grab a wine bottle from the barn and fill it with brandy from one of the vats. But as I bring it out into the sunlight, it's too obvious. I need something more discreet.

It reminds me of the day when I came home from a fight at school. I pulled my cap away to show my father the bruise on my forehead.

"Put it back on," he said, shoving the hat down on my head. "You don't announce your troubles."

"But you already knew it happened."

"Doesn't matter."

He followed the same rule with wine. Even the truck doesn't have the winery's name on it. My father put it on there when he first bought the vehicle, but two years later, he removed it. Because when you're carrying something people want and will do anything to get, you don't advertise it. And although it has been scrubbed from the sides, I can still see HART WINERY when the sun hits at a certain angle.

I place the bottle on the driver's seat and head back to the house.

My mother smiles as I enter the kitchen, the truck keys in my hand. "Are you going out?"

"I am. But I'll be home before dinner."

Her smile fades. "What are you up to, Letty Hart?"

"Just looking out for the farm."

"Why do I think you're being dishonest?"

"Me?" I say as innocently as possible. "Not at all." My stomach clenches at the lie. She can't know I'm going to see a bootlegger. I'm all she has, and I don't want her to worry, even though the lie weighs on my shoulders.

I'll tell her as soon as the sale is over. When we have the money and this is all in the past. But I still need something to carry the bottle in. "I'm looking for a bag. Not a purse but a bag. One that can take some weight."

She stares at me silently, an expression I can't quite read on her face. "There's one in his closet. Richard's closet."

The mention of my father is like a punch to my gut. She never says his name, never talks about him. She closed the closet door the day after he left and hasn't opened it since.

"A leather bag," she continues as she stands at the sink, shaking her head but making no movement toward the closet. The thought of riffling through his belongings will bring back too many memories for her, I know that. And it will for me, too. But I don't have a choice. I need something to transport the bottle.

I enter the bedroom and open the closet door, the scent of his shaving soap still clinging to his belongings. He took only one thing that day—a canvas bag filled with some clothes—and walked away from everything in this life. I push the remaining clothes and memories aside and search until I find my father's leather satchel. Slung over his shoulder nearly every day, as he carried his tools in it while walking through the vineyard. The feel of the cracked leather against my palm brings a wave of conflicted memories. My time tending vines with him was good until the day he chose another family over us.

"Will that work?" My mother stands at the door, her arms crossed as she leans against the frame, her eyes marked with sadness.

I nod.

"I wish you would tell me where you're going." But she leaves the room before I have a chance to answer. Probably knowing I won't.

The moment leaves me feeling unsettled, and I follow her. She's back to working on the potatoes in the kitchen. I can't lie to her again. "I found someone who will buy some of the brandy."

The potato drops out of her hand, rolling around in the sink. "Letty, no. We talked about this. You were going to hammer it closed."

"One barrel, that's all. And it's safe." The lie stings, but I swallow it away like thick cough syrup.

"No." She picks up the potato and scrubs at it, her jagged and forceful movements revealing her emotions. "I don't like this."

"I know, but if we don't do something . . ."

She looks up at me, her eyes glistening and wet. "We'll get by."

"On what? Peaches? They won't pay the bills, and you know it. And I'm not going to let everything slip out of our fingers, everything that you and I have worked for."

She doesn't look up at me again, and I know it's time to leave. I can't be late, but I still don't like the idea of taking the brandy in a bottle, even with the leather satchel to hide it. My eyes land on the cans of peaches on the shelf and the small size of their metal containers, which hide the contents. "I'm going to do some canning before I go."

She doesn't reply, and her silence increases the pain in my stomach.

I leave the house, catching the screen door with my foot, even though there's no reason to hide the noise. But still, I want it to be quiet. For her.

The area where my mother cans is perfectly organized, empty cans on the left, their fronts adorned with the painted labels she creates every year. This version has a large yellow peach in the center, the leaves still attached, and the words FRUIT OF THE HART FARM above it.

The lever to seal the cans is on the table in the middle of the area. The one she bought when the winery was thriving years ago, as a way to can tins like the ones at the grocery store. She wanted the peach business to be bigger. We both did. But nothing turned out how we planned.

I pour enough brandy from the bottle into a can to almost fill it and place it under the lever, lining up the lid. My hand grips the lever, but I don't move. I've never canned before. It is her project. But I've watched it enough times.

Except the cans are never this full. And this is all liquid, not peaches. I pour some of it into another can, leaving a small gap at the top.

I ready the lever and slam it down, sealing the can, waiting for the brandy to spray out. Except it doesn't.

I pick it up and shake it, the liquid sloshing about inside, the contents completely hidden. The perfect way to move the brandy without anyone knowing what it is.

I can four more and slip all five into the leather bag, along with some of the cans containing peaches, just in case.

The house is silent, the screen door still closed. I step back inside and into the kitchen to say goodbye.

My mother looks up, her face drawn, as if the last few years have been a culmination of tragedy and today is the final straw.

"I have to. If I don't try, we'll lose everything."

"Who are you going to see?" she asks.

"A friend." I look at her, our eyes locked on each other. "Do you really want to know?"

She shakes her head and doesn't look up again.

This time she doesn't wait in the driveway for me to leave.

CHAPTER FIFTEEN

FORMAN

Forman didn't speak to any of the other officers at the morning roll call. Even when Warrenson seemed to wait for her to give him an update, she stayed silent. Because there was nothing to update. Not yet.

But now the shifts have begun and she's still here, the weight of failure pressing heavily on her. She glances around the station: two officers dealing with phone calls, another one taking a public complaint from a well-dressed couple, and then there's Beaucamp at his desk, a newspaper in his hands. Beaucamp, the one who made the comment about her failing at the case so she wouldn't bother Warrenson anymore. But he's also a detective who sometimes helps Raymond with Prohibition detail.

"Beaucamp, if I wanted to find out about a bootlegger, would you be able to help me?"

His attention remains on his newspaper, his flat cap, the one he says he prefers to wear as it's easier to chase suspects, though Forman hasn't heard of him chasing one yet, pulled down close to his face. "That's Raymond's territory," he replies.

"Yes, but he's not here right now. And you are."

Beaucamp keeps reading, the paper balanced on his bloated stomach. "Aren't you supposed to be finding some jewels or something?"

"Working on it. But I need to know where a certain bootlegger lives. Or works. Or whatever they do. Can you help?"

He glances up. "What's in it for me?"

Forman curls her upper lip and then realizes it, pressing her lips together instead. "Helping out a fellow officer. And when you needed that paperwork filed last year, I was the one who did it." She'd done it for a few of the officers during a particularly busy week, staying late to get it done, the excitement of closing cases taking precedence over preparing dinner for her father and aunt. They'd celebrated during the delayed dinner, knowing that the crimes were solved and the victims had resolution.

Beaucamp doesn't move, but his eyes remain on Forman.

"I'll do next week's paperwork, too," she offers, knowing that this is her best lead at the moment.

He folds the newspaper down and tosses it on the desk. "Current bootlegger or former bootlegger?"

"I don't know. I only know his name is Thomas."

"They don't go by names like Thomas. They have other names. What else do you have?"

She pauses, but she doesn't need to reach for her notebook. She knows the answer. "Only Thomas."

He picks up his newspaper. "You're out of luck, Forman."

"Please. I need this."

Beaucamp looks up and then frowns, his green eyes becoming obscured by his brow. "Get me another name, his nickname. Preferably a full name, too. Then I'll help you out."

Forman waits, but the conversation is over, Beaucamp's attention back on the news of the day. She needs someone who knows people, knows the major players in Hollywood, and knows how to take a clue like "Thomas" and get a full name.

She walks away, passing Warrenson as she does.

"Find the necklace, Forman?" He flashes a fake smile, taunting her.

"Not yet. But soon." She grabs her bag and moves toward the door.

❦

It's a little too early for patrons to visit the Rosewood, the taxi dance hall where women are paid to dance with men, but a line has already formed outside the building. Tickets are sold for ten cents each, and the women earn money on every ticket they collect, spending their afternoons and evenings spinning around the dance floor.

But Forman isn't here for the hall. She's here for the surrounding area. She's patrolled these streets for the last two years, and she knows the girls and their routines. When Forman joined the force, her duty was to interview female suspects and female victims. For two years, she's done just that, and she's hoping that time will serve her well now.

She leans against the Rosewood building and stares at the narrow street off the main Hollywood thoroughfares, not far from the movie studios. There's a bakery on this side next to the hall, the scent of freshly baked bread filling the air, and across the way is a hardware store, a bank, and a family diner, the front windows of which advertise coffee, doughnuts, hamburgers, and soup.

It only takes an hour until Ruthie shows up. She lives on the street and was beat up a year ago by a still-unidentified man who robbed her of the money a kind passerby had given her. Forman was the one who took the report and the one who helped her get back on her feet.

Ruthie trusts Forman, or at least she used to.

This time she's not alone. A taller blonde girl is with her. She looks as rough as Ruthie does, their hair tangled, their clothes slightly torn and smudged with dirt, yet both wear red blush and lipstick perfectly applied.

Forman waits until they're closer, standing near the dance hall, before she approaches. "Ruthie." Her voice cracks as she says her name.

Ruthie looks up, the scowl on her face disappearing as she recognizes her. "Annabel Forman. Nice to see you."

Forman smiles at the other girl and then refocuses her attention on Ruthie. "How are you holding up?"

"I'm doing fine. Some days are better than others."

Forman nods. Ruthie's healed from the wounds inflicted that day last year, eye shadow where the black eye used to be, her nose unswollen and uncut. But Forman knows not all scars are visible on the outside.

"We're still searching for him, you know. Following the clues."

Ruthie shakes her head with a laugh. "There aren't any clues. It's done. Don't worry about it."

"You know I do."

She stares at Forman. "Is that why you're here? Checking in on us?"

"Not exactly." Forman pauses. "I have a favor. I'm looking for someone."

The blonde friend moves to the other side of the street, her exit silent and quick.

"You scared her away," says Ruthie.

"Apparently."

"Girls don't like cops around here. They think they're trying to help by finding us for our families or people from a while back, but the truth is, most of us don't want to be found."

"I'm not here about any of them." Forman retains eye contact with Ruthie, hoping to keep the connection going. "I'm looking for a man named Thomas, and I thought you might be able to help."

"Thomas? Don't know him."

"He goes by a different name. He's into"—she pauses as she thinks how to phrase it—"illicit liquor."

"I thought you investigated women crimes, Forman."

"This is different. Can you help? I need to know where he is or, if not that, at least the name he goes by. The nickname."

Ruthie glances around the area, her fingers running up and down the piping of her faded dress. "Why did you come to me?"

"Because you know people. And you tell the truth."

Ruthie shifts her eyes to the ground. "I'm not a snitch."

"Never said you were." She's thinner than Forman remembers. "When was the last time you ate?"

Ruthie shrugs.

Forman pulls out the little money she has, a few coins from her bag, and places them in Ruthie's hand. "Get something to eat."

Ruthie stares at the coins. "Is this for food or because you want information?"

"For food." Forman's statement is clear and strong. She doesn't break the rules. Not ever. "If you can't find out who Thomas is, that's fine. But I want to make sure you're OK and you get fed."

Ruthie folds her fingers over the coins. "Thanks." She glances back at her friend, then meets Forman's eyes. "You have anything besides a first name?"

"He did deliveries at a mansion near the Hollywoodland sign. Beachwood Canyon. They throw lots of parties." She looks at Ruthie. "Please eat. You have the money now. Come on, we'll go over to the diner together."

"I can't be seen with you, Forman. You'll ruin my reputation. After all, it's a swell one." She winks. "Will you stick around?"

"I'll be here for a bit."

"Be a while. I'll be back." She steps away but turns around. "Don't follow me. Stay right here."

"You know I will."

"I know, Forman. You're a good one." She smiles and walks down the block, disappearing behind the diner.

Forman returns to her lean against the wall of the Rosewood as she keeps an eye on the people walking through the area. It's a stark contrast—those with money mingling with those who have none. Like Ruthie. And her friend, who hovers in the doorway of the hardware store, watching her from under the side of her torn fascinator. Forman doesn't blame her for staying away from her. It's tough out here, and she wishes she could help. And maybe she can. Once she makes detective.

The dance hall is open now, and gentlemen in their pressed suits move through the line, ready to enter.

"You stayed. I'm glad."

Forman turns and there's Ruthie, already back, her hands empty.

"Did you eat?"

"I will." She pats the small bag she carries around her wrist, the coins moving inside it. "In a few minutes, I promise. With my friend."

Forman nods and glances at the hardware store. "She's pretty wary of me."

"Of course she is. She's smart."

"Put in a good word for me, OK?"

Ruthie smiles with tight lips as she lowers her head, her eyes focused on Forman, a mischievous glow to them. "Why, Forman? You trying to make friends now?"

"Something like that." Forman looks over at the young woman and then back at Ruthie. She takes the last coin out of her pocket, a nickel, and hands it to Ruthie. "This is for your friend."

"Thanks." She keeps it in her palm. "The man you're looking for is Rudy."

"Rudy? I said Thomas. Give me my nickel back." She jokes, but the idea of another dead end makes her stomach turn.

Ruthie steps back, a grin on her face. "Thomas 'Rudy' Rudinsky. He delivered to the Michaelses' place. That's the one you mean in Beachwood, right?"

"Yes. How did you find out so fast?"

"I have my ways, Forman. You have yours."

CHAPTER SIXTEEN

LETTY

The truck hums along the road, and though I'm used to carrying grapes and wine, this time it's different. I have a certificate for the wine, but I don't have anything for the brandy. If I'm caught, I could end up in jail, my mother without the money to bail me out and our chance of keeping the farm gone before it even began.

I've left my rifle at home, the chamber still empty, but I've brought the small club I started carrying when I deliver wine to the church. It's about a foot long, with woven leather covering the piece of wood inside and a looped strap at the end. It fits inside the deep pocket of my pants, along with my pocketknife, which is always with me. Although no match for a gun, they are at least something, and I'm not about to walk into a bootlegger's garage empty handed.

Hollywood approaches, as does a police car waiting on the side of Cahuenga. The cop stands next to it, watching as I pass, and a surge of adrenaline goes through me. The cans of brandy are mixed in with the cans of peaches, and they are out of sight, but the thought of having an illegal substance in the truck makes me nervous.

The address Shorty gave me is not far from the center of Hollywood, and as I continue along, the number of restaurants and hotels increases, as does the number of people. If this is his territory, he has all of Hollywood in his hand.

I pull onto Vine, park near the corner, and sling the leather satchel over my shoulder and across my body.

The red sign out front reads QUADLING GARAGE. Quadling, a reference to the southern division in *The Wonderful Wizard of Oz*, where Glinda, the good witch, lives. It makes me smile, but my hands tremble, the nerves still evident. I squeeze them together as I walk toward the garage.

Inside is a maroon 1926 Cadillac, like the kind celebrities own and drive slowly down the boulevard to give fans a view of the luxury their movie ticket purchases afford.

This car won't need repairs for years, and even though the walls of the garage are lined with tools, probably from a previous owner, the vehicle is angled in a way to hide whatever is behind it.

I take a deep breath and move past the Cadillac, its slick sides free of any dirt and grit. It doesn't travel the types of roads I do. It stays in the city or perhaps barely moves at all.

Behind the car is a larger room with some more untouched tools and Shorty sitting at a desk. The large man from last night is at his side and stands as I enter, a gun in his hands.

I reach for my club, but I know it's no use, and I weigh my options: stay or run away. But I keep my feet firmly planted on the ground. This is what I came for, though it's hard to convince my racing heart of that.

"Down, boy," Shorty says as he motions for the man to sit. "This is the one from the Nine. I asked her to come."

It takes a few seconds, but the guard slinks back into his seat.

"You're here," says Shorty.

"I keep my word."

"So do I." He glances at my satchel. "Did you bring a sample?"

I pull out a can of peaches, though I can tell by the weight—this one has the booze.

"Only one?"

I take out another can. "Don't flatter yourself."

He smiles, the gap between his front teeth showing. "You're going to do well. Take a seat."

I sit down in the chair and place both cans on the desk, keeping my satchel across my body in case I need to run.

Shorty picks one up and shakes it. "Hidden in a peach can. Clever." He pulls a screwdriver from the desk, one that looks sharper than it needs to be, pierces the can, and sniffs at the new opening. "Did you make this?"

"I came by it legally, if that's what you're asking."

"I'm not. Only wondering if you're the maker." He pours the amber liquid into a glass.

"I can be."

Shorty takes a long drink, the guard watching his every move. He leans back and looks at the glass, swirling the brandy around as it climbs the side. "Not bad."

"You know it's better than that."

He grins. "Apparently you do, too." He pours the rest into the glass, tossing the can into the trash bin a few feet away. It lands inside easily. Shorty takes another sip, swirling the glass again after it's left his lips. "This is good. I approve."

I lean forward. "So we have a deal? You'll buy it?"

"I didn't say that. Yet." He looks at me as if he's calculating the price of the brandy or how easy it would be to kill me. I can't decide which. "If you're going to become one of us, you'll need a nickname," he says. "What do people call you?"

"I'm not one of you. I'm just making a sale. And people call me Letty."

He nods. "Do they call you anything else?"

A smile crosses my lips. "Someone last night called me Bootsy."

"No, not that. What do you do for fun?"

I give a half shrug, thinking of the wine, tending the vines. "I shoot cans."

"You good?"

"Not bad."

"You're lying."

I relax my jaw. "I don't miss."

"I thought so," says Shorty. "You're a marksman. Now you're Marks."

"I prefer Letty."

"Whatever you say, Marks." He reaches into the desk and pulls out a thick green ledger book as long as his forearm and about half as wide.

"The way things work here is that trust is important. It's key in this business. Without it, you're out of luck. You trusted me to come here today. Now I need to know if I can trust you." He flips open the ledger until he reaches the middle of the white pages.

"What do you mean you can't trust me?" I glance at the guard next to him. "How do I know I can trust you?"

Shorty writes something on one of the lines in the book. "You can't, but that's not the issue here. You're new, I'm not." He leans back in his chair and puts his feet up on the desk, the bottom of his shoes faded and worn, a squashed cigarette on the heel of the left one. "But here's what's going to happen. I'm going to give you a simple test. If you pass, I'll know I can trust you. And I'll buy your barrel of brandy."

A test. Like hitting the cans off the fence posts as a kid. Or like my dad wanting me to shoot the birds. A test that I failed.

"If you don't want my brandy," I say, "I'll find somewhere else. You're not the only game in town."

Shorty laughs, the sound echoing through the empty garage. "You have spunk. I like that. And there are less options than you think. No one will work with your ilk. You think the others will buy from a woman? Try again. Trust, Letty. Trust. No one is going to trust you walking in somewhere, trying to sell. They'll think you're a setup, a plant from the police. But I see something good in you. It's a simple test. If I can trust you, then your one barrel, or"—he pauses—"however much more you decide you want to sell to me, we'll proceed and things will be good."

I don't like the amount of time this errand is taking. I thought it would be easier and I would already be on the way home. "What's the test?"

"Good." He nods. "I'm going to give you an order. I have a delivery for a friend in town. He's a new customer and wants a few cases for a party this afternoon. You'll deliver it for me. Help me out and I'll help you."

"I don't need that much help."

He pulls some bills from his coat and tosses them on the desk. "I'll bet ten clams you don't."

The bills are slightly unfolding, the stack of them fanning out. Ten dollars would go a long way right now. But delivering alcohol is a lot riskier than simply selling at one place to a bootlegger. I reach for them, but Shorty grabs them from the desk.

"Ah, not yet. That's for when you get back. After you do the delivery."

"What if I get caught?"

Shorty smiles, though it's more of a smirk, his lips closed as he looks at me with his beady eyes. "You won't. You're a woman. Only a woman cop can search a woman, and we only have a few of those."

I look at the money and shift the cans in my bag. Extra money would be nice.

"Where do I have to go?"

CHAPTER SEVENTEEN

LETTY

A guard is waiting outside the gates as I arrive at the address Shorty provided. There's a clipboard in his hands as he approaches the truck, and I go through the rehearsed dialogue from Shorty. "I'm bringing the meat and potatoes for Mr. Michaels."

The guard nods, his gaze not even falling on the clipboard, and opens the gate. "Sure. Enjoy the party."

I pull into the driveway, my truck sputtering as it climbs the steep slope next to the manicured lawn dotted with fruit trees. The noise strikes worry in my chest, but I reach the house without issue, the ionic columns coming into view.

The front door is wide open, ready for the afternoon guests to arrive. I climb out, leaving the delivery in the truck.

In the event that this is a trap, either by Shorty or the police, I don't want to risk being seen with the bottles. All three cases of gin, rum, and whiskey are in orange crates, and two bags of bottles are stowed in potato sacks. The code should have been "oranges and potatoes."

I stop at the entryway threshold, my pants and cotton shirt making me feel even more out of place in contrast to the mansion's lavish interior. I have a dress or two at home but haven't worn them in years, the winery work taking over my life and my wardrobe. I have no desire to change that.

I knock with two quick raps, as if I'm doing the secret code of the speakeasy, and wait, looking out at the view.

Catalina, the island off the coast, is visible from here, as is a lot of the city. Whatever Mr. Michaels does, it pays well. Soft music plays from another room, the crackle of the record accompanying the notes.

But no one comes.

I don't want to enter uninvited. I don't know the routine. But if I wait longer, the guests might arrive, and Shorty's specific note was to make sure I was gone before they got there.

I worry the music is drowning out my knocks, so I do them again, louder this time, in hopes that Mr. Michaels hears me.

A woman wearing dark eye makeup appears from one of the far rooms. Her hair is pinned in curls that remind me of an actress I saw when I snuck into the pictures last year.

"Yes?" she says, looking me up and down. My baggy pants are a far cry from her corseted dress and tapered sleeves. I am clearly not a guest. "What do you want?"

"I have a delivery for Mr. Michaels," I reply calmly, though I'm feeling anything but. I don't belong here.

"Nick? You have, um, a visitor!" she yells upstairs. "Take care of this quickly. Guests will be here soon, and you know I don't approve of these distractions before my party."

"Who is it?" asks a distinguished man in his sixties coming down the stairs in an expensive suit, freshly pressed. He stops in the middle of the staircase as his eyes lock with mine. "Who are you?"

"I'm here for Shorty."

"Oh, you. You should have been here earlier."

I worry I've lost the sale by arriving late, though I came here right from Shorty's and don't think I could have driven any faster. "I'm here before the guests, and I have your delivery, Mr. Michaels." My voice is flat and strong.

He grimaces. "Bring everything around to the back. Follow the driveway to the far side, leave it by the garage." He turns away, and I know I'm not supposed to follow him.

I drive the truck around to a garage, which I'm sure is filled with expensive cars, and line up the delivery along the wall.

The guests have arrived, at least a few of them, as I can hear their singsong voices as they exit their cars at the front of the house. I move around the side, catching a peek at the women in their long gowns and the men in their tall hats that add a few more inches to their height. They might even be film stars, though it's too hard to tell from this distance.

This is the life. Opulent parties in luxurious settings. But what I'm jealous of most is the easy way they have about them. No worry of losing their home or not having enough food.

"Recognize anyone? You should," says a male voice.

I turn around and stop at the face in front of me. "Otto. What are you doing here?"

He smiles, his full beard moving as he does. "Working. I saw you talking to Mrs. Michaels at the front door. I figured you'd be out here."

"Is this right?" I motion to the cases alongside the garage.

"Yep. I'll move it in now." He picks up a case and I do, too.

"You're working the party?"

"Mr. Michaels owns the speakeasy. I work for him wherever he needs me to. Besides, I grew up just down the street. It's easy for me to come here."

I follow Otto through the open door and into a giant kitchen, where two cooks are preparing steaks.

"Margaret didn't say you would be here tonight," says Otto.

"She doesn't know yet," I reply. "You see her often?"

"We go to the pictures together a lot." His voice is softer now, and I try not to smile at the thought of them dating. "I stopped by the dress shop today to say hi. That kind of thing." He points to the larder. "Stack it up here, and don't go through that door." He motions to a swinging door that most likely leads to the front of the house, where the guests are probably already mingling.

"Makes sense that Shorty is supplying the party, too," I continue. "Since he does the speakeasy."

"Oh, Shorty? He's new this week. The last guy didn't work out," Otto replies, picking up one of the potato sacks. "I guess your talk went well with him last night, then."

"You could say that."

"Is this your stuff that you wanted to sell?"

"No. This is all Shorty's. A trial run to see if he can trust me."

Otto laughs, the deep sound emitting from his chest as if he doesn't care who hears. "Sounds like him." He glances back at me as he carries the next bag in. "I'd love to try yours."

"Actually, I have a can in the truck."

He raises his eyebrows. "Go get it."

I help him move the rest of the cases inside and then remove the peach can from the satchel. "I need something to open it with."

"Don't worry about that." He takes a knife from his pocket and pokes two holes in the top, then pours some into his mouth, only an inch from his beard. He swishes it around and swallows, taking a moment before speaking. "You made this?"

"Not exactly."

"But you have a lot of it?"

I shrug.

He looks at the can. "Best I've ever had, and over the past few years, I've tried a lot." His beard hides some of his age, though he can't be much older than I am, but this is his world. "You meet the right people, you can do your own stuff."

"No, this is just a onetime thing."

Otto smiles, a sly look on his face. "I've heard that before. We'll see." He hands the can back to me. "But don't worry. Shorty is a good one. Stick with him and you'll be fine. Other ones out there?" He shakes his head. "Stay away. It's a dangerous game."

His words hang in the air, but I place my hands on my hips. "What if I'm not afraid of a little danger?"

He shrugs. "In this town? You should be."

CHAPTER EIGHTEEN

FORMAN

Forman arrives back at the station, Thomas's full name not only on her mind but also in her notebook.

Beaucamp's desk is empty, the chair pushed in as if he's gone for the day.

The station has other officers, but she needs to talk to Beaucamp and only him. If he's out on a call, he could be hours, and if it's one with Raymond, he may not return until after dark. Forman doesn't have that kind of time.

Today's newspaper is in the trash can next to his chair, and there's a ring from his coffee cup on his desk, the liquid circle still not dry. She puts her hand on it, pressing her palm down in the middle of the circle. It's still warm.

He was here not too long ago, which means he might still be somewhere in the station. She glances around, taking in every officer in her line of sight, but Beaucamp is not one of them. She moves past the desks and heads outside, studying the parked police cars in case Beaucamp is getting into one.

The cars are empty, and there are only unfamiliar faces on the street, except for Captain Warrenson, who is shaking hands with a gentleman in a brown hat. They are saying their goodbyes. If Beaucamp's left on a case, Forman's only missed him by minutes, if that.

She has no idea when he'll return. She could be waiting here for hours, and she knows Warrenson won't put up with that. He's probably a moment away from ordering her to check out a penny arcade. There have to be other ways to find out more about Rudy, but she doesn't know them yet.

As the man in the brown hat takes his leave, Warrenson turns his attention to her.

"You look nervous, Forman," says Warrenson, a twinkle in his eye.

"On the contrary," she replies, approaching him. "I'm looking for Beaucamp. Have you seen him?"

He grins. "Not getting him to do your work, are you, Forman?"

"Not in the slightest." She pulls her shoulders back and stands tall to get closer to Warrenson's height.

"Good. He's around here somewhere. Back inside."

Forman nods, even though she knows he's not at his desk. She stays a few inches ahead of the captain as they walk back inside the station.

Beaucamp's desk is still empty.

"Something I can help you with while you wait for him?"

The offer is tempting, but Forman doesn't think Warrenson will know where Rudy is. Nor does she want him to think she can't handle the investigation. "No. Just getting to the bottom of the case."

"The jewels? Of course," he says, his voice jovial, as he walks to another part of the station, not bothering to ask any more questions.

Forman waits near Beaucamp's desk. She needs him to come back now. She glances at the door to the station, but another door opens instead. The one to the men's restroom.

Beaucamp saunters out, doing up his belt as he does. He makes eye contact with Forman, drops his hands to his sides, and beelines to his desk. "You have a name, don't you?" he asks.

She tilts her chin down slightly, keeping her gaze fixed on him.

"How did you get it?"

Forman stays silent. It's not a question she will ever answer.

"OK, then," says Beaucamp finally, as he sits in his chair. "What is it? What's the name?"

"He went by Rudy. Thomas 'Rudy' Rudinsky."

Beaucamp's demeanor changes at that. He's no longer amused.

Forman feels herself lean back as her breath catches in her throat. Beaucamp doesn't move.

"I thought we had a deal, Beaucamp."

Beaucamp slowly shakes his head and puts his hands palms up on the desk. "I'm sorry."

"You said get a name, and I did. You said find out the entire name, which I have, and you would help me. We had a deal."

"That's not it." He stands up and moves over to the large wooden drawers that line this side of the station. He flips through the files as Forman watches, her heart pounding as she waits for his answer.

It takes a minute for him to find what he is looking for. "Thomas 'Rudy' Rudinsky," he says, handing her the file. "You don't have to open it if you don't want."

"Why not?" The papers feel cold against her fingers.

Beaucamp stares at Forman, the air heavy between them. "Because he's dead."

CHAPTER NINETEEN

Letty

I park on Selma Street instead of Vine, not wanting my green truck to advertise that I'm working for Shorty. Or with him. Or that I'm here at all.

I look at the people I pass on the street and wonder what they would think if they knew that I was working for a bootlegger. An unassuming farm girl who is about to earn money for an illegal product.

Otto's words—that I can do this on my own—go around in my head. I'll sell this one barrel and then see after that.

Shorty's car still sits proudly in the garage. At least he didn't leave and take the money he owes me. I'll be brief, a quick trip inside to get the money, and then go back to the farm, ready to load up the rest of the liquor.

But the place doesn't feel like it did before.

The air is heavy with a stillness after turmoil, that sinking feeling that you've walked into somewhere you shouldn't be. I move past his car, into the main room, as a strong odor of cigarette smoke lingers.

I see the guard first. He's flat on his back, his feet flopped to the side, the gunshot wound evident on his chest, a small trickle of blood still leaking onto the concrete below him.

This is recent. Moments ago, if that.

My eyes scan the garage, taking in everything as if in slow motion, like staring at a photograph, a frozen moment I shouldn't be privy to.

Shorty is still at his desk, his chair pushed back at an angle. He's slumped over the ledger, his face pale, his expression suspended in time.

I've never seen a dead body before, let alone two, the shock settling in as I stare at both of them. But there's no blood around Shorty.

Maybe he's not dead.

I tap his shoulder. He's still warm, but he doesn't move, the red marks around his neck indicating a struggle he lost. A bullet took out the guard, but Shorty's murder was more personal.

I feel heat climbing up my arms as everything inside tells me to run.

The sound of a faucet comes from the back.

My eyes flick to the noise, a small door near the rear exit. The faucet stops. My whole body freezes.

And there it is. Footsteps.

I'm not alone.

The small door is only a few feet away, but the exit to the garage is a distance. Uncovered, and sure to be seen, I won't make it in time.

The handle turns.

My only option is to hide under the desk of a dead man.

I push myself into the space beneath the wood desk, Shorty's lifeless leg against my shoulder, and pull the chair in front closer. The chair I sat in earlier, when I made this deal and entered this world.

The footsteps are nearby, a heavy, efficient clip to them.

There is no pause, no moment of shock. Whoever it is, they've already seen this scene, with two dead men. Because they're the one who created it.

CHAPTER TWENTY

LETTY

The footsteps shuffle around the garage, accompanied by the sound of tools being handled, the rustle of fabric, and the moving of other heavy items I can't see. Whoever it is, they're looking for something.

Black shoes come into view as the intruder stops in front of the desk, the well-polished oxfords less than a few feet away, a small scuff on the toe of the right one.

I flatten my back to the side of the desk, hoping it will swallow me. If I try to get closer to Shorty, it might move the body, giving away my location. The chair in front of me provides a small amount of coverage, but if he pushes it to the side or sits down, he'll find me under here for sure.

He's close enough now that I can almost hear his breathing and smell the reek of tobacco coming off it.

My leather club and knife are in my pocket, but seeing what he did to the others, I don't think I'm strong enough to fight him off. I know I'm not.

He stands over me now, rustling through papers on the desk. If he knows I'm here, then this is a game to him. Like a cat playing with their prey. It seems like minutes, but it's probably only seconds, as he waits. I wait, too.

Shorty's legs shift behind me, and I clasp my hand over my mouth to stifle any noise. The killer is moving the body. I could take this opportunity to make my escape—sprint toward the garage opening or chance it and run for the back exit. Neither plan seems particularly appealing.

As I weigh my options, the movement behind me ceases, Shorty's lifeless body once again still. Whatever the man needed from him, either under his body or on the desk, he now has.

The black oxfords turn and walk toward the front of the garage, the sound of each footstep ringing in my ears.

I can see now that it's a guy in a gray suit, but that's all I can see, the seat of the chair blocking my view and, in turn, his view of me.

He stops and looks back at the desk, as if he's taking everything in. I still can't see his face, but I don't want to turn my head to get a better look. The movement might make him notice me, and at the moment, I'm hoping he's still unaware of my presence.

But now he's coming, the footsteps approaching quickly.

I raise my club, ready to try to fend him off.

But he goes to the right of the desk instead.

He picks up something from the top, the scraping sound above me.

A can drops to the ground.

My can.

It's a few feet away, rolling around, a dent in the side from the fall. But it's keeping the brandy inside. For now.

He leans down and picks it up, his gray sleeve and white shirt visible. I want to close my eyes, as if looking at him will make him see me, but I force myself to keep my eyes open. The outline of his face comes into sight for a moment before it disappears along with the can.

And then he's gone as quickly as he came, his footsteps leaving through the back, the rear door slamming behind him.

I scramble out from under the desk and look around.

I'm alone.

I need to leave in case he comes back, but I want to find the can, the dented can, full of brandy, with our farm's name on the label. But it's nowhere to be found, and neither is the ledger. The one that Shorty wrote my name in when I made the delivery to Mr. Michaels.

CHAPTER TWENTY-ONE

Letty

I run to the back door of the garage and peer through the window. The man in the gray suit is getting into a black sedan, tossing the ledger and can into the backseat behind him. He killed Shorty, but now there's a link to me. And he could come for me, or my mother, next.

I sprint to my truck and climb inside, waiting until the black car passes before starting the engine and following it onto Hollywood Boulevard.

There are enough vehicles between us to avoid suspicion, or at least I hope there are. He sits at a traffic signal a few cars ahead, his windows open as if he were out for a leisurely drive and hadn't just ended the lives of two people.

The signal changes, and the line of cars moves forward.

A turn here. A turn there.

I stay a couple of car lengths behind as he traverses the city.

We're moving along Wilshire Boulevard now, passing department stores and even a park, rowboats dotting the lake on what to everyone else seems like a quiet Sunday afternoon. The black sedan continues weaving past other vehicles, and I follow as closely as I can without being spotted.

We arrive downtown, the buildings taller here, replacing the houses of the residential areas we just left behind. The city is cluttered with construction, new hotels and theaters popping up on nearly every block. He takes two more turns, and I wonder if he's trying to lose me, if he knows he's being tailed.

I watch him turn onto Broadway, and I follow, only a few cars behind, as the street reveals dual-lamp streetlights on both sides and the new city hall in the distance. Due to open next year, the massive metal skeleton dwarfs everything around it as crews work to complete the largest structure in the city, with twenty-eight floors.

But Broadway is crowded, parked cars lining the sides and trolleys coming down the center lane, and I fall behind.

The blocks get denser as he gets farther ahead, the vaudeville theaters and movie palaces replacing the stores, their marquees bigger and flashier than those built in Hollywood the last few years.

The signal changes, and pedestrians step into the street, forcing me to stop. They stroll across the intersection, and I watch the black sedan recede into the distance. All this way and I've lost him. I wait for the signal to change and race past the other cars, but there's no sight of him by the time I reach the city hall's construction site.

My only chance is if he has stopped in this area.

I drive a loop around the block to the right and then go to the left on Hill and First.

I'm about to give up when I notice his black sedan in the parking lot next to the Central Police Station.

He's going into the *police station*. Is he turning himself in for the crime already? Not likely.

I pull into the lot across the street next to a hot dog stand and stare at the station. I've never been to the two-toned building before, its lines defying the slope of First Street. And I hope I won't need to come again after today.

He's still inside the building, the car alone in the parking lot. I quickly move across the road and stand below the large advertisement for Southern Pacific trains on an adjacent building. A man in a dark hat holds a newspaper, and I pretend to read along with him.

"Can I help you with something?" he says, folding the paper back.

"Not at all."

I glance over at the black sedan. There's no one near it, but it doesn't mean there won't be. "Say, are you done with that paper?"

He glances up. "What's it worth to you?"

"Nothing. I'll go get one." I step past, but he stops me.

"Here. Take it."

I tip my hat to him, and he strolls away. I refocus on the sedan. I need to move now.

I open the newspaper and pretend to read it as I approach the car and lean against it like I'm reading and look around. No one seems to be paying any attention to me, which is perfect.

I hold the newspaper up and glance in the back window. There, on the floor, is my can. Next to the ledger.

I pull the door handle on my side. It doesn't open.

I try again, this time harder, with the nerves and adrenaline increasing my efforts.

The door swings open, and I grab the can, ready to slam the door, but on second thought, I pick up the ledger and open it, flipping through the pages until I reach the last one with writing. Relief floods through me. Shorty didn't write my name. He wrote "Marks." No one would ever know.

But still, don't leave evidence. I slip the ledger into my waistband at the back, the thick paper against my spine with my shirt over it, and attempt to close the car door quietly. Except the noise is louder than I expected. I walk away swiftly with my head up, like I belong here. If I run, I'll draw attention. I don't want to be noticed.

I cross the street and join the line at the hot dog stand, my eyes again focused on the car. I don't have to wait long. The man with the gray suit has exited the station, his unmistakable swagger the same as in the garage, his diamond-shaped face barely hidden by his hat. But now he's with an officer.

They talk as if they're old friends, and I know I should leave, but I can't. I'm focused on his movements as he approaches his sedan.

He's going to see that the ledger is missing. That the can is missing. He's going to find out. My feet finally start moving.

I make it back to my truck, glancing only one more time at the lot before I drive away. He's still talking with the officer. He doesn't know yet.

My heart is racing as I drive back toward Hollywood, panic subsiding with each block I pass. I am alive, and I have my can. I have all the evidence.

But there is no money from my delivery this morning. And there is no longer someone trustworthy, like Shorty, to sell to. But I now have two cans left.

The ledger is on the seat next to me as I wait at the signal, my new passenger the key to everything I've wanted to avoid and everything that I could become. The choice is mine.

I open the ledger.

CHAPTER TWENTY-TWO

RAYMOND

Raymond reaches his car, the black sedan the same as always, but he notices a nick in the paint near the driver's-side door. He clenches his teeth. He doesn't like scratches on his car.

His fingers touch the area, the paint missing, the metal underneath. He probably did it on one of his nighttime errands. He'll need to be more careful.

Officer Peterson is still nearby, smoking a cigarette, as if waiting for Raymond. But Raymond's already spoken to him, the normal conversation about wives and movies, the same topics Peterson always brings up, along with the routine questions that Raymond already knows the answers to, which have already been covered. Now Raymond wants him to go away so he can get the ledger. He never should have left it in the car, but he was in a hurry to get inside. In a hurry to be seen.

Raymond waits, checking the tires of his car, willing Peterson's cigarette to burn itself out quickly so he can be alone. Peterson will ask questions about the ledger as he carries it in. He'll want to know what's inside and where it came from. Raymond's not in the mood for questions. Not now. Not ever.

He moves to the next tire, flicking a small pebble from the rubber tread.

"Tires OK there, August?"

Raymond stiffens. It's Peterson's habit to occasionally call him by his first name. He's the only one who does it, besides Betty and Warrenson, and though Raymond has reminded him that he prefers his last name or, better yet, Detective Raymond, Peterson won't listen.

"All fine, Clarence. Would you mind grabbing me a pencil from inside?"

"What's the matter, your legs broken?"

"Not last time I checked."

Peterson laughs but walks back to the building. Raymond waits until he disappears inside before pulling open the back door.

It swings wide, and he reaches in for the ledger, keeping an eye out for Peterson's return. If he can tuck it under his arm and get inside before Peterson gets back, he can avoid any questions.

His fingers graze the floor, the rough, empty surface and nothing more. He moves farther into the car and tries again, eventually shifting his attention to the vacant space.

The ledger is gone. All of Shorty's information on whom he sold to and where he bought from, gone.

Heat rushes into Raymond's throat and across his temples. He checks the rest of the car, but the ledger has vanished.

He spins around, his eyes scanning the strangers walking along the street, on their way to jobs, meetings, anywhere else but here. Their hands clutch small purses, paper lunch sacks, and shopping bags but not the faded green book he needs.

He was only inside the station for a minute, if that.

Someone knew he had it.

Someone was watching him.

Someone wanted it back, and he knows it's not the ledger's owner. That man's dead.

"August, you OK?" Peterson is back, a cigarette in one hand, a pencil in the other. "You have that look on your face when someone's moved the coffee on your desk." He puts the cigarette between his lips but doesn't pull a smoke. "Or when someone's taken your new gal and you can't complain because your wife will find out." He holds up the pencil. "Still need this?"

"Mind your own business, Peterson. Everything is fine."

Peterson's sporting that smug smile of his, but the cigarette and pencil are the only things on him. Raymond knows the ledger wouldn't fit under his jacket—a few too many Sunday roasts this year. Besides, Peterson wasn't near the car without Raymond.

Raymond glances around once more, gazing across the street at the hot dog stand and then over to the coffee shop.

Someone is onto him.

And he's going to find out who.

CHAPTER
TWENTY-THREE

FORMAN

The morgue holds the same constant chill it has the few other times Forman has been here; the tile on the walls and floor keeps the room as cold as the lifeless bodies on the tables.

Walter Glick looks up as the door closes behind her, his white coat stiff as he stands near a body, a sheet hiding the identity. "You here for this one?" He pulls the sheet slightly up, face as unmoving as the departed individual's in front of him.

Forman shakes her head, staying near the door. "No. One last week."

The sheet drops from his fingers, landing at an angle and revealing the head of a man with short auburn hair. "That's a shame. This one's a good one. Gunshot wound."

Forman steps to the side, farther into the room but not any closer to Glick. "There was a gentleman brought in last week named Thomas 'Rudy' Rudinsky. Do you remember him?"

"I see bodies every day. You'll have to be more specific." He turns to the sheet and pulls it back, continuing his work on the auburn-haired man.

Forman leans closer to the wall, using Glick to block her view of the body. She doesn't mind seeing dead bodies. She's seen her fair share over the years, the first one long before she joined the force, but bodies in the morgue are different. They are in their prepping stage. A stage not to be viewed or remembered.

"He was found in the river," she continues. "Strangled. Not sure the day, but it was last week. I don't have a description on him, but he was a bootlegger. Did deliveries to Hollywood parties and such."

Glick glances up. "Last week? Yeah, I remember that guy."

Forman breathes a sigh of relief but still wants to make sure he has the right guy in mind. "How do you know it was him?"

"Don't get many river killings in here, and besides, he had the classic marks of a bootlegger." Glick looks at Forman. "Old burn scars on his arms, as if he'd had trouble with the still at one time. I've seen it on a few of them."

She moves forward at this news, though she still keeps Glick between her and the table. "I'm looking for an item that he had. Or, rather, that he stole. A diamond necklace. He had it in his possession not long before he was found in the river."

Glick chuckles. "You think a body would come in here with that?"

"You never know. I thought it was worth checking. It's not in evidence—I already looked."

Glick furrows his brow. "You're the woman cop . . . What's your name again?"

"Forman. Annabel Forman."

"That's right. Listen, they all come in without possessions. I don't mean what you're thinking, about removing the evidence before they arrive." He picks up a sharp knife from the set of tools near him and pulls the sheet back more. "I can guarantee you that that necklace was long gone before an officer even arrived on the scene. And you might be thinking it was because the body was left for a while and people scavenged, but I have my own theories about that."

Forman steps closer to the table, the body in full view, but keeps her focus on Glick. "Care to share those theories?"

"Not really."

"Whatever you tell me can stay out of the report."

He glances at her sideways, his left eye hidden by the bridge of his nose. "People like him, bootleggers, they got no reason to hang on to fancy jewelry. It's all about the money. My guess is he stole it and pawned it right away. You want to find this necklace of yours? Check the hockshops."

"But bootleggers make a lot of money already—"

"Some do," he interrupts. "But there's something to be said for more. The need to get ahead in this town. They all come in without possessions. Him and all the others."

"Others?"

"They all meet their end and usually land on my table. We get bootleggers in here all the time. Even more so recently."

CHAPTER TWENTY-FOUR

I arrive at a mid-city address listed in the ledger, expecting to find some-place discreet, except it looks like a regular bar, the kind that was shut down years ago. Yet here it is.

No one looks up as I enter. The bartender wipes the surface of the counter with a cloth, and three men sit at a table in the corner, their suits finely pressed and their faces expressionless. Two are my father's age, early fifties, and the younger one looks like he could be in his thir-ties. They sit there without talking, and the thought crosses my mind that they are federal agents. But I push it away. I haven't done anything wrong here. Yet.

I sit on a stool at the bar, the wood in front of me well worn and clearly the place to be before 1920.

"Good afternoon," I say, the leather satchel still across my body. The bartender nods to me. "Where does a girl get a drink around here?" I'm not sure how to ask him about his supplier, but buying a drink is probably the best way to ease into the topic.

"We have soda, water, fizzes, highballs, and sours."

So they do serve alcohol. I glance back at the men at the table. They can't be officers. The bartender wouldn't talk like this in front of them.

Sal's drink comes to mind. "I'll take a gin rickey." It's the one he often made at his house, the name always sounding funny to both me and Margaret back then.

"I didn't say we had those."

I'm not about to let him go that easily. "Try."

A slight smile crosses the bartender's face, and he sets to work. The room is eerily quiet. I feel the eyes of the other three occupants on me, but I don't turn around to check. Instead, I watch the bartender make the drink, his movements fluid and practiced, like Otto's.

He puts it in front of me, the glass of clear, bubbly liquid with a lime on the rim. "A gin rickey. Special for the lady."

"Thanks." I lift the glass and take a sip. But I can only taste the lime. I haven't had a gin rickey before, but I can tell there's no booze in this. He's trying to trick me. "I don't think you mixed it correctly."

His eyes narrow. "You grilling me?"

"It's not the recipe." I push the glass back toward him. "You're missing the gin. It's supposed to have gin, lime, and club soda." I remember Sal rattling off the three ingredients one day as Margaret and I helped her mother in the kitchen.

The bartender laughs, the gaps in his teeth showing as he does. "Haven't you heard? This whole town's dry." He lowers his head. "Or have you had your head in the sand these past seven years?"

"Shame," I reply, my pulse quickening but my manner still calm. "I heard this was the place to get a good, stiff drink. A cocktail with booze. Maybe even a glass of wine."

The chairs at the table behind me move. I fight the urge to look.

"You heard wrong."

"You're missing out," I reply.

"Is that so?" he asks in a tone that's not a question.

I mask my nerves with a small smile. "There's a lot of speakeasies in this town. They make nice money. You could, too."

He leans forward, and I can smell sweat and musk. "You know a lot about this?"

"I know what I know." I'm not sure when I should say that I can provide him with brandy. I feel like I need to earn his trust, but I'm not sure how to do it. "If you want to change, I might be able to help."

His attention shifts to the table behind me. I follow his gaze.

One of the men, the youngest one, is standing, his fists clenched. "We don't want trouble here. Especially a rat."

"She's with the temperance," says the second man.

"Or she's working with the feds."

The barstool feels unsteady beneath me, but I don't stand. "None of the above."

"Why should we believe you?" the youngest man says, stepping forward.

"You have no reason not to." I slide off the seat, relieved to feel my feet land solidly on the ground. "I'm only saying that I know where you could get some high-quality brandy if you wanted any." The words fly out of my mouth so fast that even I barely understand them, but they make the intended impact.

"You the fuzz?" asks the young one, now in front of me.

"No. Are you?"

A smirk crosses his face. "No. You an agent?"

I shake my head. "Are you an agent?" Now it's become a kind of game.

"Are you one of Shorty's guys?"

"I have nothing to do with Shorty."

"Is that right?" He steps closer to me, only an inch between us. He's towering over me, and I know this is a challenge. I have to prove my toughness.

"Shorty is dead," I reply, reporting the news as casually as the day of the week.

He doesn't react.

"And it doesn't mean a thing to me," I add.

The two older men laugh. "Doesn't mean a thing to us, either," says one.

"So why are you here?" The young one is still in front of me, but he doesn't seem as threatening anymore.

I grit my teeth and then relax my jaw. "As I said, I can get you brandy."

"Is that so?"

"Are you grilling me?" I repeat the words the bartender said earlier.

He waits to reply. "What if we told you we already get everything we need?"

I glance at the nondescript bottle on the table. It's glass, but I'm not sure what's inside. "You serve gin rickeys without gin. Are you sure you have everything?"

"You can get us gin?"

"No." The word tastes sour as I say it. "But I can get you brandy. And wine. I'm only letting you know there are options."

"You're out of your territory," says one man.

"Shorty doesn't have a territory anymore," I reply. "Not after today."

"No, but our guy does," says the older man on the right. "And you're in it. Not sure he'd be happy about you coming in here. Your type." He pauses as he looks me up and down. "He took over this area a few weeks ago when our last guy left. Shorty did the same thing you're doing right now. It didn't work."

"Your guy—" But I stop before I say more. I don't know who it is, and Otto's warning rings in my ears.

"You're a tough broad," says one of them. "Our guy might not like that, but I do."

"Agreed," says the man on the far end, his white hair jutting out from underneath his hat. "You'll go far in this business. And you're a looker to boot."

The comment turns my stomach. "I'll go far in this business because I'm going to work hard."

All three men laugh at that.

"I like her," says the young one, his stance now shifted back a few feet, as if admiring me from a distance. "She has nerve. Hey, gal, if we ever decide to get rid of our guy, we'll let you know. In the meantime, I suggest you watch your back. We won't tell him you were here, but word spreads fast in this town. One of you already ended up in the river last week." His tone is threatening, and I know I should leave, but I don't want to show them they have that much power.

I return to the stool and finish my dry cocktail, my focus on the worn wood of the bar and the paintings of horses in the room. The bartender doesn't come over, and I'm certain the three men are still watching me from their table, but I don't bother to check.

When the glass is empty, I put money down on the bar and stand up. "Thanks for the gin-less rickey."

The bartender doesn't reply, just picks up the money. I don't look at the other men as I leave.

As I reach the sidewalk, without a sale or a customer, the realization of the situation hits me. Our winery contract is gone, we won't be able to pay our bills, and I'm trying to sell something illegal that no one will buy.

I climb into my truck, ready to head back home, but I don't move. I watch the street ahead, cars passing on their way to places and homes with money. I have to accept that I've failed.

"No." I slam my hand on the steering wheel. "Never."

I didn't nearly lose everything to give up. I pull the ledger out of the bag and open it, going down the list once more as I start the engine.

CHAPTER TWENTY-FIVE

FORMAN

Forman flips through the file on Thomas, or Rudy, as she sits at the station. Her only lead on the necklace that was lost, or rather stolen, from Mrs. Michaels came to an end at the morgue, but that doesn't mean there's not something else to find in the file. She had glanced through it before going to visit Glick, but now she takes a closer look, searching for additional clues. And yet there's nothing. The dead don't share their secrets. And if Glick is right, the necklace was long gone before Rudy met his demise. It's time to hit the pawnshops.

Forman's about to close the file when one word jumps out at her from the article clipped to the inside of the front cover. The first word of the story: *Another*. A simple word, but it becomes complex when put next to the following word, *bootlegger*. *Another bootlegger*. Like Glick mentioned, there's been even more of them recently. The article goes on to state that this death by strangulation and discovery in the Los Angeles River is assumed to be the work of a fellow bootlegger over a turf war, but all Forman needed was that one word.

Beaucamp was out on a call when she arrived, but now he's back at his desk, doing the paperwork. He doesn't look up as she approaches.

"Where are the others?"

"What do you mean the others?" He keeps his attention on the page, his scrawl almost illegible and a stark contrast to how she filled out paperwork for him last year, decipherable to anyone who could read. This would be legible only to him.

"The other bootleggers that died. I want to know about them."

Beaucamp shrugs, refusing to look up at her. "They choose a dangerous life. Sometimes they die. They bump each other off. It's part of the business."

"Then there shouldn't be any reason I can't see their files."

Beaucamp gives her a sidelong glance before shifting his head, his eyes remaining focused on her as he does. His gaze is unnerving. "What are you up to, Forman?"

"I'm following a lead that can get me the promotion I deserve. Now, the others?"

"Does this have to do with the Michaels case? What did she lose, anyway?"

"Her patience."

Beaucamp, who has always been pleasant but not exactly nice, nods, his head barely moving up and down, like an empty rocking chair in the afternoon breeze. "Be careful, Forman. Stick to what you're supposed to."

"I will." She holds her hand out. "But first, the other files."

"You really owe me."

"I told you; I'll do the paperwork for you next week."

Beaucamp sighs and gets up, his legs heavy as he walks to the cabinet. "How many do you want?"

"All of them."

He shakes his head as he searches through the cabinet until he has four files in his hand. "If anyone asks, you didn't get these from me, OK?"

"Of course." Forman takes the files back to an empty desk and flips through the first one, several pages thick. Two months ago, a bootlegger,

Wiley Whitey Daniels, was found in the Los Angeles River near Los Feliz. The autopsy determined he drowned, though speculation continues that he was strangled. It goes on to detail his crimes, but Forman moves to the next file.

December 1926. Bootlegger Harold Sugar Malone. A few children fishing in the river found his body on the banks near Elysian Park. Strangulation is listed as the cause of death.

Next file. Bootlegger, found in the river close to Long Beach, body too battered by the storm currents to identify the cause of death.

The final file, and the earliest one, pertains to a man in his fifties, a bootlegger from the San Fernando Valley who died in a car accident a couple of years back.

Forman shakes her head. Such a dangerous line of work, and yet he died in a car accident. Except the car was found in the Los Angeles River. Just like the others.

But with Rudy, there are five. All within a few years. It's something.

Forman picks up the files and carries them to Captain Warrenson's office, placing them in front of him on his desk as he watches. "Five bootleggers, all killed and dumped into the Los Angeles River."

Warrenson doesn't move.

"This isn't a coincidence. You know it isn't."

He flips through the files, slowly, methodically, as if perusing the newspaper.

Forman waits, doing her best to keep her feet still. She feels that same excitement that she felt during the holidays, when her father would bring home wooden puzzles, a homemade gift from a client, and she would do them with her mother and, later, her aunt.

He closes the last file and leans back in his chair. "What do you want me to do about it?"

"It needs to be investigated."

Warrenson puts his hand to his chin. "I don't see a problem here. Someone is killing those who leave a stain on our great city, and I'm supposed to care? If they're sorting this out themselves, then it's even better for all of us. Best to leave things as they are."

"Captain . . ."

"Don't you have something else you're supposed to be working on? A burglary? Good detectives keep their focus and solve the case at hand, Forman."

She shifts her weight back onto her heels. "This is connected."

"You're distracted and unfocused. You can either solve the Mrs. Michaels case or you need to return to your penny arcades and leave the real police work to the men."

Forman tightens her fists but keeps them to her sides, out of view. "It's connected. It was a bootlegger—"

"I don't care, Forman. You're not investigating a murder. You're investigating a jewel theft. You can't even handle that." He removes the silver watch from his breast pocket, the one he looks at when he starts the morning meetings, but this time he barely glances at it. "And you're almost out of time," he reminds her. "Tomorrow morning, the deadline arrives."

"It was a bootlegger who stole the necklace. He's one of the files there. He's dead, like the rest of them, all in the river."

Warrenson shakes his head as he slips the pocket watch back into his shirt. "We had an agreement. Find it or give up. Things like this are better left status quo, Forman."

Forman has more to say, but she knows Warrenson isn't going to listen. She picks up the files from his desk without a word and walks back into the station room. It's not even the necklace at this point—it's that she sees the connection no one else does, and yet she's not allowed to do anything about it.

"Homicide!" shouts Miller, his hand covering the mouthpiece. "Wallace, you want to take this?"

Wallace looks up from his desk, his cheeks their usual pink, his face continually stubble-free, as if he couldn't grow a beard if he tried. "OK." His voice wavers a little. "What is it?"

"Quadling Garage in Hollywood. Wallace, it's an easy one. From what I hear, it was just a front for a booze ring. One of the customers probably got a bad case of hooch. Killed the guy."

Forman stops, the words still floating in the air and then landing. *Another bootlegger.* Her attention shifts to Miller. "How?"

Miller looks at her, a squint in his eyes, and directs his focus back to Wallace. "You taking this, or do I need to assign it somewhere else?"

"I'll take it," Wallace says a little tentatively. He pulls on his coat over the suit that still looks awkward on him, unlike the uniform he wore recently. He grabs the paper from Miller, glances at it, and walks out the door.

Forman sits back down at a desk, flipping open the first file again. It's already late. Her aunt and father will be waiting for her to start dinner, but more so, they'll be waiting for an update on her progress. She considers checking pawnshops for the necklace, but the idea is overshadowed by something bigger. The mysterious deaths of all these bootleggers. And now another one, still at the scene.

Forman grabs her coat and follows Wallace out the door.

CHAPTER TWENTY-SIX

LETTY

The streets of Hollywood welcome me back with a sense of comfort, as I know I'm clearly in Shorty's territory. Someone won't have taken this area already. He's only been dead for a few hours. Besides, after looking at the ledger some more, I feel like I have a better understanding of Shorty's codes and who his current clients are.

Quadling Garage looks the same as I drive by, the door open, the car in view, but now a few people stand nearby, staring in as if they see something. The garage is about to reveal its secrets. I park two blocks away and stroll down to the Sampson Hardware store, the site of a delivery two weeks ago, according to the ledger. The shop is empty as I enter, one man behind the counter, a bow tie close to his chin.

The store has a similar layout to the one I go to in the valley when I need supplies for the house or the barn. Metal bowls, buckets, rakes, and the occasional mop on the one side, hammers and saws line the back wall, and a counter to the right with packets of seeds, drawers of nails, jars of turpentine, and a smiling owner standing proudly by them.

"What can I help you with today? Running an errand for your husband?"

"No husband." I glance around. "And even if I had one, I've built a barn and know how to use tools." I smile politely in an attempt to hide my irritation at his assumptions. "I'm here to see if there's something you'd like to buy." I touch the can in my satchel but decide not to bring it out. "Do you know Shorty Paulson?"

The man slowly nods. "He may have been in here a time or two."

"Good. I'm taking over his line of work. You need something, you come to me. I can even offer you a product today, since I know it's been two weeks since your last delivery."

"Already have my supply . . ." He pauses. "Does your father know you're doing this?"

"Does your wife know you buy alcohol?"

He grits his teeth and smiles. "If I can get you anything for your house or barn, let me know. In the meantime, good luck. It's a tough business you're entering."

"It's a tough world, no matter what business." I pull on my cap, give him a nod, and walk out the door.

Two strikeouts. Two customers who already have their own stashes or suppliers. So far, the risk of taking the ledger was for nothing.

Across the street, Anderson's Drugstore sits empty, the counter and barstools bare, waiting for customers. I know the feeling.

I look around at the surrounding buildings. There's Hotel Lamar, a two-story brick building, which would have guests who might want a drink but employees who might not want to take the risk of serving it. On the corner is a gas station where a gentleman stands near the TURN OFF YOUR MOTOR sign as an attendant in a crisp white uniform and red bow tie fills up his car.

But there's a man sitting on the ground nearby, a silly smile on his face, singing a barely comprehensible song. There's a tin cup in his hand, and while I don't want to add to his intoxication, I'm also tempted to see if this will work.

I wait until I'm close enough to make a side comment that won't be heard by others, finally feeling comfortable when he's only a foot away. "Might you be in the market for some brandy?"

He raises his eyebrows. "Brandy? I'll take some brandy."

"Two dollars."

"I don't got that."

"Then that's not going to work."

"Wait, wait, hold on." He lifts up his foot and takes off his shoe. He pulls out two quarters from the inside. "I have this."

I look back over my shoulder. There are enough people around that this is dangerous, but then again, it will just look like peaches. I take the sweaty coins and hand him the can.

"Hey! I thought you said it was brandy."

"It is. Open it."

He holds the can out to me. "I want my money back. I can't open this."

I take another look around, then take the can back, remove the Remington from my back pocket, and poke two holes in the top. I pour some into his cup, and there's still a good amount in the can for my next stop, wherever that might be. "Here."

He takes a swig, raises his eyebrows as he looks at his tip cup, and then grins. "Wow, you weren't kidding!"

"I never kid. Enjoy. Tell your friends. There's a new option in town."

I stroll down the street, but footsteps approach from behind me. I don't like the sound of them, along with what I'm carrying in my hand, a peach can with holes in it and brandy still inside.

I move to the side to let the person pass, but the footsteps stop and wait. I turn around to face the owner of them.

It's a tall man, towering at least a foot above me and full of muscle, the thick smell of whiskey emanating from him.

"You." He points at me. "I want what you gave him."

I try to step past him, but he blocks me. With a liquor-induced sway, he leans toward me intimidatingly, his filthy coat moving with him.

"You give me what I want," he demands, a slur to his words.

I step back but keep my guard up. "I think you're mistaken. I have nothing for you."

"I need whiskey. I want whiskey." He stumbles forward. "You need to give me what I want."

"I don't have whiskey."

He clamps on to my arm and stares into my eyes. "Can you get some?"

I yank my arm away. "No. I can only get brandy. Do you want that?"

"You don't have brandy." His eyes stare at the can in my hand. "Or do you?" He lunges for it, but I step back.

"Easy now." I glance around, but only two people, both men, have stopped to watch this interaction, and neither of them looks like they're going to step in to provide assistance.

"Give it to me!" He grabs my right wrist and tries to yank the can from my grip with his other hand. "It's mine now."

"Stop." I raise my left hand as a warning. "I have nothing for you. Let me go."

"Give it," he repeats, his nails digging into my skin as he frees the can, but his hold on my wrist remains.

I swing, my knuckles cracking against the side of his face. I'm right-handed, but the muscles in my left arm are strong from the work on the winery over the years, and the punch is delivered at full force.

He stumbles back, letting go of me as he does. He falls to the ground, his face registering the pain and surprise of the impact, the can releasing from his grasp, brandy dribbling onto the sidewalk. "You hit me?"

"Yes," I reply, comforting my aching hand. "And I'll hit you again if you try anything like that," I warn. "You want something? You can pay like everyone else. But don't you dare threaten me or think you can get things for free. Do we have an understanding?" My heart is pounding, but I try to stay as calm as possible. My left hand is throbbing, but my right is free and ready to strike if necessary.

"A woman shouldn't hit a man. It's not right." He's rubbing the side of his face.

"Then you need to treat women better." I step closer so that I tower over him now.

He crawls back away from me before standing up, swaying as he does. "This isn't over."

"No, it's not," I reply. "And if I hear about you grabbing another lady's wrist when she tells you to stop, I'll come back to finish the job."

He glares at me, his hand to the side of his head where I hit him, as he grabs the can from the ground and stumbles off in the opposite direction. There should be barely any brandy left in it after the spill, so I decide not to chase him.

Only when he's gone do I look at my hand. It's red, swollen, and hopefully not broken.

The two men are still watching from the side, their faces barely hiding their surprise. But there's a woman nearby with a stronger expression, one conveying that she was privy to the events of the past few minutes.

"What are you selling?" she asks. She opens her purse. "Doesn't matter. I'll buy three of whatever it is, after seeing that show right there."

I look at her, her green dress and coat with matching hat. There is no white bow around her neck and no white pin on her suit, the kind that temperance workers across the country wear to show their allegiance to the cause. I remove the last brandy can from my satchel, the remaining ones containing only peaches.

She stares at the can; then her eyes flick up to meet mine. "Peaches?"

I smile softly but don't break eye contact.

She raises one eyebrow. "Or not peaches?" she adds. I don't respond. She looks at the can again. "What is it?"

"If you're dry, it's peaches. If you're not, it's the best brandy you've ever tasted in your life. Though I have real peaches, too." I pat the bag.

She takes the can from my hand and looks at it. "This kind. I'll take five."

"Five it is, but I don't have them right now. I can get them to you later tonight. Where should I meet you?"

"Right at the corner." She points to a café with a red-and-white awning. "I own the place. My name's Thelma. Feel free to bring more than five."

"Letty. And I'll be there."

Thelma nods, a slight curve at the corners of her pressed lips. "Perfect."

CHAPTER
TWENTY-SEVEN

FORMAN

Wallace is quiet in the car, but he has a small smile on his face. She can tell her presence is a comfort to him. That he's not on this case alone. He didn't even say a word when she got into the passenger seat, catching him before he pulled out of the station. He took only a quick glance to see her get in, and once she was settled, he started driving.

Forman thought of asking about his wife or if he had kids. They'd barely talked in the year that he'd been on the force, and although she knew that he was married and that his father worked upstairs at the station, this was about the extent of what she knew. Then again, he didn't know anything about her, either.

They pull up outside Quadling Garage, a patrol car already underneath the red sign, blocking the view from curious onlookers.

Wallace turns off the engine but doesn't open his door.

Forman waits, too. She wants Wallace to go first. This is his case. Except he doesn't move. "Are you OK, Wallace?"

He nods, but his cheeks have lost their color as he stares ahead at the garage.

"It'll be fine. Let's go inside. One step at a time."

Wallace exhales, keeping his eyes forward. "You shouldn't be here."

Forman nods. Wallace has a point. "But I am here, and I'm not leaving."

"I thought you were supposed to be doing your own thing. The test the captain gave you."

"Yes, but there's this, too." She looks at Wallace. "I'm not taking it away from you. I only want to see what's there. Understand?"

He doesn't reply.

"Wallace—"

He gets out of the car and walks toward the garage. Forman follows.

The scene feels static, even with the two officers in the room. A man is slumped over the desk, his hat on the floor in front of it, and there's a second body to the side, near the shelves.

Wallace is frozen, not even removing a notebook from his coat, as if it's the first time he's ever seen a dead body. And maybe it is.

The other officers look at him, waiting for him to say something, but he's staring at the man on the desk.

"What's his name?" asks Forman, breaking the tension in the air.

"Shorty Paulson," replies the attending officer, whom Forman recognizes as a man named Leaman.

"And him?" She points at the deceased on the floor.

"Probably his protection. A lot of good it did Shorty."

Wallace finally takes out his notebook. While he makes notes, Forman moves closer to the victims. The man on the floor has been shot, a bullet to the stomach, but there is no blood around the man on the desk. Shorty. She walks around, staring at the scene until she sees the deep-purple marks on Shorty's neck. Strangled or a broken neck, like some of the other bootleggers. Except this one didn't end up in the river.

"Wow. Is that a dead guy?" A man in a long black coat is standing inside the garage, swaying slightly, a can in his left hand, a dazed look on his face. "I saw your cars out there, but I didn't think it was because there were dead people."

"This is a closed scene," barks Officer Leaman.

The man doesn't move, just puts the can to his mouth and takes a deep drink. Wallace is still taking notes, Leaman is not moving, and the other officer stands at the side of the garage protecting the crime scene.

The man in the coat steps forward. "Wow," he repeats.

"Come on, let's go." Forman grabs the man's arm and pulls him toward the door. He doesn't resist but follows her lead like a submissive child.

"But that was a dead guy," he says as they step outside, the late-afternoon sun glaring off the car windows as they pass.

"Yes, and you will be soon if you don't get a move on." She releases his arm and waits for him to walk away, but instead he stays and takes another sip from his can. "What are you drinking?" she asks.

His palm is blocking most of it, but there's a large peach on the front, the brand logo of some farm. Except it's not like a normal can of peaches, where the entire lid is off so you can get to the fruit; rather, it has two small holes in the top to drain the liquid.

Forman reaches for it.

He pulls it back. "Mine."

"What is it?" But she can smell it on him, the thick, sweet scent of brandy or whiskey.

"It's mine," he repeats, and Forman waits for him to take another sip.

He smiles a goofy grin, a red mark visible on his face, and puts the can to his mouth. She grabs it out of his hand and steps back quickly.

"Hey."

"Calm down. You'll get it back."

"Really?"

"No." She sniffs the can. Brandy, but there's barely any left, a few drops, if that. "Did you buy this from here?" She points back at the garage. "From Shorty?"

"Nope." He looks at her. "But if I say yes, can I get it back?"

"Highly unlikely."

Another patrol car pulls up. She can see it out of the corner of her eye, but she stays focused on the task at hand: keeping the can of booze away from this man.

Even still, Forman sees Detective Raymond step out of the car and adjust his hat as he closes the door. He falters for a moment when he spots Forman. "Didn't think I'd see you here." He glances at the building. "I hear it's a homicide."

"Yes."

"Then what are you doing here?"

Forman pauses for a moment, choosing her words carefully. "Helping out."

"Interesting." His eyes drift to the can, now at her side in her hand. "Doing a little grocery shopping while you're at it?"

"Not quite."

"It's mine," says the man. "Mine. Not hers. Mine." He reaches for it again, but Forman keeps it away from him, pressing her hand against his chest. He eventually gives up and leans back against the wall, sliding down until he's sitting on the sidewalk. "It's mine," he whispers.

Raymond is still staring at the can. "What is it?"

"Not what you would think."

He puts his palm out for it, and Forman hands it over. Raymond's face twists as he reads the label and then sniffs the can. "This isn't peaches."

"No, it's not."

"What was in it?"

"You'd have to ask him." Forman points to the drunk, who is looking dreamily up at the sky. "What was in here?"

"Stuff to help. My wife ran off with another fella, and then I got punched today." The drunk reaches out his hand for the can Raymond's holding.

Raymond keeps the can just in front of his outstretched fingers. "What was in it?"

"Magic." The drunk grins.

Raymond swats his hand away and grabs his arm, crouching so he's at his level. "Where did you get it?"

"A new friend. Who is not very nice."

"Who?" He shakes him, his grip tighter now on the man's upper arm. The drunk peers at Raymond, as if trying to see through him.

Raymond smacks him on the shoulder. "Where?"

"Detective," says Forman, "we don't hit suspects."

He glares up at Forman, the anger in his eyes slowly dissipating. "I want to know where he got it." Raymond stands up and brushes his hands off, as if the invisible dirt from the drunk will stain his palms. "Did he say anything?"

"I asked him if he got it here, from Shorty, but he said he didn't. That was all I got before you pulled up."

Raymond doesn't comment, his eyes racing back and forth as if the wheels are turning in his mind. He focuses on the label. "I'll take care of this."

"It's OK. I can handle it."

"This isn't your case, Forman." He steps closer to her. "You need to leave the tough cases to the big boys."

"It's connected to my case."

"To Mrs. Michaels?" He laughs. "I don't think so." He leans forward, the odor of baloney and mustard thick on his breath. "Be careful there, Forman. You're treading where you don't belong. A wrong step in this town can get you killed."

"Are you threatening me, Detective?"

"Not at all. Just making sure you appreciate the consequences."

CHAPTER TWENTY-EIGHT

FORMAN

Forman jumps off the Red Car near Westlake Park, her journey the same as it is every day, her police badge granting her free rides to and from the station.

There are rowboats out on the lake, mostly couples enjoying an early evening on the water, the surrounding palm trees swaying in the breeze. But as Forman slings her bag over her shoulder, she's reminded that her hands are emptier than they should be. She was meant to pick up groceries but spent that time at Quadling.

Hopefully there's something in the icebox she can make for her aunt and father for dinner.

Forman heads toward the Victorian house with two turrets and a large garage where horse buggies used to be kept. Her aunt bought it nearly twenty years ago. Although she's a spinster who never married or owned a car, she chose a house big enough for a family. Forman and her father moved in after her mother's death, unable to stay another night in the bungalow. They've been here ever since.

The house is silent as Forman enters, but she can see her father in his chair by the window, a view of the lake in the distance. He's looking at the boaters. He spends his days there now, watching the world go by after taking an early retirement.

He looks up as she comes into the room, his salt-and-pepper hair smoothed to one side, and grins. It's the same warm smile that greets Forman every time she returns home. "Annabel, did you capture the bad guys today?"

"Always," Annabel replies.

"Good girl." He's in his red vest tonight, his cane to the right of him. He's had it ever since he hurt his knee a few months ago after a fall on an afternoon walk, a daily routine that has now ceased.

She knows he'd rather be back at work. His early retirement wasn't planned, but after a younger dentist with the look of a film star who fights swashbuckling pirates opened a practice a block away and leafletted the neighborhood, her father found his practice in sharp decline. It took only a few months before he had to permanently close. He attempted to become one of the factory-contracted dentists after that, cleaning the workers' teeth, but everywhere he tried, the position was already filled. Now he sits at the house and counts the ducks on the lake, the number always changing, as they seem to migrate back and forth around the city.

He folds his hands in his lap. "There were eleven of them today."

"One more than yesterday," says Annabel as she puts her bag down and heads to the kitchen.

But her aunt is there already, a blue apron over her knitted shawl, the oven on behind her.

"Aunt Caroline, what are you doing?"

Her aunt looks up and smiles. "Dinner's almost ready, my dear."

Annabel is taken aback. Her aunt hasn't cooked for *years*. Cooking is Annabel's job when she comes home from her police shifts. Her aunt is young by all standards, only a few years into her fifties, but suffers from a lack of energy she blames on the Great War, keeping her daily activities to crocheting and not much else, especially leaving the house. But she must have today.

"Your father mentioned you're up for a promotion," she continues. "I decided it was time I made my specialty. This used to be your father's favorite, and I know you liked it, too."

The metal timer near the stove buzzes, and Caroline turns to the oven, grabbing the yellow-and-green mitts she crocheted. While her aunt takes the meal out, Annabel looks around the kitchen. A pineapple upside-down cake, Annabel's favorite from when she was little, sits on a stand on the counter. An item that wasn't there this morning.

Caroline puts the roasting pan on the stove and steps back. "Crown roast of lamb with broiled potatoes."

"Aunt Caroline," she exclaims, knowing the time and money it took, "you shouldn't have!"

"It's my privilege, my dear. Promotions are a big deal in this household." She wavers a bit, her shoulders swaying. "Now, if you don't mind, I'm going to sit down."

Annabel holds her delicate arm and leads her to the dining room, which has already been set with china. It's the plates they've had since she was young, inherited from the paternal grandparents Caroline shared with her brother.

"I'll take care of the rest."

"Thank you, my dear. I'm fine; it just got a little hot in the kitchen." Caroline cools herself with her favorite black lace fan. "Well, did you?"

"Did I what?" she asks, halfway back to the kitchen.

"The promotion, my dear."

Annabel pauses, looking into her aunt's eyes, which hold so much hope. "Not yet. It might take a little more time."

The fan moves faster. "Why don't they promote you already? You've been there two years. Wasn't that the agreement? Two years and then you could move up?" Her aunt shakes her head in rhythm with the fan. "I still don't understand why they won't give you a gun. A girl has to arm herself." If Caroline could have, she would have drawn her pistol right then for effect, as she'd done at dinners years ago, but her niece knows it's up in the closet, no need for protection now. It's no secret in the family that her aunt was quite the markswoman but gave it up the day the Great War ended.

"She's doing it," replies her father from his chair in the living room. "One of these days, Annabel, you're going to walk in here as a detective, aren't you?"

"Of course." She smiles and steps into the kitchen, but her shoulders feel heavier than before.

❧

After dinner is over and Annabel has cleaned the dishes, she retreats to the living room and takes out her notebook. Her father is already asleep in front of the radio, dozing to the evening music programs, and her aunt is crocheting in the front room, the start of a light-pink shawl in her hands.

Annabel sits on the sofa and opens her notebook. She flips through the pages, eyeing all the details about Thomas, the necklace, the boot-leggers, and now Quadling Garage.

But it isn't adding up. She knows she's missing something, but she can't put her finger on it.

She closes the book, her father waking as she does.

"What? What is it?"

"Nothing, Dad. Just working on a case."

He looks at the large grandfather clock in the corner, its dark wood contrasting with the shiny brass pendulum that swings inside. "It's late."

"I know. But it's on my mind."

Her father smiles with the same pride he displayed when she would visit him at his office after school, his patients always paying him compliments in front of her, and the walls lined with thank-you cards from neighborhood families.

"Good girl. See? You're already a detective in my mind. Keep up the hard work—they'll reward you. I always rewarded my employees at the dental office. Hard work and dedication. That's all it takes."

She nods, but she knows it isn't that simple.

CHAPTER
TWENTY-NINE

LETTY

The morning sun barely illuminates the horizon as I sit with my mother at the kitchen table, the money from yesterday's sales in front of us. Only one day, but there's already a stack.

My mother flips through the bills. "If I didn't see it with my own eyes, I wouldn't believe it." She glances up at me as she puts the money back down, shaking her head. "You were safe?"

"Of course."

A knock at the front door makes us both look up, except it's more of a pounding than a knock. Our eyes meet, and she grabs the money off the table, shoving it down the neckline of her dress. It's the fastest I've seen her move in years. I wait a beat before I open the door, worried they'll break it down before I get there.

"Morning," says a man as he adjusts his round glasses, though his focus doesn't shift from me. Two officers stand behind him in their olive-green suits, brass buttons down the front, their badges on the left side of their chests.

"I assume this is the Hartman residence?" the bespeckled man asks, though it's more of a statement and a formality than a question.

"Hart," I reply. "My father changed it."

"Why?"

"Why not?"

"The Hart residence," he repeats as he takes his notebook out of his coat pocket while keeping his gaze unflinchingly on me. He has a slanted scar in the middle of his chin. "And you must be Loretta."

"Letty." But a jolt of terror surges through me as I realize this isn't our first interaction. The scent of cigarettes, the highly polished oxfords, the black sedan in the background. I'm face-to-face with the man who killed Shorty. The one I stole the ledger from.

I keep my outward calm. "Do you have a name, too, or shall we just go with Nameless Stranger?"

"August Raymond. Detective August Raymond. May we come in?"

A cop. Shorty was killed by a detective. The police.

I glance at my mother, the color draining from her face. I look back at Raymond. "I'd rather you didn't. My mother and I are sitting down for breakfast."

"Your mother . . ." He pauses as he looks at his notes. "Virginia Hart. And Richard Hart—"

"He's dead," replies my mother.

"Yes," says Raymond, a small smile at the corner of his mouth. "Yes, he is. This won't take long. I think you know why we're here."

I whisper to my mother behind the door to give her a heads-up that we'll be OK.

"What did you just say to her? Mrs. Hart, what did she say to you?"

I narrow my eyes. "I'm telling her that you're here to ask some questions."

"Next time you speak to her, you need to tell me what you're saying."

"Don't trust people, Detective?"

"Never have, never will." He glances around. "What is it you do here? Those look like grapevines. Do you have wine on the premises? More than two hundred gallons?"

"Of course."

Raymond grins like a hungry kitten who's just found a huge bowl of cream. "Are we in violation of the Prohibition law? Looks like someone is about to lose their family business."

"We're official sacramental wine producers," I reply. "We have the certificates."

"Then how come I've never heard of you?" His lips curve into a smile, but his eyes remain cold.

"You weren't listening," says my mother. Sass runs in the family.

"We have a deal with Father O'Leary at St. Nicholas of Myrna," I continue, even though I know the deal is ending. "If she needs to, my mother can go get him for you."

"I can check on it myself." Raymond pauses and looks at us. "You sell to anyone else? Anyone ever drive up here and offer you money for a couple of bottles?"

"No."

"If you have, I can arrest you for a liquor law violation."

"I already told you no. Is it the habit of the LAPD to ask the same questions over and over? Seems like a waste of time."

"It's not why we're here." Raymond stands up straighter, his shoulders back in an effort to look taller. "Who else is on the premises? How many staff?"

"None."

He laughs. "I like a broad with a sense of humor."

"Too bad I'm not being funny. The four of them left after my father did. I guess we weren't their number-one choice anymore. It's surprising how fast loyalty fades once the status quo changes."

Another black car comes down the driveway, rocks flying as it races along the gravel road.

Raymond is momentarily distracted by the noise but turns back to me. "The games are about to begin. May we come inside?"

I hold the door with my right hand, blocking the three of them with my body. "I don't think you should. The man of the house isn't home. It's not right for you to enter if he's not here." I let a small smile escape with my comment, playing into the modern decency.

"What man? We already know your father's never coming home again." Raymond's eyes are cold and lifeless. "And you have no staff. It's only the two of you." The men shift behind him. "I suggest you let us in. It's only going to get worse if you don't."

My legs start to shake with the realization that this isn't going to end well, but I stand my ground. "Tell me what you want."

Two men exit the car that has just pulled up, guns in their hands, yet they still take the time to button their suit jackets. One wears a brown suit and the other a gray one.

Raymond's expression doesn't change. "We have it on good authority that you've been bending the rules. Selling booze."

"Bootlegging," adds one of the other officers.

Raymond gives him a look.

"Loretta, what is he talking about?" My mother's soft voice drifts toward the door, but it's the same one I've heard before when she needed to feign innocence.

"You beat us here, Raymond." The man in the brown jacket is now on the porch, the one in the gray suit only a few steps behind. He meets my eyes, his own void of emotion. "Federal Agent Douglas."

It's clear what's about to happen. There's no use delaying it. "Please don't break anything," I say as I release my hold on the door.

It only takes minutes for them to ransack the house in search of the illicit liquor they're accusing me of selling. The beds are flipped, holes are punched in the walls, and everything we own is emptied out of the cabinets. I sit with my mother on the steps of the front porch, every noise making both of us jump, but we know what they're going to find. Nothing.

My pinkie is intertwined with hers, the same thing she did for me years ago when I was scared, but now my pinkie is on top, protecting her.

I try not to let the tension flow into my fingers, but every moment I wait for them to exit the house, my muscles tighten.

My other hand rubs my mother's back as we wait, the front porch getting colder beneath us. "They'll leave soon."

"What if they don't?"

"They have to. There's nothing here." But as I listen to them rustle around in the house, the thought of the cellar under the barn remains at the forefront of my mind.

One at a time, the officers walk out of the house in frustration, their hands empty, their disappointment visible.

Raymond is next, his shoes kicking up dirt in the driveway as he glances around for another place where we could be hiding the brandy. His eyes finally meet mine. "We didn't find anything," he admits.

"Of course you didn't," I reply, trying not to show the relief I feel that they're about to leave.

"Can't win them all, Raymond," Federal Agent Douglas says, joining him in the driveway.

"Even checked the basement. Nothing," says the man in the gray suit, his gun finally back inside his coat.

"It's not over yet. I have more planned." Raymond focuses his attention on my mother. "I have a couple of questions for you."

I shift closer to her. "Anything you need to ask, you can ask both of us."

He glances at me, his lip curling in anger. "Excuse me." His voice is louder this time. "You have to answer me when I ask you questions." He's like a child about to throw a tantrum. He steps toward her, his arm extended, but I stand up and move in front of him.

"Don't touch her."

He sneers at this. "I'm an officer of the law, and I can arrest her right here and now if I want. Both of you if you'd like."

"On what grounds?"

"Any grounds I want." He stares at me, the threat heavy in the air between us.

It's almost amusing seeing him like this. A man clearly used to getting what he wants and now being denied that. My mother stands from her seated position on the porch, ready to head back inside.

"Today is far from over for you. We're not leaving yet." Raymond smiles. "Where are the peaches?" he asks calmly.

CHAPTER THIRTY

RAYMOND

Raymond waits for an answer as he stares at the two ladies in front of him. Mrs. Hart flicks her eyes at Letty, but Letty doesn't look away from Raymond. Interesting.

"Peaches?" she asks. "You want to buy something while you're here?"

Raymond presses his lips together, holding back the smile. "Not exactly." He waits for the fear to appear on their faces, but it doesn't. He casts a glance at Douglas and Overson, but they're watching him from the side, their arms crossed, unamused at the situation. As agents, they're supposed to take the lead on raids, but this was Raymond's tip. And he needs to deliver.

Raymond shifts his stance, reaches into his coat, and produces the can he's been keeping. "This is yours, correct?"

Mrs. Hart squints her eyes and nods, the movement so slight, it's barely noticeable.

"I'll take that as a yes."

"Where did you get that?" asks Letty.

"A suspect we arrested had one of these in his possession. That's what led me to you."

"You came all the way out here because he bought peaches from us?" Mrs. Hart shakes her head. "Could have saved you the trip. We sell a lot of canned peaches."

"Is that so?" Raymond holds the can closer to them, though neither of them looks at it. "But not peaches. Alcohol."

"I think you're mistaken." Letty crosses her arms.

"Oh, I bet you think I am. But I can guarantee I'm not. So let me ask you again. Where are the peaches?"

Letty wipes her hands on her pants and brushes a strand of hair from her face. "This way," she says, showing a lack of fear or worry.

Her mother reaches for her shoulder, but Letty pats her hand. "You can stay here."

"On the contrary," replies Raymond. "I need both of you."

The two women hook arms, and Raymond follows them toward a carriage house that sits about twenty feet from the house. He feels the same adrenaline rush he gets when he visits bootleggers, though that's often alone. And he's missing his cigarette.

"The canning station," Letty says as they enter the carriage house.

It's a large table with a lever press on it and empty cans in crates to the left, with a basket of full cans to the right.

He moves around the table, sniffing like the basset hound he had as a child. But there's not the slightest scent of alcohol. They're better at this than he thought. Even the best bootleggers he's visited over the years couldn't conceal that whiff in the air from alcohol spilled on their clothes and invisible drops in the dirt.

He picks up a can from the basket, the weight heavy, the label matching the one he brought. It's exactly like the one that was filled with alcohol. Raymond's fingers twitch for the cigarette papers and the tobacco tin, but it's not time yet.

"Here we are, the moment of truth. You're charged with violation of the Volstead Act. Both of you."

Mrs. Hart steps back, but Letty doesn't move. "On what grounds?"

Beaucamp and Miller stand by Douglas and Overson, waiting for Raymond's signal to proceed with the arrest, but he doesn't give it.

He holds up the sealed can he pulled from the basket and shakes it. "This is everything I need."

Letty puts her hands on her hips. "You have nothing."

A challenge. Raymond enjoys challenges. Especially one he's about to win.

He takes the can opener hanging on the wall and opens the can, staring at Letty as he does. Her gaze is unflinching, but so is his.

He dumps the contents onto the ground, waiting for the scent of whiskey and the look of fear and defeat in her eyes.

Instead, she smiles.

He looks down.

Peaches, their quartered light-orange slices, lie in the dirt at his feet.

"Looks like peaches," says Beaucamp, his tone nearly a laugh.

"Close your head, Beaucamp." He turns to Letty. "This isn't funny, Letty Hart."

"I never said it was."

It has to be here. He opens another can, pouring more peaches onto the ground.

The agents stay to the side, shaking their heads, but Beaucamp and Miller join Raymond until every single can is empty and discarded, the fruit mixing with the dirt in a pulpy mess on the carriage house's floor.

"Where is the whiskey?" His fingers are gripping the last empty can so hard that his wrist aches.

"We don't have any," replies Mrs. Hart. "We're a winery."

He picks up the can that the drunk had in his possession, the one he brought here today, and holds it in front of them. "This can was full of whiskey."

"Why do you think it was whiskey?"

Raymond tilts his head. "Because I have a nose. Anyone who does could smell it."

"OK," says Letty. "A man decided to fill up one of our empty peach cans with whiskey and use that as his cup and that's why you're here?" She shrugs, an amused smile on her face. "Seems like a load of baloney."

Raymond throws the can down. "This is far from over. I'll find where you're keeping the liquor."

Letty's smile doesn't fade. "There's no liquor. It's time to focus on more important things, Detective. Like unsolved murders."

Raymond narrows his eyes. "What murders?"

"Any of them. Surely you have more important things to do than bother a farm that legally produces wine."

"Indeed," responds Raymond, but he knows something else is going on. "You may not have alcohol, or at least none that I can find right now. But where do you keep this supposedly legal wine?"

"In the barn." She motions to the other building on the property.

He nods to Miller, who turns and walks to the car.

"I'm going to need to see it," continues Raymond.

"Why?"

Raymond tilts his head and smiles. "You can unlock the winery, or we'll break the doors down. But either way, we're getting in. And I won't be feeling as nice that way. There'll be arrests. Both of you."

Douglas takes out his watch, ready for the show ahead, but Raymond doesn't need to look at the time. He knows it will only be minutes from now. He walks alongside Letty to the winery. Though she keeps trying to move ahead of him, he keeps pace.

After she unlocks the door, Raymond strolls inside, the wooden barrels stacked against the wall, two vats on the other side. "Not bad. But who makes it?"

"I do."

Raymond laughs. "I find that hard to believe."

"Why?"

He scoffs. "Do you really need me to say it?"

"Women are excellent winemakers. We would make excellent detectives, too."

Raymond looks at the uneven lines of the barn doors, the large barrels no woman could move, the grape crates breaking at the corners. "You need a man here." He nods at Letty. "Maybe you'll find one someday."

"We get by just fine on our own," she replies. "The two of us, working together." She looks at Raymond and then at Beaucamp to his side. "There were three more of you. Where are your friends?"

Raymond doesn't answer, enjoying the moment as Miller completes the task they discussed earlier. Raymond can't do what he really wants to do right now, but at least he can enjoy this. He glances at Letty and Mrs. Hart, his eyes moving back and forth between them. "I'm feeling a little generous today. I won't arrest you. I'm not low enough for that. Arresting a broad when she's played nice. But about her mother . . ."

"We're legal, and I'm the only one who makes wine here." Letty puts her hands on her hips. "If you have to arrest someone, take me, but leave her out of it."

"A tiny thing like you? You wouldn't last five minutes in jail. Besides, the boys downtown will never believe a woman was bootlegging."

"You never seem to listen, Detective Raymond. There's no bootlegging going on."

"Seems we have a difference of opinion. And that's fine. But remember, you're not in jail because of me."

Letty tilts her chin up. "I don't owe you anything."

"Sure, you don't." But Raymond's tone is jovial, a switch from just moments before. He turns his attention to the barrels and starts counting.

"What are you doing?" asks Mrs. Hart.

"Completing the process. There's been suspicion of bootlegging here, and we need to follow through on it, which includes investigating your wine."

"We have the certificate," Letty replies.

"I'll get Father O'Leary," says Mrs. Hart.

"You're not going anywhere. We can go speak to him ourselves, and if it's verified, you'll get your barrels back, but for now"—he pauses at the sound of the trucks, led by Miller, rolling in on the dirt driveway—"we're confiscating everything here until we can confirm that you're legal."

CHAPTER THIRTY-ONE

LETTY

When the last truck leaves our winery, only two barrels remain in the barn, left behind due to lack of space. The federal agents are long gone, as they accompanied the first trucks, but Raymond is still here.

The fact that an officer, Beaucamp, is still with him provides some solace. When he took care of Shorty, he was alone, as far as I know.

Raymond turns to me and adjusts his round glasses, a look of triumph on his face. "Next time, you should really be careful who you sell to in this town. Even if it was just peaches."

"Next time you come to our house, you should watch where you walk." I point to his shoe, which is covered in a horse chip from the neighbor's filly, who occasionally wanders through our property. I don't bother to hide my smile.

Raymond takes a handkerchief from his pocket and wipes off his shoe. "I'll be watching you, Ms. Hart."

"I have nothing left to watch. You've taken it from me."

He grins, his head moving slowly up and down, clearly pleased with himself. He presses his lips together, as if there's more he's going to say.

"Ready?" asks Beaucamp.

"If we must." Raymond tips his hat at us. "Ladies." He walks out of the barn and toward his car with Beaucamp. I step outside to make sure they leave, watching as the black vehicle races down the driveway, dirt flying up around it.

I wait until the sound of the engine is a distant memory before returning to the barn and staring at the mess in front of us.

My mother is softly weeping, and I put my arms around her.

Our entire inventory is depleted. There is no wine revenue left. Two barrels won't get us far with the church, and they've taken all the bottles.

"They've gone. It's OK now," I say, trying to comfort myself as much as my mother as we leave the barn.

"I can't go through another one of these." My mother's voice is weak, as if any energy she had left has vanished. "Knowing that they could come again at any minute and arrest us. We did everything right. Everything as we were supposed to, and this still happened. This is because of what you've gotten yourself into. Letty, this happened because of you."

"A man stole a can out of my hand yesterday. It won't happen again. Also, no more advertising. Our label was on the can. That was my mistake. Never again."

"You have to stop."

"And do what? We have no money and no product." My attention drifts to the vineyards. It would take years to replant the ground with something else that could be harvested, and we don't have the time or the funds. "If I don't continue, we lose everything. That can't happen."

She rests her head on my shoulder. "We've already lost everything."

"There was a winery that got their barrels back after the trial. In the city. It was in the paper." My words fail to assure her. My mother doesn't lift her head.

I hook her pinkie again, and we stand there as the light changes in the sky. I thought they wouldn't come to the winery. I thought it was a safe place to hide from the dangers of the boulevards. Today showed me that it isn't. I have a choice: to fight back or let a corrupt cop take away my freedom, my safety, and my family.

"We can survive," adds my mother. "We'll go live with my sister in Salt Lake. We'll be OK."

But that means leaving everything behind. The land her father bought years ago when he came out to California, the land she kept when she married my father and they grew the vineyard, doubling it in size. The one he left behind when he left us. The only land I've ever known.

I stare at the Verdugo Mountains in the distance, at the way the eucalyptus trees sway in the breeze at the edge of our property, and at the peach trees my mother planted when I was little. I was nearly ten when they reached full size and I was able to swing off some of the branches, the peaches falling to the ground as I did, a midday snack for me and the neighboring kids in the area.

"OK, that does it." I walk toward the house, but my mother stays back, a note of fear and worry in her eyes.

"What?" she asks.

"I'm making a plan." I cross the threshold and look at the state of the house. The kitchen table is upended, the cabinets open, their contents strewn, and the bread box on the floor, the remaining loaf squashed by a shoe. They looked everywhere for the brandy, in every space they could. Even the icebox is open, the meat on the floor, already thawing.

"A plan to go to Salt Lake?" my mother asks from the doorframe of the house. She hasn't entered yet, as if she's afraid to see the full extent of the damage, but she knows me well enough to know there's more to my statement.

"No." I step back onto the porch and look past her to the barn. The sagebrush plants are undisturbed on the side near the back. Where they need to remain intact. "They've destroyed nearly everything and taken everything they haven't. We'll barely be able to eat tonight, let alone tomorrow."

"We have enough for a train ticket." My mother pulls the money from her dress, the bills I gave her earlier folded up neatly, hidden in the one place they didn't dare look. If they had seen the money, they surely would have taken it, too.

"You want to leave the winery? Our home?"

She shakes her head. "You know I don't."

"Good. Because we're not going anywhere."

"But we have nothing left," she adds.

"Not exactly." I stare at my mother, her eyes almost hopeful as they wait for my next statement, hanging on to whatever solution I'm about to offer. "They didn't find the cellar."

CHAPTER THIRTY-TWO

FORMAN

"Your two days ended last night, Forman. I'm guessing it's back to the penny arcade today?" Warrenson stands not far from her, but he's loud enough that his voice carries throughout the station. "Unless you have a necklace to show us?"

Jacobs and Miller look over, but Forman focuses her attention on the captain. "My work will continue, no matter the deadline. I'm going to do whatever I can to improve this city."

"Don't worry, Forman. You can't solve them all." Warrenson steps forward and taps her on the shoulder. "Maybe in another year or two, we'll give you a second chance."

"Maybe," replies Forman as Warrenson retreats to the other side of the station. But she's not letting this case go, her mind racing with all the information she's gathered.

Shorty makes the sixth bootlegger in the past few years—the sixth bootlegger to die in the same way as the others, even if he didn't end up in the river.

Sounds of scuffling erupt as three suspects brawl in the lobby. Officers run over to help, but as Forman watches the men fight to control each other, she makes a different choice. She slips over to the filing cabinet near Beaucamp's desk, flips through the drawer, and pulls out the file she's looking for. Pressing it close to her to keep it out of sight, she heads over to a desk on the other side of the station.

It's a file she's already looked through, but she knows she's missing something. And she's not ready to return to her normal duties, not just yet.

Forman turns the pages, DECEASED stamped in red ink under the photo of the bootlegger. If they're all being killed by the same person, the killer might have the necklace. But this one, the first one, isn't like the others. It was a car accident, with no signs of foul play or strangulation.

Yet this file is different in another way. It's thinner than the others, as if there's something missing.

She looks again. She doesn't have the other files to compare it with at the moment, but she knows they were detailed, containing reports on their bootlegging businesses and their crimes against the law, followed by information about their deaths.

This one is only on his death, with a brief reference to his bootlegging, like a postscript on his life. And pages of the report are missing.

"Forman, why are you still here?" asks Warrenson. He stands over her shoulder imposingly. "You should be out on your patrol."

"Going now." She closes the file and stands as the scuffle erupts again.

"Settle down, boys," he hollers to the three suspects, all of them now cuffed. "We'll get you processed soon."

Forman takes this opportunity, while he is distracted, to slip the file into her bag.

He turns back to her and snarls, "Well, what are you waiting for?"

"Of course." She moves past him and out of the station, but she knows she won't be doing her normal beat. She'll be checking the pawnshops in case the necklace is there. The opportunity for a promotion may have passed, but there's still a necklace to find. She doesn't believe it's at Mrs. Michaels's house. It has to do with Thomas. It must.

After that, she'll find out what happened to the bootlegger in the file in her bag. Nicknamed Winks.

His real name: Richard Hart.

CHAPTER THIRTY-THREE

LETTY

The steady rattle of the truck engine fills the air as I wait in the driveway for my mother to join me. She's a few feet away, her hands twisting the pale cloth she was using in the kitchen. It's the same movement she made seconds before my father walked away. When she had said all she could say and waited for him to put the final nail in the coffin of their marriage. A marriage that, to my young eyes, had seemed fine only the day before.

She said more than I did that day. And now, once again, I'm silent, wondering if she will join me on this journey. I can do this alone, but I'd rather not.

The twisting continues.

When my father left, I took over the winemaking, learning as much as I could through trial and error. She helps me harvest, the vines too numerous to pick on my own, but other than that, she leaves me to it. At first, I didn't think she wanted to help, but as I watched her over the years, I saw the way she'd reach out to do something and then pause. The way she'd open her mouth to make a suggestion but then stop herself. It wasn't that she didn't want to help. She wanted me to learn on my own. To be strong. And I am.

But now the time has come to see if we can be strong together.

"You don't have to," I finally say, a heaviness between us from the destruction wrought today.

She wrings her hands harder. "I don't know if I like this idea."

"If you have any other ones, I'm open to them. But we need to move fast. If there's anything I've learned from this week, it's that we have to be quick."

"Letty . . ."

"Stay here. I'll take care of it. You don't have to know."

My mother shakes her head and opens the door of the truck. "As long as this isn't dangerous."

"This part? Not yet."

She gets into the passenger seat and closes the door, the sound magnifying the silence between us.

I turn right out of the driveway, the Santa Monica Mountains in the far distance, with the city behind them, as the truck chugs along, the road uneven underneath the tires.

We approach the local gas station, the truck nearly yearning to stop, but I know we have enough. I filled it up a few days ago. Before everything changed.

"Where are we going?" Her voice is quiet, hesitant to ask but compelled to try.

"A little errand."

She twists the kitchen towel again, like a child clinging to a blanket, hoping it can protect them from the evils of this world. "Where?"

I keep one hand on the steering wheel as I turn to her, my hand touching her shoulder. "Do you really want to know?"

She shakes her head, but a small smile comes to her face, the first I've seen today and one that surprises me.

"Why are you smiling?"

"Because of you."

I take my hand away, trying to focus back on the road, but still look at her every chance I get. "Why?"

"Because everything is gone and yet here you are, still moving forward." She looks at the towel, her hands relaxing. "There's nothing you can't handle."

I swallow hard, letting my doubts go. "You raised me well." I glance over at her. "I'm sorry I brought this on you. And I'm sorry they destroyed your supply of cans and peaches. Soon we'll be able to afford more. I promise. And you'll go back to canning, and I'll go back to . . ."

"Whatever it is you're doing now," she replies. "I'll keep canning. Today won't stop me. I'll can more. Peaches, that is."

"Like mother, like daughter."

"And you? How are you going to sell the brandy?"

"I think we should hide it in plain sight."

"What do you mean?"

I turn to her. "They were looking for cans, right? Let's do bottles."

"Letty." Her tone is one that I've heard throughout my life when she feels like I'm on the wrong path.

"Father always said to make it simple—don't label the bottles, and don't drink the product. We labeled them before. Now we won't. And as for the simple, well, it will be simple."

"Letty," she repeats, "your father wasn't always right."

"No, he definitely wasn't," I agree. We're close to our destination. The goal of this errand. "This is going to work. The big sales didn't, but individual sales did. I have an idea."

"Care to share it?"

"Not yet."

"You are your father's daughter."

I flick my eyes to her. "No, I'm not. I'm your daughter, and I'm me. That's all I need to be. Trust me on this. It will work."

I slow down outside Carter's Dairy Farm, the white fence lining the road, a small herd of black-and-white Holstein cows in the bare pasture.

"Why . . . ?"

"You'll see."

The driveway is short, the wooden barn right near the road. The smell of the cows permeates the truck.

"Letty, but aren't they the ones who came to the winery the other night?"

"Yes, they are." I stop the truck near the main barn, my mother silent as I close the door, leaving her inside.

The milking area is in front of me, a long open building with cows lined up inside but no people around.

A man in a straw hat exits a small barn to the left, a bucket in his hand.

"Hey," I shout. "I'm looking for Billy Carter."

"We don't allow visitors during working hours."

"Not a visitor. Tell him a friend is here to see him."

The man wavers for a moment and then disappears back inside.

I glance at my mother, but she's still sitting in the truck, the reflection on the glass blocking my view of her face. I know she's worried, though. I don't want her to be.

I return my focus to the building, my hands on my hips. I don't have a gun this time, but I don't think I'll be needing one.

Lawrence, the younger of the intruders from that night, stumbles back at the sight of me. "Billy!" he yells, frozen like a raccoon caught in the light, his hands almost raised, as if I'm armed. The sight makes me smile.

Billy walks out of the barn, his overalls muddy. He stops when he sees me, but he doesn't react.

"Remember me?" My hands are still firmly on my hips.

"We don't want no trouble."

"And you'll get none. But I'm here to make you an offer."

"We don't take offers from people like you."

"No, you just come and try to rob me in the middle of the night." I don't move, my stance the same. "I didn't shoot you that night, so the way I figure it, you owe me one. I want to buy some of your bottles. Right now."

CHAPTER THIRTY-FOUR

FORMAN

The pawnshops end up being an errand akin to navigating roads that have no end, where you can drive miles into the desert in search of a town and come away with only sand in your teeth.

Forman visits two, both in the Hollywood area, where Thomas could have easily gone after coming down from Beachwood Canyon. Neither owner had seen the necklace Forman described, and both tried to sell her other necklaces, saying they were similar or would look pretty on her.

Ending up empty handed, Forman returns to her normal beat for the day, patrolling the streets, though her mind stays on the case.

At the end of her shift, she returns to the station, but unlike the other officers leaving for the day, eager to get home, she waits near the wall of the main room, her focus on Beaucamp's empty desk.

"It's late," says Warrenson. "Time for you to get home to your family."

"Soon."

He's standing behind her now, as if deciding what to say. "What are you up to, Forman? There's no longer a case assigned to you."

She looks up at Warrenson, at his graying hair, his weathered face. He's been here for a long time, working his way up to captain, and Forman is certain that he's stayed late more than a few times without thinking twice about it, his wife at home waiting. And he's never commented on any of the guys staying after their shifts.

"Closure, Captain. Closure. I'm following up on a lead." But her eyes move past him. Beaucamp has entered, and her hand grips the file from her bag.

He's with Raymond, and they're both smiling. She can hear snippets of their conversation, recounting a big raid and the barrels of wine now in the police storehouse.

"Home, Forman. You had your two days, and you didn't solve it. I'm sure any other closure can wait." Warrenson moves past her, patting Raymond on the shoulder as he disappears down the hall. Raymond stops to talk to Jacobs, but Beaucamp returns to his desk.

Forman approaches, even though Beaucamp has not yet taken a seat, and holds up the file.

His eyes drift to the file and back to her. "What is it?"

"The same file from the other day."

The realization dawns. "You took it from my cabinet?"

"Borrowed it. You let me look at it once; twice shouldn't matter. But it's missing pages."

Beaucamp crosses his arms, his height almost even with Forman. "I keep clean files."

She opens it to the first two pages and then the third. "See? Where's the rest of the file on this guy"—she looks at the name—"Richard Hart?"

"Why do you want to know?"

"Can't an officer be curious?"

He narrows his eyes, which are already shaded by his cap and hard to read. "Not if it's dealing with a case that has nothing to do with her work."

"It's an old case from years ago; no one will care."

He doesn't shift his gaze. "You care."

She nods.

"You're letting this take your attention away from your chance at a promotion."

"Haven't you heard? The promotion already passed."

"Then why are you digging?"

"What's this?" asks Raymond as he saunters over. "Your promotion? Did you solve the thing for Mrs. Michaels?"

Forman gives an almost imperceptible shake of her head.

"Sorry to hear that, Forman. Better luck next time. In fact"—he pauses as he pulls a bottle of red wine out of his bag—"here, from me to you."

Forman doesn't reach for the wine. "That's against the law."

"You *are* the law, Forman. Wake up. Besides, this was confiscated in a raid today. It's ours now." Raymond puts it on Beaucamp's desk. "Here, it'll be waiting for you when you're ready."

"I won't touch it."

"Lighten up, Forman. This job is a lot more fun when you learn to bend the rules."

Warrenson reenters the station room. "August, in my office. I hear you did good today."

Raymond grins and adjusts his glasses. "I did, Captain." He struts over to the office, his gait wide, and Forman is alone with Beaucamp once again.

She closes the file to prevent the pages from slipping out. "I want to know about this guy."

"It's not your territory." He holds out his hand to take the file.

"It might be."

He raises his eyebrows but keeps his hand out, his head tilting. "Let's see."

She hesitates, worried she's not going to get it back, but gives it to him anyway. He opens it to the second page and then flips through more. "Huh."

"What?"

"No photos. There should be some in here from the autopsy."

"I thought you kept clean files."

He glares at her. "I do. They were in here."

"Who has them now?"

"No idea." He flips over a page and then closes the file, pausing for a moment with an air of frustration before leaning toward the drawers.

Forman holds out her hand. "I want to keep looking at it."

"Forman, the information you're looking for isn't going to just magically appear." He holds it closer but still slightly out of reach.

"We'll see." Forman takes the file back from him and tucks it under her arm, moving toward the door.

"You're taking it home?"

"Not exactly," she says as she spins on her heels and looks at Beaucamp. "I'm going to the morgue."

"You're wasting your time."

"Maybe. Maybe not."

🦋

The morgue looks and feels the same as the day before. The only changes are different bodies gracing the tables, but even they look similar covered in sheets. The ones without coverings have the same lifeless stares.

Forman doesn't bother to keep Glick between her and a body this time as she approaches. "Glick."

He looks up from his current project. "You're spending a lot of time in here lately," says Glick. "I thought you stuck to all of the women stuff."

"I used to. Not anymore." She points to the file in her left hand. "I'm looking for an autopsy report from two years ago. Richard 'Winks' Hart. He was a bootlegger, died in a car accident."

"Well, there you have it. Car accident." He busies himself organizing the instruments on the table, as if neatness counts in a profession where the patients no longer care.

"I don't think a car accident was all of it."

"Care to elaborate?"

"Not really." The temperature in the room feels colder than it did yesterday. "Do you keep files here?"

Glick motions at the folder in her hands. "After everything is finished in here, all reports go back to the boys and end up in files like that."

"Not this time. They're missing."

He turns back to the body. "Sounds like someone doesn't want you to know."

"That's not going to stop me."

He smiles, keeping his head down. "You remind me of my wife."

"I don't know if that's a good thing."

He glances up. "It is." He takes a moment and puts down the blade, removing his gloves and leaving them on the tray. He walks over to the sink and washes his hands in hot water, the steam rising up from the bowl.

Glick turns off the water, dries his hands with a white towel, and heads to a metal rolling cabinet. He pulls out a long drawer, flipping through the folders. "Richard Hart, you say?"

"Yes, July 1925." Forman tries to contain her excitement, which is tinged with unease at the thought of a break in this case.

"Richard Hart, July 1925," says Glick as he pulls up a file.

"Yes!" she says a little too enthusiastically but quickly corrects her tone. "That's it."

He flips the pages, the thin paper crinkling in the stark air. "You say car accident?"

"Yes." Forman crosses her arms.

His eyes remain on the paperwork. "Maybe he died in a car accident, but something else was going on."

"What do you mean?"

He slides a paper forward on the cabinet and points to his notes. "See that right there? His neck was broken. One swift movement took him out."

"During the accident?" Forman reads along the handwritten line.

"Well, it could have been part of the accident, but he wasn't alone. That twist of the neck? That was done with human hands. The victim had bruises on his neck, indicating finger impressions." He looks up at her from the paper, a softer paternal look on his face now. "Can I give you a piece of advice?"

"Sure."

"Stay away from all this. There're people involved in this that you don't want to cross."

Forman steps closer and looks him in the eyes. "Tell me. I want to know."

"Certain people to stay away from. People who won't appreciate where you dig. Even when some end up in here, there's always other ones to take their place. Not to mention the ones who end up untouchable."

"Like who? Give me a name."

Glick takes a moment, his eyes moving back and forth as if he can't decide to speak, but then breathes out. "If you ever come across someone named John Corizano, or Blue, you run, not walk, the other way."

CHAPTER THIRTY-FIVE

RAYMOND

It's been three days since the raid, and Raymond hasn't heard a word from the Hart Farm. They haven't come in, as far as he knows, to file an appeal to get their wine back. It's the easiest takedown he's ever had, even though he was unable to prove that the brandy came from there. But his methods, this time, were clean and honest. And yet they worked.

The ocean breeze rustles around him, and Raymond touches his right pocket to feel for the outline of the folded piece of paper. It's still there, the address written in a small scrawl, waiting for him.

"You OK, Raymond?" Beaucamp adjusts his cap, wiping his forehead before putting it back in place. "You seem distracted."

"Doing fine," replies Raymond. He touches his pocket again.

They are standing next to the docks in Long Beach, where rumrunners have been rumored to moor at times. An old sailor leans against one of the pilings, not impressed by Beaucamp's questions.

Beaucamp continues with his interrogation, but Raymond's view is on the ocean, the navy-blue waves moving back and forth, forming peaks, and then dissolving as quickly as they appeared. The metal case of tobacco is in his other pocket, the weight pulling on him as if begging to be used. Soon.

"I told you they don't come here no more," says the sailor, his yellow coat folded up near his collar, his gray hair a month past needing a trim.

"Sure, sure," says Raymond. "If they do, we'll be back."

"You'll be here for nothing." The sailor spits to the side and returns his focus to Raymond.

"Well, that was disappointing," Beaucamp says, closing his notebook, as they walk back to the parking lot. "Drive all the way down only to reach a dead end."

"You know they come here," says Raymond. "They pull their boats up to the docks and unload the crates, then motor back out to sea before the fish even realize they've been gone. Don't worry, we'll get them."

"Maybe." Beaucamp looks more tired than usual. "Sorry you came in your own car. I should have waited for you."

"No, no, it's fine." Raymond adjusts his glasses, using the movement to hide his smile.

"Come on, I'll follow you back. Maybe it can still be a better day."

Raymond puts up his hand. "Beaucamp, you go back by yourself. I'm going to stick around and check on something."

"A lead? What is it?"

"Nothing like that."

"No, I'll stay with you."

Raymond moves his head. "Not this time. This is something else."

Beaucamp grins, his eyes sparkling. "You have a gal on the side, don't you? What would Betty say?"

"This isn't about Betty."

"Sure it's not." He kisses his two fingers and holds them up. "Scout's honor, I'll never tell."

Raymond shifts, pulling his coat closed as he does. "It's not like that. It's just a small errand. A follow-up on a case from the other day. That guy who said some kids stole candy from his store."

"A follow-up," says Beaucamp. "That I can't join you on."

"No."

Beaucamp nods again, his grin remaining. "OK, then, lover boy. I'll see you back at the station."

Raymond tips his hat and waits for Beaucamp to drive away, not moving until the black sedan is a speck in the distance.

He slips into his own car and pulls the paper from his pocket. A house in San Pedro, just seven miles from here.

His hand stays on the silver cigarette case as he drives, his fingers tracing the familiar engraving.

The address is a two-story Craftsman with dark clapboard siding, white trim and eaves, a veranda supported by stone columns, and a porte cochere with a lawn in front. Like any other house in the neighborhood.

Raymond puts his hat on as he gets out, the felt sitting firmly on his head. He moves into the driveway, his shoes clipping on the concrete, but he stops at the gate to the backyard.

The scent is in the air, one that he can smell from ten feet away, and he's surprised the neighbors haven't complained, but maybe they're all in on it, too. A house close enough to the docks to move product from the boats, and yet this guy wants to make his own. Interesting.

Raymond stands near the house and opens his cigarette case. He pulls a paper out, and with a flick of his fingers, he's laying tobacco in a fine line on the white sheet. The anticipation makes his hand shake as he rolls up the cigarette and licks the seam.

A boy cruises by on his bike and looks up at Raymond. Raymond waves and smiles, and the boy continues on. People don't remember the nice man who smiles. They remember the one who looks like he shouldn't be there. The one who is uncomfortable. The one who looks out of place.

Raymond removes the gold lighter from his pocket and lights the cigarette, drawing one short drag as he slips inside the gate.

It's time.

CHAPTER THIRTY-SIX

FORMAN

Forman's been back on her regular patrol for the last few days, but it's not regular in her mind. Not after the information she learned about the bootleggers.

A girl in her early twenties walks down the street in front of Forman, a canvas-covered suitcase in her hand, as if she's just arrived in Los Angeles, dreams of the silver screen filling her head. When she turns around, Forman swears she looks familiar. A young woman she has seen on her patrols. And this is the second girl with a canvas-covered suitcase in as many days.

The girl, her blonde hair bobbed, barely showing under her black hat, is in a black-and-white dress, far fancier than the suitcase she carries. But that's not what's piquing Forman's interest. It's that she keeps looking over her shoulder every two steps, like she wants to make sure no one follows her. The girl yesterday had the same air to her, a carefulness, as if she held a secret no one should unlock.

She turns down a street, the suitcase awkward in her hand, as if it has some weight to it. Forman moves to the corner to watch the girl, keeping her distance.

The girl stops outside a grocery store and glances around, her attention landing on Forman. Forman maintains eye contact until it's clear the girl is not going to move. Forman glances back to the main boulevard, watching the cars go past, then returns her attention to the store. The girl has gone inside.

Forman takes her time walking toward the store, wanting the girl to be in the middle of whatever she's doing in there as Forman enters.

Fruits and vegetables are lined up on the left-hand side, and a long counter to the right likely served as a bar before the law was enacted.

"How can I help you today, madam?" asks a friendly-looking man, gray hair at his temples, a white apron in front. "Officer," he corrects himself.

She glances around; the store is empty. "I was looking for someone who just came in here. Black-and-white dress, blonde hair."

He shakes his head. "Nope, haven't seen her."

Forman stares at the man, but his smile remains. "It was about a minute ago. She had a suitcase."

"Take a look around if you like." He picks up an apple that has rolled onto the floor, replacing it on the stack with the others.

Forman strolls to the back of the store and checks the side room, but the entire place is empty. The girl has vanished.

🦋

Forman waits near the street, unsure if she should phone in this event. She has the call-box key in her bag, but she wants to find out more.

And then like magic, the girl appears, walking out of the grocery store, the suitcase seemingly lighter in her hands.

Forman nods to her as she approaches.

The girl flashes a smile back, continuing on her way.

After a moment, so does Forman, the whole event puzzling. She arrives at the Rosewood dance hall, part of her regular beat.

Ruthie and her friends are nearby, except they're different from when she saw them last week. They're more confident—different makeup, even new clothes. Cleaner. Better groomed.

Ruthie smiles as Forman approaches. Her hair is neatly pulled back, and she's wearing a blue dress. A new blue dress, unmarked and untorn. "Is this going to be a new habit of yours, Forman? Coming around here more often?"

"It's part of my patrol."

"Not this much. You worried about us?"

"Not as much as I used to be. Life seems to be looking up for you."

"It might be," says Ruthie, her smile the same one she always gives, no matter the question.

Ruthie's friend, the blonde who was so skittish before, stands close, no longer afraid of the uniform. "What's it to you?"

Forman directs her attention back to Ruthie. "Girls have to stick together. I've been worried about you, but it seems you're getting money again." She gives them the side-eye. "Prostitution is illegal, too. The men won't always be so nice. And some of you may end up in the morgue. I've seen it myself."

Forman thinks back to one of her first days at the station. A girl, not more than fifteen, was nearly beaten to death in a hotel after the man who hired her decided he wanted to rough her up instead. Warrenson had given Forman the task of trying to get information from her. They figured a woman would have more luck than any of the male officers. But the girl stayed tight lipped. Never gave a clue as to who had done that to her. She lived for two days before she finally succumbed to her injuries.

"We don't have time for that," says the shortest girl in the group, the one who looks closest to Ruthie's age, her brown hair cut in a bob. "We get by on our own and don't listen to any coppers."

"Agreed," says the blonde.

"She's one of the good ones, Dorothy." Ruthie nods her head toward Forman. "She's on our side."

"Doesn't sound like it," replies Dorothy.

"I am," Forman says, looking at the three women in front of her. Girls, really, one of them possibly not more than a few years into her teens. Ruthie looks to be the oldest of the group at nineteen. But all of them look better than Forman's ever seen them in the two years she's been patrolling the streets. "How are you getting by, then? What changed this week?"

"There are other ways to get by in this city than turning tricks," says Dorothy.

"Such as?"

Dorothy tilts her head and puts her hand on her hip as she looks around at the people passing by and then back at Forman. "Why should we tell you?"

"There's no need. I'm just curious. I really do want to help." Forman's learned during her time on the force that there's no way to make a victim, or a suspect, talk if they don't want to.

"We don't need help," Dorothy says defiantly, then turns and walks away, soon sidling over to a man in a top hat at the far corner of the block, next to the bakery.

The shorter girl with the bob moves a strand of hair away from her face, her cheeks pink from some type of cheap rouge. "Let's just say a deal came along and we knew how to take advantage of it."

A deal. A situation. Something to put them more in harm's way.

Forman reaches into her pocket and pulls out the few bills and coins she'd put in there for groceries on the way home. "Here."

"Is this a bribe?"

"Never." Forman glances at Ruthie. "You know I'm not like that." She holds out her open palm, offering Ruthie the money resting there. "Here, take it. It'll keep you from whatever you were going to do tonight."

Ruthie looks at the money but doesn't move. The other girl picks up the bills and the five coins from her hand. "Pleasure doing business with you," she says, walking away from Forman, but Ruthie stays.

"What is it, Ruthie? What's the change? Are you working for someone?"

Ruthie pats her shoulder. "Believe me, you don't want to know. Leave us be. But know that we're safe and things are swell." She smiles at Forman with the same genuine expression of trust she has worked so hard to gain. "We're doing OK."

Forman nods, but her attention is distracted by Dorothy walking down the street, a suitcase in her hand. A canvas-covered suitcase.

CHAPTER THIRTY-SEVEN

LETTY

A large clock sits on the shelf, its size hiding the outline that the last one left due to years of sun bleaching the wallpaper around it.

My mother is on the couch in the living room, her dress made of silk and velvet. Her first new one in years but not the last.

Even her hands seem more able as she knits, the finest lavender thread forming into a square. "I'll make strawberry Bavarian cream cake for dessert tonight."

"Have you made that before?"

"No, but there's a first time for everything." She's the happiest I've seen her, the stress of the past few years melting away in the past few days.

I turn my attention to the deliveries for tomorrow and calculate how many bottles I'll need to fill, making notes in the ledger. Fifteen in total. Not fifteen bottles, but fifteen deliveries. Everything is moving much faster than I anticipated.

The ball of yarn drops from the couch and rolls toward me. I pick it up to hand it back to her, but she's not looking at me. She's looking out the window. "Someone's here." Her voice has a note of fear in it, and an ice-cold wave washes over me.

I slam the ledger shut. It's all in code, all names and addresses illegible to the untrained eye, but still, it's proof. I don't push it back in the bookcase—it's too obvious. I glance around, my heart pounding as I look for a place it can go. Somewhere they didn't look on their raid last time.

My eyes land on the floorboard near the bedroom, the one that creaks when we step on it. I grab a knife from the kitchen and place it between the floorboards, prying the loose one up to reveal a small space a few inches deep and wide enough for the ledger.

"How many?" I ask, shoving the green book into the cubbyhole.

"One," my mother replies, her focus still out the window, the knitting needles in her hands frozen.

I pull the velvet-covered chair—the one my mother recently bought, a pale pink to match her new bedroom set—over the space. It looks awkward, out of place, as if it's hiding something, but it will have to do for now.

"Police?"

"I don't think so."

I grab the rifle—the chamber loaded with bullets—off the mantel, and move to where my mother sits.

The figure is walking up the driveway, a suitcase in their hand.

The gait is familiar, confident. Not afraid of what might be inside the farm. Of who might be inside.

I recognize her now that she's out of the trees. Curvy and determined, she has a walk that shows she knows what to do in any situation. Including this one.

"It's fine. She's one of us."

My mother doesn't move her unflinching gaze from the window. "This is why I don't like things happening here."

I lean the gun against the sofa and go out to the porch.

"What are you doing here, Dorothy?"

Her blonde hair is bouncing on her shoulders as she makes her way up the drive, ruddy cheeks glistening from the walk and her heels no match for the gravel road.

"I told you not to come to the farm." It was one of the first rules I told the girls when Margaret introduced me to them two nights ago near the dance hall.

She stops and sighs. "I was out of bottles, and there's a big order."

"You don't come here."

"I know. But . . ." She shrugs. "Besides, I'm in the area to visit a friend."

"I thought you weren't doing that anymore."

"I want to do both. Earn twice the money." She smiles, showing the gaps in her teeth, her eye makeup smudged from a late night. "I'll stop when this pays enough."

"It will. Keep selling." My attention is on the suitcase. "Come on. Let's get you filled up and out."

She follows me into the barn, and I lock the door behind us. She puts the suitcase on the table and opens up the bottom section, only accessible from the outside of the case, and only if you know where to find the secret latch. The four flasks are lined up perfectly, the fabric bands keeping the bottles in place. She hands me one.

"Do you want to take some milk bottles with you?"

Dorothy leans against a bale of hay, not sure whether to sit or stand in what is surely a foreign environment for her. "I like the flasks. I can sell a little at a time. Some boys only want a sip."

"That's not all they want." I fill up a flask from a bottle of brandy I keep hidden in the hay. I hid it the night after I met the girls and offered them work. A precaution, so if they ever did end up at the farm for more brandy, I could refill them without revealing the secret room below. A rule I will never break.

Dorothy decides to sit, crossing her legs as she watches me pour the liquid into the flask for her. She picks a piece of straw from the bale and pulls it apart in her fingers. "People have been asking about you."

I fill up the next flask before I glance at her. "They want a sale?"

"No," she replies, the shreds of straw falling from her hands. "They want to know about you."

I place the third flask under the bottle, my hand not as steady as before. "Such as?"

"Who you are. Where you are. What, exactly, it is you do." She's working at a new piece of straw now.

I focus my attention on the fourth flask as thoughts race through my mind. Questions are never a good thing. "What did you tell them?" The flask is full, but I wait to put the cap on.

"Nothing." She leans back against the wall. "I know to keep my mouth shut."

I screw the top on the flask and place it in the case. "Good." I close and fasten the suitcase and hold it out to her. She reaches for it, but I move it back. I motion with my other hand, my fingers hitting my palm.

She removes a wad of bills from her chest. I take them as I give her the case and count the bills. "It's all here?"

"Yes."

"You did good."

She grins again. "I always do."

I hand her a bill back. "A tip, for keeping your mouth shut."

She takes it. "Thanks, boss."

I shove the empty bottle into the hay, and we walk outside, Dorothy waiting as I lock the door securely behind me. I'm careful to never leave it open for a second, not ever, but especially now. "I'll come to you next time, Dorothy. If you need me to deliver more often, I'll do that."

The same sly smile I've gotten to know appears on her lips. "OK."

"You need a ride?"

"No. I'm meeting my friend. A customer out here in the valley."

"Be careful."

She puts one hand on her hip. "I always am." She moves toward the street before she turns around. "Are you worried? About someone asking?"

"Not at all. They won't bother to come all the way out here." But the words feel heavy on my lips, and I'm not sure if I even convince myself. Dorothy had no trouble getting here, and neither will anyone else. Friendly or not.

Dorothy heads down the driveway, but the unsettled feeling that arrived with her visit won't go away.

I need to do something. I survey the house. The outside is still unassuming, with its faded paint and splintering wood. We don't need to change that. You don't advertise when you come into money. Even the truck remains untouched. Everything looks the same, and yet nothing is. Especially now that someone is asking questions.

I pull the truck up to the barn, backing it up until it's right near the doors.

"They aren't supposed to come here," says my mother, coming down the front steps while I unlock the barn once again.

"I know. It won't happen again."

"What are you doing?"

"A little insurance, just in case." I flip down the small panel at the back of truck, revealing the empty compartment I built in the bed to house several bottles of liquor. I grab one from the barn and slide it into the space, its location now secure and hidden.

"In case of what?"

I look up at her, her eyes squinting in the late-afternoon sun. "In case of anything."

CHAPTER THIRTY-EIGHT

FORMAN

Forman leans against a eucalyptus tree, as if she's waiting for a bus, except one won't stop here. She watched Dorothy as she went inside the farmhouse, meeting a girl with brown hair and a beige cap. Then both of them entered the barn to the right of the driveway. Forman didn't mean to follow Dorothy all the way out here, so far from the city, but her curiosity got the better of her. Even when Dorothy took the different Red Cars into the valley, leaving the line and walking nearly a mile to the farm, Forman followed.

Yet Dorothy is walking back along the driveway now, her whole visit less than ten minutes. Barely enough time to eat or get clean, and she doesn't look any different. Only the suitcase seems heavier as she walks, her body angling to the side with the weight.

Forman stayed back during the interaction, as the last thing she wanted to do was spook Dorothy. She needs her trust.

The line of eucalyptus trees may shade Forman from sight for the time being, but they won't do anything once Dorothy gets closer, and now she's nearly to the road.

While on the Red Car, Forman prepared what to say if Dorothy noticed her, a spiel about how she was working on a separate case and how it was a surprise to be heading in the same direction. But Dorothy didn't look back during the journey, the suitcase her only concern. Yet being on the same train car, or even on the same street, isn't the same as standing right outside the farm where Dorothy clearly added something to the suitcase.

She reaches the road, and Forman moves behind a tree, the thin bark flaking off as she brushes against it. She has less than a minute until Dorothy passes.

Forman doesn't want to stop her to ask what's inside the suitcase. She needs to keep her connection to the girls, and searching them won't do any good. It won't get to the root of the problem, or whatever it is that they're up to.

But Dorothy'll be here soon.

If Forman moves into view, she'll risk losing whatever trust she's built, but it will be worse if Dorothy notices her behind the tree.

Forman takes a breath and steps onto the road, dreading the interaction.

Except Dorothy is heading the other way, walking toward the Verdugo Mountains, away from the city and away from Forman.

And now Forman's alone.

She shifts through the trees and examines the farm from a distance, looking for the girl in the beige pageboy cap. She's by the barn, a green truck moved beside it.

It sits there for what feels like several minutes as Forman tries to see what the girl is doing, but one of the barn doors blocks her view.

The girl closes the door, brushes her hands on her pants, and gets in the truck, moving it to the house.

Except she's not. It's heading down the driveway.

This is her chance. Forman removes her badge from her jacket and slips it into her bag in case the truck comes this way down the road. If it follows Dorothy, it will take a while for her to catch up, and the truck will be long gone before she finds out where it's going.

The truck turns onto the road in Forman's direction.

She steps out and puts up her hand.

The truck slows to a stop, the passenger window open. The girl in the driver's seat is only a few years younger than she is, maybe in her midtwenties. She is not fashionable like the girls in the city, always donning the latest styles. Instead, this girl's clothes are really simple, well worn, and sturdy enough for farmwork.

"Lost?" asks the driver.

"Something like that," replies Forman, realizing she has to speak up to be heard over the hum of the truck engine. "How did you know?"

The girl looks toward the road. "We don't get a lot of walkers out here."

Forman nods. "I didn't realize I was so far from the Red Car Line, and it'll be dark soon. Any chance you're heading to Chandler? I can pick up the trolley there." Forman knows it's a different direction from where Dorothy headed, so they likely won't run into each other.

The girl looks at the road in front of her, tapping her fingers on the steering wheel as if she's debating between trying one of Houdini's death-defying tricks and giving a stranger a lift for a few miles.

She looks at Forman, her brown eyes searching and calculating all at once, and motions to the seat. "Get in."

CHAPTER
THIRTY-NINE

RAYMOND

Raymond pulls his car into the driveway, a package of veal cutlets on the seat next to him wrapped in crisp white paper from the butcher near the station.

Betty will already be cooking dinner, but this is for tomorrow. She'll be thrilled. That's the key with marriage. Surprises. Always the good kind.

He steps out of his car, a small ache to his hip as he does, the errand from earlier taking slightly more energy than planned. They don't always fight back. They don't always know it's coming. But this time, this one did.

Raymond stretches his arms before reaching for the veal. His left arm is tight, too, but he got the job done. He'll have Betty massage his shoulder later. He'll make the usual excuse—that a suspect got a little out of hand. It's always the basic truth, even when details are erased, removed from the story as if they were never there in the first place.

He slams the car door, the veal in his hand, but a recognizable sound makes him stop. The familiar rattle of the engine, the slow crawl of the tires.

A trickle of ice slides down his spine.

It must have been following him, to be here so soon after he arrives.

Raymond knows the car before it even stops in front of the driveway, before he even looks back at the street. It's the one he's heard for the last two years: a 1924 Rollin Touring. The owner went so far as to have it driven out from Chicago, an homage to his roots.

Raymond pivots, the wrapped veal nearly falling out of his hands. There it is, the black box frame, the five-passenger car with the beige interior.

And the twins, the only ones who ever drive it. Because the boss has a bigger car. A better car. But this is theirs, and as usual, one twin sits in front, the other in back, too big for the small vehicle, their matching black bowler hats nearly touching the roof.

These visits are rare and only occur when there's trouble.

The back door swings open.

Raymond doesn't move. He knows he has to get in, but he wavers for a moment, drops of perspiration forming on his temples. Officers don't ride in the backs of cars. Criminals do.

"He wants to see you," says Frankie, the twin sitting in back.

"Apparently," replies Raymond.

"Now."

Raymond moves to return the veal to his car, as there's no time to take it inside the house. He also doesn't want Betty to see the twins.

"No," says Frankie as he climbs out of the car and waves a gun in the air. "Bring your things."

Raymond hesitates. He doesn't like to be the one out of control. The one sitting in the back of the car. The one who will be trapped. But he knows if he doesn't take the meeting, things will only get worse. He glances back at the house, his wife inside, his child most likely sleeping. Worse for everyone.

He gets into the car, sliding onto the beige fabric, and pulls the door closed behind him.

"That took long enough," says Eddie from the driver's seat, the dark-gray shoulders of his suit dwarfing the seat. Although identical, the twins are wearing different suits, Frankie in dark brown.

Raymond leans back on the bench. "You can tell him a cart spilled its apples and blocked the road."

Frankie moves his shoulders in a small laugh, catching the reference to one of Blue's earliest bootleggers. "I always liked you, Raymond. You're a funny guy."

"Let's hope it stays that way. Didn't think I'd see you boys for a while. What's the boss want today?"

Eddie looks over his shoulder. "You'll find out."

"Don't worry, you'll be home before dinner," says Frankie.

"Promises, Frankie," says Eddie. "We don't make 'em."

"Right," replies Frankie, his goofy smile shifting as he realizes his mistake. They've been working for Blue as long as Raymond has, even longer. The smile fades. "Drive."

Raymond glances out the window as the car pulls away. He can see Betty in the kitchen, a red-and-white apron around her waist as she prepares dinner.

He stays silent, feeling no need to continue the conversation, and apparently the twins feel the same. They wouldn't tell him anything anyway. They aren't privy to details from the boss. They're almost useless, but their brawn makes up for their stupidity.

There's nothing to say as the weight of an invisible clock settles in the car, the seconds ticking by as they pass streets filled with people on their way home.

Instructions always come in phone calls, not meetings. Meetings mean trouble. Meetings mean disapproval. Meetings mean danger.

CHAPTER FORTY

LETTY

The lady sidles into my truck as everything inside me screams that I shouldn't be doing this. I know she's a cop, even though there's no badge on her dark clothing. Her outfit resembles a uniform, but that's not what's tipping me off. There's something about the way cops move, the way they study things. And right now, she's studying me.

But I'm hiding in plain sight. This is the new way.

"What brought you out here?" I glance at her. "We don't see many of you around. They usually leave the farms to themselves."

"They?"

"Officers. Like you." I've decided to play the card early. No use keeping it to myself.

The lady smiles. "It's that obvious."

"Don't worry, it's a compliment." I press the gas, a flutter in my stomach as I think of the hidden brandy only inches from my new passenger. "It's nice to see women on the force. I don't think we have any in the stations out here."

"No." She pauses. "There's only a few of us, so I don't think you do." Her tone indicates there's no thinking about it, she knows, but she leaves it at that.

The sputter of the engine is the only sound as I drive along my familiar route, each building we pass another step closer to Chandler. These are the same roads I've driven for years, but they're changing, new construction all the time, more stores and more houses. I see them now with a fresh eye. Everything can change.

We're only a few minutes away from her stop, but I worry that her reason for being out here in the first place is because they're looking for the exact thing I'm afraid they might find. I keep my hands on the steering wheel, aware that any bump in the road could make the bottles bounce in the back, and my grasp gets tighter and tighter. I take my foot off the gas.

"Everything OK?" She's looking at me now, a slight tilt to her head. "You slowed."

"The truck," I lie. "It does that sometimes." I press the gas again, trying to keep a steady amount of light pressure on the pedal. "So the valley—what brought you out here?"

"I was on a call." She smooths her skirt. "But it turned out to be a false alarm. So now I'm on my way home." She smiles, though it's a reserved one, as if she can't show too much emotion.

I don't know if it's her personality or the job that makes her that way.

"Alone? I thought you had partners." Maybe she does and he's already back at the farm, where my mother is inside the house. Except they won't find the brandy. Everything is covered now. Everything is hidden.

"Sometimes we do." Her attention stays focused on the road in front of us. "But I don't. Not at the moment."

"Sometimes it's better without a partner. Better on your own." I don't mean for the bitterness to come out, but it's there in my voice, a nod to my father. My mother and I do fine by ourselves. If he'd never been around at all, if he'd left when I was a baby, the gaping hole of his absence, the empty weight of his betrayal, and the void he created would have filled in years ago.

"What do you grow at the farm?" She's looking at me, her hands folded in her lap, an air of informality now, as if she's out for a drive with a friend.

I motion to the back, where two bins of peaches are tied to the sides of the truck. "Peaches." I wait, uncertain whether I should say more, especially with what's hidden in the bed. "And until a few days ago, we were a sacramental winery." I look at her, her hair tucked neatly under her cap. "One of your friends took care of that."

She nods. "I'm sorry to hear that. They're cracking down on illegal alcohol."

"It was legal."

She looks at me as if she understands. But I know not to trust anyone.

"You can try to get it back," she adds.

"We'll see. Detective Raymond—"

"Raymond?"

"You know him?"

She nods, but I don't like the turn this conversation has taken. This was a mistake, but it's too late to back out now.

"Chandler, you said?" The boulevard is coming up, a mock city of the one over the hill, the farmlands far behind us. Many don't bother to go to the city, as everything we could need, from supplies to gas to food, is right here. I could even sell my wares here, too, but I know to keep it far away from home.

"Yes," replies the officer, as if she can read my thoughts. "I'll pick up a Red Car." Her attention shifts to me. "Unless you're heading to the city. I'm on my way back to Hollywood."

I clench my teeth for a moment but relax my jaw just as quickly. I don't want her to notice the tension in my jaw. The longer an officer is in my truck, the greater the chance that she'll discover what I have in the back. Still, if she thinks I have nothing to worry about, then that will be to my favor. "I can do that," I reply.

"Great. It'll save me the wait." She looks out the side window.

Otto had said most of the cops were paid off, but I also know there are officers like Raymond. Ones who will take out people like Shorty. And I've invited one into my car.

I reach into my pocket and slip my fingers around my club. The eucalyptus trees are gone now, the flat land of the valley stretching out into the distance, with buildings huddled together every mile or so.

"I didn't get your name," says the officer. "I'm Annabel Forman, though the guys at the station call me Forman."

"Nice to meet you, Annabel." I keep my attention on the road as I drive toward the Cahuenga Pass alongside the Red Cars. "I'm Letty Hart."

The chill in the car is immediate. I look over at Annabel, but her mouth is slightly open, her eyes frozen on me.

CHAPTER
FORTY-ONE

RAYMOND

The car stops outside a metal warehouse in Vernon, a city a few miles past downtown Los Angeles and known for its negligent Prohibition enforcement.

Except Raymond hasn't been to this warehouse before. Blue owns several and moves the product, and himself, around all the time. The best way to stay alive is for no one to know where you are, and he does it with ease. Except the twins know. And why or how he trusts them, Raymond doesn't understand.

"Get out," says Eddie.

"Not going to join us for the party?" asks Raymond, a lack of humor in his voice.

Neither twin moves.

"We'll be here when you're done," adds Frankie.

"Somehow I doubt that." Raymond steps out of the car and straightens his coat. When he visits the bootleggers, they don't know the fate that awaits them. They're fine one moment and dead the next. But this is different. He knows exactly what is waiting for him.

He pushes his hair back, puts his hat on, and opens the metal door. Time to get it over with.

The warehouse is cold, sacks of flour lining the sides of the building until the crates of alcohol appear, their wooden boxes barely masking the contents.

A sole line of lights illuminates the area, ending at Blue, leaving him in the shadows and Raymond in the light.

John "Blue" Corizano is sitting at a table, steak and potatoes in front of him. He's tall and solid, his salt-and-pepper hair hidden underneath his white Panama hat, a blue feather tucked into the right side of the band. Raymond's never asked if that's how he got his nickname, though more likely it was from his strangling of the first few bootleggers after he came here from Chicago, their faces turning blue as he held them underwater.

He's clean shaven, his dark-blue suit impeccably clean. He has more money than he knows what to do with, and he pays Raymond well to make sure it stays that way. Until today. Depending on what Raymond says in the next few minutes.

Behind him stands Tommy, nicknamed after the submachine gun, a tommy gun, that he holds in his hands. Raymond's never learned his real name, but he's always near Blue, ready to protect him.

Blue looks up as Raymond arrives at the table, clearly interrupting his dinner. "Well, well, well, look who the chickens have managed to bring in."

"You can call, you know. I can come on my own."

Blue flashes a crooked grin. "Now, what's the fun in that?" He sneers, pulling a long gold chain out of his jacket and flipping open the pocket watch at the end, the gold cover swinging as he does, the engraving on the back hitting the light. "You're late."

"Apple cart."

Blue nods, amused by the reference. He slips the watch back in his pocket and returns to his plate, cutting into his steak, the knife slicing through the meat with ease. "I hear you've stopped paying attention."

Raymond lifts his chin and pulls his shoulders back, his left one still aching. "I disagree. I took care of one this morning. I've been cleaning up this entire time."

"Really?" He puts a piece of steak in his mouth and chews, continuing to stare at Raymond as he does.

"Listen, Blue—"

"This is not *your* meeting." He slams his hand on the table, the silverware rattling as he does. Silence follows, only broken by the sound of him swallowing. He cuts another piece, his movements forceful and ragged. "You're supposed to be taking them out. That's why I pay you."

"I am."

"You've let a new one in." Blue looks up at Raymond and moves the knife to another portion of the steak without breaking his gaze, slicing into the meat like the slow note of a violin. "You're getting lazy. I don't like lazy." He holds up the cut piece and looks at it. "Can you imagine how I feel when I hear someone new has moved into my territory, taking customers that are meant for me? Shorty's customers were supposed to be mine."

Raymond leans back. "I took care of it. I raided her already. Three days ago. Checked the house, checked the basement. She's nothing, and she's got nothing."

"*Her?* It's a dame?" Blue laughs. "You're worse than I thought. I don't know why I don't finish you off right here."

"Because I'm police. Because you need me. Because I'm worth it."

"You." He points the knife at Raymond. "Are." Jabs again toward him. "Nothing."

A tremor rocks through Raymond, starting at his head and shaking down to his toes. He shifts his stance in an effort to hide it from Blue. "She doesn't have any more product. I checked."

Blue stands, the screech of his chair echoing from wall to wall, his glass of red wine spilling over the table. "Is that how you think we take care of things? Remove their product?" A laugh starts in his stomach and rises up to his shoulders as he removes a gun from his holster and checks the barrel.

Raymond reaches for his waist, but Blue already has the gun aimed at him. "That would be unwise, Raymond. You ever point a gun in my direction and I'll make sure you and your family are never heard from again. We clear? I'm sure Betty wouldn't look so pretty with a bullet in her blonde head."

Tommy also has his gun aimed at Raymond, but he won't shoot unless given the go-ahead by Blue.

"And I hear you have a daughter now. Few months old."

Raymond drops his hand to his side. "How did you—"

"I know everything. Everything. Don't you forget it." He turns the gun sideways. "Now, this new bootlegger, this woman, she's a problem. You're messing up, Raymond. I'm paying you to make sure I'm the only one left. If you can't handle the situation, I'll find someone else who can. But you won't be alive to see it."

"I'll take care of her." Raymond's voice is stern, but even he can hear the waver in it.

Blue raises his left eyebrow, his reaction when he doesn't believe something. "What's her name?"

He doesn't want to give away the details. To show his hand. "Marks," he replies, the name in Shorty's ledger.

"Give me one reason not to take care of Marks myself?"

Raymond swallows hard. "Because you can trust me. I'll handle it."

"Now," says Blue.

"Now," repeats Raymond.

"Good." Blue slides his gun back beneath his coat and sits down, his large hands grabbing his fork and knife. He again cuts into the meat but motions to the empty wineglass in front of him, still on its side.

Tommy reaches over and rights the glass. He pulls a bottle from the cabinet behind Blue and fills it with red wine, the edge of the bottle accidentally hitting the glass. The wine spills, and the glass rolls across the table, then falls to the concrete floor below, breaking as it lands.

"Do you see this?" Blue is staring at Raymond as he speaks. "Do you see what happened here?" He pulls out his gun and shoots Tommy in the head, his attention back on Raymond as soon as the bullet is fired.

Tommy falls to the floor, his lifeless eyes gazing into nowhere as his submachine gun slips down his chest, the noise reverberating through the warehouse.

"This is what happens when you make a mess in my business. You understand?"

Raymond nods, the lump in his throat making it hard to swallow.

"Good. Now take care of her, and get out of my sight before I change my mind."

Raymond's footsteps echo through the cavernous warehouse as he walks away, each step anticipating the bullet that is sure to come for him, even though Blue has put his gun away. He used to be in awe of the moment when Blue took care of business, whipping out a gun and finishing people off, but now that he's a potential target, shivers run down his arms and into his fingertips.

He reaches the cold night air unscathed, the car nearby, with the twins waiting inside. Raymond puts his hands on his knees, taking a moment to steady himself.

Blue was serious. Take care of it.

All cases and police investigations drain from his mind. His only goal now is to take care of Letty. But she doesn't deserve a simple twist of the neck and disposal in the river, like the others. No, this will be much worse.

CHAPTER
FORTY-TWO

FORMAN

Forman directs her attention back on the road, leaving everything she's discovered about Richard Hart unsaid. They're passing the amphitheater in the hills now, the Hollywood Bowl, which means the ride will be over soon. The city is near and their brief interaction almost over. Something inside Forman urges her not to leave it alone.

"Your father . . ." Forman's voice fades away as she focuses on all the details she can't say, and doesn't want to say, right now. "He was Richard Hart, correct?"

"Yes."

"My condolences."

"Thanks." Letty glances over at Forman; her eyebrows rise and there's a slight shake to her head. "How did you know?"

"I read the report. About him in the river."

Letty focuses her attention back on the road. "I didn't think anyone cared."

Forman smooths her skirt out again. "Some people do." She looks up at the buildings ahead, Hollywood coming into view. "It's never easy to lose a parent."

"He left us long before that. He wasn't part of our family anymore." Letty shifts in her seat, but Forman can feel the tension in the air. The awkward silence when someone is trying to push away the pain that's still inside them. Still part of their daily life. She's seen it in the girls on the street. And in herself.

"When I was sixteen," begins Forman, "two men robbed our house. My mother was home alone, my father at work. I was at school." She pauses for a moment, steeling herself, but the words don't hold emotion anymore. She's said them too many times. "We think they expected the place to be empty. A bungalow near the studio. Maybe they thought she was an actress." The memory weighs heavy, even after all this time. "They beat her to death before leaving with the only item worth anything in the house. The radio."

Letty stops at a traffic signal and looks at her, but Forman doesn't meet her gaze. She can't. She can only tell this story if she doesn't see the pain reflected in someone else's eyes.

"All that over a radio." Forman takes a deep breath, the exhale carrying her sorrow and a hint of frustration. "A neighbor described the two men in detail. The clothes they wore. The car they drove. They never found them."

"Why? Why did they never find them?" Letty's voice is soft.

"No one ever investigated," replies Forman. "More important cases, they say."

The air in the cab of the truck is stagnant, stilling the moment.

"I'm sorry," Letty offers, the car not moving even though the signal has changed. "Is that why you became a policewoman? So you could investigate?"

Forman shakes her head, looking out the window. "It was thirteen years ago. There was barely a report. They didn't even take a photo of the scene. That was a mercy. The mental picture is hard enough, but for other people to see how she looked, what happened to her? I'm glad it's not in there."

"You looked at the report?"

"First day on the force." Forman smiles, but it's the same one she makes when she doesn't want the other person to know what she's thinking. "But that's not the reason I joined the force. I wanted to make sure no one else experienced that void. I wanted to make sure that every case was investigated and, hopefully, every case resolved. That every victim, every family member, was treated with dignity and honor. That people who cross that legal line end up behind thicker lines of iron and steel, the key thrown away."

Cars move around them, eager to get on their way, and finally Letty does, too, joining the throng of vehicles as they enter the city.

They're both silent as Hollywood Boulevard approaches.

"Anywhere up here is fine," says Forman.

"You live in Hollywood?"

"No, but I don't want you to have to drive any farther than you already have. The Red Cars won't take long from here." Forman keeps her hand on the door, waiting for the truck to stop. It eventually does, right near a bank building, the tracks of the Pacific Electric Red Cars in front of her. Forman almost doesn't want to leave the bootlegger's daughter, but the journey has come to an end.

"Thank you for the ride, Letty Hart."

Letty smiles. "You're welcome, Annabel Forman."

Forman hops out and closes the door, leaning on the window ledge before Letty can drive away. "One last question that I have to ask."

Letty stays facing the road but flicks her eyes at Forman, as if any trust they just formed has vanished. But Forman pushes on, the information Glick shared with her top of mind now.

"What does Blue mean to you?"

"Blue?" Letty shakes her head. "A color?"

"Good. Leave it that way."

CHAPTER FORTY-THREE

LETTY

Mrs. Wilson's Dress Shop is quiet and void of customers as I enter, the racks of dresses lined up, ready for those who can afford them. I always feel out of place here, and it's not just the pants and button-down shirt I've worn since the day I started helping my father with the winery. My closet contains older dresses, but I have no notions of changing my style, even though I can now afford these clothes. I don't fit into this world of fancy fabric and bejeweled outfits. Nor do I want to.

"Letty!" exclaims Margaret, standing next to the glass case containing gloves and ostrich-feather fans, at least ten hats displayed next to it, all resting on a row of pegs. Margaret is not Mrs. Wilson, but she might as well be. She's the only one ever here. "Do we have new friends with us today?"

I squint my eyes. "I never thought of bottles of brandy as friends."

"You didn't think of bottles of brandy at all until recently."

"True."

"But they are friends. It's much more fun that way." Margaret tilts her head to the side and grins, her left eye almost closing in a wink.

"Want to go to the speakeasy again tonight? Or maybe a different joint? I know several."

I think of the empty bottles back in the barn and the deliveries lined up for tomorrow. "Not tonight."

"What's going on with you, Bootsy? You seem not yourself."

Her comment makes me smile. Margaret has known me a long time and can see through whatever facade I try to put up. "I'm all right, but it's been a strange day. One of the girls came to the farm."

"I thought they knew not to do that."

"They do." I glance out to the truck, the peaches still in the back. I need to bring them inside. I don't like them exposed out there, where someone can take one as they pass by, though the real prize is hidden underneath. Four bottles in each crate, the straw surrounding them and the peaches on top. There are more in the bed of the truck, but those are a precaution, though I could give them to Margaret. "A cop was with me this afternoon. A lady officer."

"You get pinched?"

"No," I say with nearly a laugh in my voice as I think about the situation. "I gave her a ride."

Margaret grins. "You sly girl, you. I never knew you were such a risk-taker, inviting the enemy into your truck." She puts her finger to her chin as she looks up at the ceiling. "Actually, never mind. You've always been a rebel; you just didn't show it all the time. Only on a select few occasions." She leans forward. "The cop," she says in a whisper. "Did she search you? They're the ones that can, you know."

I shake my head. "I was giving her a ride to the city. We just talked. That was it."

"About bootlegging?"

I laugh. "Of course not. I don't keep . . ." I point to her leg, where I know she has a flask tucked into a band beneath her dress.

"You can pay them off, you know. A lot of the big guys do."

"Not this one. She's straight as an arrow and formidable. Nothing's getting past her."

"Don't worry about it, Letty. There'll be others you can pay off, but for now, you have everything you need. Where are the bottles? Some of the girls said they would stop by tonight, so I'm staying open late."

"What about Mrs. Wilson?"

"What Mrs. Wilson doesn't know won't hurt her. I'll help you carry the crates in." Margaret hops out from around the counter, wearing another new dress I haven't seen before, the gold fringe falling in uniform angles just below her knees. "Otto says the deliveries for Shorty are coming in soon. You going to pick them up?"

"Of course."

She puts her hand on her hip and lowers her chin. "Look at you. Not only brandy."

"With Otto's help, no. Brandy for now, but soon, everything." I nod, but as I stare at the truck on the street, Annabel's parting words go through my mind. "Margaret, what does the color blue mean to you?"

Margaret shrugs, her brown bob dancing as she does. She points to a pale-blue dress with a ruffled skirt on a mannequin at the front of the store. "Are you thinking of changing it up? A bootlegger in a swanky dress? Can you imagine? I love it. Let's do it." She strolls over to the racks, but I don't budge.

"No, it's not about clothes." The words repeat in my mind. There was something about the way Annabel said it. "The color itself. What does blue mean to you?"

"The color of the sky. The ocean." Margaret grins. "The blue seal on dollar notes. But green is my favorite color." She rubs her fingers together. "Those Federal Reserve notes. Why?"

"I don't know. The officer asked me about it as she stepped out of the truck, and there was something about the way she said it. The tone in her voice."

Margaret stops moving around the store, her head shifting slowly to the side as she looks at me. "Did she mean the color blue? Or Blue?"

"What's the difference?"

Margaret crosses her arms as she leans against the glass case. "Because if she said 'Blue,' she's asking about Blue, the bootlegger. He's the biggest one in Los Angeles. He runs all of downtown, or at least that's what Otto says."

"How does Otto know?"

"Otto knows everything. Besides, I guess he wanted to take over the speakeasy after Shorty died."

"And I got to it first," I add as Otto's warning from the delivery at Mr. Michaels goes through my mind, about it being a dangerous game and Shorty being one of the only good ones. Or the only good one.

"You sure did!" Margaret's practically humming to herself as she picks up two dresses from the side hook and moves them to the middle of the store. "Timing is everything, my friend. Now, let's get those peaches inside."

I don't move from my position near the front counter. "Should I be worried about this Blue?"

Margaret shakes her head. "Keep to yourself, Letty, and you'll be fine. They'll never suspect a woman outmaneuvered them."

CHAPTER
FORTY-FOUR

Letty

The sun is low on the horizon as I reach the farm, the occasional oak tree casting long shadows on the road, with the Verdugo Mountains reaching toward the sky in the background.

I park the truck at the back of the carriage house, far away from the house and barn, out of view from the road. There are still some bottles of brandy in the truck bed, and even though Margaret could have sold them, a stirring deep inside told me to hang on to them. I can deliver more to her tomorrow on my next round.

The house is quiet, though the lamp in the living room is on. My mother's door is closed with a blue loop of yarn on the handle, her signal my whole life for when she has a headache. It's been a while since she's come down with one of them, but there's more stress these days than usual.

On the counter is a meatloaf, mashed potatoes, and peas. The meal she made and I missed because of the deliveries.

A sole plate waits nearby, ready for me, but the rest of the meal is untouched; her headache must have come on before she had a chance to eat.

I pull Shorty's ledger from my satchel and make notes of today's deliveries, the amount for next week, and the week beyond. I place it on the table and pick up my dinner plate, only a small slice of meatloaf and a tiny portion of peas and potatoes. It doesn't feel right eating without her, and I know she'll be up in a few hours. I don't want this new job to create a rift between us. Or let it widen into a ravine.

I take the plate to the table and sit down, the ledger only inches away. But I'm done with it for tonight. I'll put it in the hiding place under the floorboards after dinner.

My eyes turn to the barn through the window as I eat, the twilight creeping in. I'll have to fill more bottles tonight for tomorrow's deliveries. Business is booming, the need—or, rather, the desire—for brandy in the city far greater than I could have imagined. One day I'll run out of brandy. There is only so much beneath the barn. But I'll learn how to make more. For now, my father's stash is enough to get us through the next few months at least.

I take another bite of the meatloaf. It's cold but still delicious. Her meatloaf was always a favorite at dinnertime. She used to make it every week right up until Dad left. Now it's every so often and only when she's happy.

My eyes focus on the barn door. But not the front ones. The side one. To the secret room.

The fork drops from my hand, the metal clanging against the plate. My attention is on the panel, the black hole gaping, inviting anyone to look inside.

My heart rate climbs. I know I didn't leave it open, sometimes double- and triple-checking before I leave.

Unless my mother did.

I'm away from the table and at the fireplace, my hands on the rifle, everything moving in slow motion.

The light is fading from the sky as I cross to the side of the barn. The sagebrush looks intact, the dirt here undisturbed. Did I leave it open when Dorothy was here? No, I know it was closed during her visit.

I crouch down and listen. The tunnel is silent and dark, as always. But I don't trust the silence now. Not until I check.

I shift the gun so I can crawl into the opening.

I'm trying to be as quiet as possible, stepping carefully so that my shoes don't echo on the wood. The air has that distinct and familiar chill.

I reach the dirt floor, but instead of lighting the lamp I fixed to the wall, I decide to let the darkness protect me and feel along for the barrels instead. They're all here and all intact.

I exhale and move to the next section, where the bottles are kept. I've spent enough time in here to have the layout of the whole place mapped in my mind. Every bottle seems to be accounted for. Whoever was here didn't want anything. Or perhaps I did really leave the door open myself. Or my mother was trying to help and forgot to close it. Maybe that's when her headache set in.

I turn to leave and stop as a cigarette lighter is struck in front of me, a cold shiver running down my arms as the light dances around the room, the flame hiding the person behind it. Until it doesn't. There, to the side of the stairs, is Raymond. He's in his gray suit, the buttons of the jacket open as he sits atop a crate, a revolver on his knee, ready to fire.

"I told you I would catch you one day, Letty Hart. Turns out today is that day."

CHAPTER FORTY-FIVE

LETTY

I hold up the rifle, my finger already on the trigger.

"You think that's going to stop me?" He stands up as he moves his revolver side to side, almost taunting me. "I'll fire this so fast you won't know what hit you. I suggest you lower your gun, sweetheart." He moves forward, the glow of his lighter bouncing on the walls.

"I'll shoot."

"Go ahead. Do it."

But he's standing right in front of me. I can't do a warning shot this time. If I fire, he'll fire right back. Even if I shoot him, he'll shoot me as soon as I pull the trigger. There's no surviving this.

"I knew you were weak." He pulls the rifle out of my hands, the metal releasing from my fingers as I try to grab it, wary of his revolver only too close to me. He tosses it to the side, the rifle landing on the soft dirt in the corner near him.

I try to remain calm, at least on the outside, but I know I'm trapped. There's nowhere to run.

Raymond lights the lamp, the soft glow illuminating the area. He pulls a silver case out of his pocket and rolls a cigarette, the gun still in his hand as he does. He lights the cigarette, sits on the crate, and motions to me. "Have a seat. This will take a while."

If I dash for the stairs, I won't make it up before he reaches me. I'm caught, like a wounded animal in a trap. Except I'm not wounded. Not yet. I lower myself to the floor, the wall against my back.

Raymond stares at me as he pulls a drag from his cigarette. "Exactly how long have you been doing this? Since the day your father left?" The smoke lingers almost protectively in the air around him.

I don't answer. My time is limited. I don't need to reveal any information. I need to protect myself. And my mother.

My mother. Asleep with a headache, unaware of the fate that is about to meet her daughter. My only hope right now is that she stays asleep.

"Seems you've done well for yourself." He motions to the barn above us. "A nice place. A large supply of brandy. I've underestimated you, Letty Hart."

"Maybe you shouldn't have," I reply.

Raymond cracks a smile. He stands up, and my heart starts to race.

"I wonder how long you would last in prison." He takes another drag and blows the smoke upward before placing the cigarette back between his lips, the rolled white paper hanging out of the corner of his mouth.

I listen for the sirens, the officers responding to another raid on the farm. But they aren't coming. Of course they aren't. Raymond has no desire to get anyone else involved. He'll take care of me like he took care of Shorty.

He taps one of the barrels. "What's in this?"

"Water."

"Oh, so you're a smart one, then. That won't go over well in front of the judge." He opens the barrel and waves the aroma toward him, though I don't know how he can smell anything with the cigarette right by his nose. He dips in the ladle and takes a swig, leaning against the barrel as he does. "Not bad," he says as his dark eyes take me in. "Whiskey. Not water."

"Brandy. And there's water in it," I add, but his delay is puzzling. Shorty hadn't moved from his desk before he was strangled, and the guard was shot before he had a chance to return fire. Raymond is taking his time tonight for a reason. Which means I have time, too. A chance. "How did you get in here?"

"Now you're underestimating *me*, Letty Hart. You look for something long enough and you find it." He smiles. "It only took me ten minutes to discover this little hideaway you have down here." He puts his arm on the barrel, the gun still pointed at me. "You're getting careless. Unwise. This town isn't a safe place for people in your profession."

I cross my arms, feeling more vulnerable.

Raymond stares at me. "How many have we lost now? Four? Five?"

"Have we? I haven't heard." I wonder if he had this conversation with Shorty before he strangled him.

"You're thinking. I don't like that," he says. "Women who think are dangerous."

"On the contrary, people who fail to think are the dangerous ones," I reply. It's time for me to get out of here. If I'm going to die, I'm going to die trying. I stand, but Raymond holds up his gun.

"Don't imagine for a moment that I won't bump you off, right here, right now."

"I wasn't sure that was the way you worked. You seem more into a show."

"Is that right?" The sides of his mouth creep up. "And why do you say that?"

"Because you want it to be real clear, like a flag waving over a fort. You wouldn't kill someone in a farmhouse cellar, because no one would find out. And furthermore, no one would care."

"I can kill you and dump you in the river. The show would still be the same."

"And then what? Pretend to investigate but get nowhere?" I nod, the realization not a surprise. "The way you did with Shorty."

"Like I did with Shorty." He laughs, and it echoes throughout the room. "I wondered if that was you that followed me. Took the ledger and your peaches. That gave you away, you know."

"I wasn't trying to hide."

He laughs again. "You could almost get blamed for it. In fact, why not? Would a gal like you murder two bootleggers to get ahead?"

"Would a guy like you?" I retort.

"I'm not a bootlegger. I just clean up the messes they make." He grins.

"The question is, why?"

"My boss wants to be the only one. If you're alone at the top, you're king."

"Seems like there is plenty of room for more."

"No, there isn't. I don't need any more bootleggers in this town. He doesn't need any more bootleggers."

I shift my stance. "I never thought you would be one to have a boss, Raymond. I saw the way you were at the raid. Ordering the men around. The federal agents. This isn't like you. It must drive you mad to have to answer to someone."

"Quiet!" He raises his gun slightly, its aim now on my face.

"You won't kill me like this." I inch forward. My rifle is only a few feet away. "I didn't shoot for my reasons, but you have your own. You like to strangle. You like to have your hands on your work."

"That will be next."

His words send a chill through me, but I maintain eye contact as I move closer to my gun. "You don't need a boss. We could work together. I'll pay you whatever he's paying you."

"You couldn't afford me." He grins again. "Letty Hart"—he pauses—"the girl with all the spirit and none of the connections." His cigarette falls to the floor, and he snuffs it out with a single twist of his shoe. "The world is a dangerous place, and aligning with the wrong people can wind you up in the river."

"Is that how you're going to do it? Bump me off and throw me from a bridge on the way back home? I thought you were more original than that."

He picks up a bottle of brandy, one of the milk jugs from Carter's Dairy Farm, filled with golden liquid that sloshes around as he holds it. "You're right." But he's not smiling. His eyes, framed by his round glasses, focus in on me, and he grabs the rifle. "Sometimes the moment you think the fun is gone, it comes right back." He snaps his fingers. "Like a lamp. Pretty great things, aren't they?" He takes his handkerchief from his pocket and puts it on the glass chimney, removing it from the lamp. "We think we appreciate the light, but we don't know how much until the moment it's gone." He blows out the flame.

The darkness surrounds me, nothing stirring as my eyes try to adjust. I hear the glass break, the sound of the lamp's chimney crunching under a shoe.

I shift to my left. He might be approaching, but if I can't see, neither can he. I steady myself, my fists up, ready for a fight.

The lighter comes to life again. He's still in the same corner, the flame reflecting off his glasses.

He lifts the bottle a few inches and motions it toward me. "Be careful out there. It'd be a shame to lose someone like yourself. You never know who is hiding around the corner." He turns and carries the bottle and my rifle up the stairs, the light going with him.

My heart is racing, and my hands are shaking, but I'm alive. He's left me. And I don't know why. I move toward the stairs, my pulse slowing as I climb into the tunnel.

The moonlight is visible through the entrance.

And then it's not, the door slamming shut.

I scramble toward it, all of the light gone, my hands feeling the rough wood in front of me. I push to swing it open, but it doesn't move.

"Raymond! What are you doing?" Panic pulses through me. "Raymond!"

I push on the door again using every muscle I have.

It doesn't budge.

CHAPTER FORTY-SIX

RAYMOND

The moonlight casts a silvery sheen over the farm as Raymond stands near the barn, an empty wine barrel in front of the opening below. It was one he left behind the other day, tossed to the side near the driveway when his men realized there wasn't enough wine in it to take up the valuable space in the truck. They poured out what remained inside before they drove away. He never knew that something left behind could come in so useful.

"Raymond!" Letty's voice is muffled from inside her wooden prison. "Don't do this!"

"Don't do what, exactly?" His cheeks hurt from grinning. It's unusual for him to smile so much, but it's something he can get used to. He's not sure when he'll tell Blue how he did this. Then again, he doesn't need to. Blue can find out everything without him even saying a word.

"No one will miss a bootlegger, Letty. They only bring crime and corruption to our city." He takes a swig of the brandy. It burns all the way down his throat, but he enjoys it. "You covered your tracks; now it's time to cover mine."

"What are you doing?" Her voice is more desperate now.

Raymond laughs. He realizes that he missed all of this fun in the other situations. It was too quick, the pleasure gone too fast. "There are many ways to handle bootleggers. One is to take away their product." He motions to the barn and the nearby vineyards. "There's putting them in prison for a long time." He smiles bigger, even though she isn't outside to see it. "Or there are those times when the bootleggers make a mistake, and their still, the one element they need for this business, blows up their house." He glances around. "I don't see one of those here, but there's alcohol. And that, my friend, is flammable."

"You can't keep me in here. They'll come get me."

"Who's going to come? By the time they see the flames, you'll already be dead." His comment is met by silence. "There's enough brandy down there for a pretty big fire. I hear that when it gets hot enough, even bones burn. There'll be nothing left."

"You'll get caught."

"Who do you think you're dealing with?" Raymond slams his hand against the barn, the same way Blue did on the table during their meeting. "I am everything you fear. I am the police, I am in charge, and I am the one who is going to clean up this mess."

He moves his head to the side, cracking his neck as he does. "Accidents don't have to be investigated very closely. I can make sure of that."

He pulls the newspaper out of his coat, the headlines are about the San Pedro bootlegger who met his end, and removes the gold lighter from his pocket.

"Are you a church girl, Letty Hart? Or did you only provide the wine?" The newsprint takes a moment to light, but soon the flame is engulfing the top of the page. "A little God is good for us." He presses the paper to the side of the barn. The weathered wood should go up like kindling on a campfire, but it fails to light.

The newspaper is a ball of flame now and too hot to hold. Raymond tosses it at the foot of the barn and tries again, this time holding the paper out more as he lights it. He walks over to the doors, placing the paper in the seam and pouring brandy along the wood.

He reaches for another sheet in his coat pocket—only a few left—and moves back to the side of the barn. The side Letty is on.

But there's a glow. The fire has started, the orange-and-red flames climbing the walls. It's only a matter of time now. He repeats this twice more before standing back. The barn is now alight with the fury and anger of fire.

Raymond picks up Letty's rifle and retreats to his car, leaning against the side as he watches his latest and greatest assignment. There will be nothing left by morning. Nothing left even an hour from now.

He removes the silver case from his pocket and rolls another cigarette. He never has two in one evening, but something about this event, something about this moment, changes that.

He lights it and pulls three quick drags, the heat from the flames warming his face. This isn't his routine. This isn't his method. The cigarette comes before, not after. But everything is different now.

Raymond holds the rolled paper between his pointer and middle fingers, the ember close to his skin as he waits to take another drag and doesn't flick the ash.

The flames climb higher, the barn no match for the fire with the straw and leftover wine inside, the brandy down below. The red glow and smoke climb high into the air. People will be here soon.

He pulls a long drag from the cigarette, the relief pulsing through him as he watches the fire double in size. And Blue didn't think he could handle it.

He glances at the house.

Raymond takes the final sheet of paper from his coat as he walks over to the house and lights it, the yellow flame spreading through the print. He holds it to the flaking paint, the ends curling as the heat rises to meet them. The house won't look like an accident. There's no alcohol inside; he's checked. But he doesn't stop. He waits until the flames climb the side of the building, adding the last little bit of brandy to the walls and smashing the bottle on the porch.

He flicks the barely smoked cigarette toward the fire, the small ember disappearing in the orange glow before it falls a few feet short. If some routines are to be broken, then all of them should be.

He rounds to the far side of the barn, where he parked, the structure hiding his car from anyone on the driveway or in the house. It would have been easy for Letty to find when she came home if she had taken the time to look, but people only ever check the surface. They never bother to dive deep.

Raymond tips his hand at the barn, the roof collapsing in on itself.

Swinging the car door open, he glances back one last time before he gets in.

"Sleep well, Letty Hart."

CHAPTER
FORTY-SEVEN

FORMAN

There's a different feel in the station at this hour. A few of the officers Forman knows from when they worked the day shift are there, but it's quieter. Lonelier. Forman never wanted to work nights. She preferred to be out in the daytime, seeing the city's ills and ails in the clear light of day. The nighttime hides everything, even the good guys.

Officer Hillman looks up at her as she passes by but doesn't say anything. She's met him a few times, when she was brought in to interview battered women or the rare female suspect at a late hour, but those events were few and far between. Yet here she is again, in the station when she should be home with her family enjoying the few hours before she has to return for her next shift.

But Blue, the one Glick warned her about, and whom she then warned Letty about, keeps going around in her mind, and she wants to know more. Even if just to protect herself.

This time, she doesn't make a secret of looking in Beaucamp's cabinets. Instead, she walks straight over and starts opening drawers and flipping through case files, looking for John Corizano, as if she has every right to. Two officers stroll by, pausing for a moment, but she doesn't look up, just continues her work. They keep walking.

Officer Hillman glances at her again on his way through the station, but he doesn't stop. That's the benefit of being a female officer here. They don't care what you're doing, even if you're not supposed to be doing it. They don't pay attention, or if they do, they don't bother to ask.

Forman keeps turning through the files, but she can't find anything about Blue, or John.

She leans back and glances around the station. She's missing something.

Except there *has* to be something else here. Glick warned her for a reason.

She glances over at Raymond's desk. He might have the name somewhere, as he's always dealing with the bootleggers, and as far she knows, he won't be here tonight unless he's working a late case. But his desk looks abandoned, the chair pushed in and no paperwork on it. She stands and walks toward it, pulling open the drawers, looking for anything on John Corizano, the man known as Blue.

There's a stack of papers at the bottom of one drawer, neatly organized, with single sheets of arrest records, as if Raymond needs to remind himself of the work he does. She finds one sole mention of John Corizano written in block lettering at the top of one sheet.

It's from a few years ago, an arrest for a liquor violation that resulted in a fine, which he paid. That's all.

Forman leans back against the desk, her tired eyes glancing at the clock. It's time to go home.

She puts the paper back and closes the drawer, but then she notices the one above it, still slightly open. She pulls it out to close it properly, and the item inside makes her stop.

It's the can from Quadling, the one she took from the drunk gentleman after Shorty Paulson's murder. A can that should be in some sort of evidence box, but it's inside Raymond's desk.

Forman looks around the station to see if anyone is watching her, but the few who are still there at this hour are focused on their own activities.

She picks up the can. The label is the same as she saw at the garage, but this time she notices the name.

FRUIT OF THE HART FARM.

Her finger traces the outside of the lid, the only openings the two holes poked in the top. There were never peaches in here. If there were, they would still be in here, unable to escape through the small knife-size fissures. This was sealed with the brandy inside.

At Hart Farm.

Where Forman met Letty.

She looks up at the map on the far side of the station, and it all starts to fall into place. She was in a bootlegger's car, and not only did she ignore all the signs, she let her get away. For now.

CHAPTER FORTY-EIGHT

LETTY

It's no use pounding on the door. I also don't want to give him the satisfaction. But I can hear the growing roar of flames as they devour everything I've worked for. Everything I've built. Besides, there's no one to hear my cries, except my mother, and she's in the house.

My mother.

Alone.

The heat is intense on this side of the tunnel, so I retreat back into the room. With the brandy. More fuel to the fire.

Except there's another way out.

When my father and I were picking grapes in the vineyard the year before he left, he said, "There's always two ways, Letty. Two ways to do things. One is easy, one is hard." He glanced up at me, the look in his eyes usually reserved for the moments when he scolded me, except this time I hadn't done anything wrong. "Always two ways, and the one you choose is up to you."

There are two ways, even now. I found it the second day I was in here, a lengthwise cut in the wall, the size of a barrel on its side, where they could be rolled in from outside. There was a barrel in front of it, and since I had the other entrance, I never bothered to move it. But now it's time.

My fingers graze the barrels in the room as I move around to the far left wall, searching for the one blocking the exit. But it's not the brandy I need to focus on, with my lack of sight. It's the walls.

My speed increases as I search the wall, feeling for any variation, my heart racing, my hands shaking. There's no way to find this in time, and yet I have to. Or die.

A thin breeze crosses my face as I move along. I shift back.

There's a stream of air coming from the wood here. From outside. I search for the rest of the line that marks the door, following the fresh air in a square. This is it.

Now to move the barrel that's in front of it.

My hands grip the top, the round wood piercing my palms when I pull it toward me, pivoting it on its circular bottom as the weight of the brandy sloshes inside. I know it's easier to move a barrel when it's on its side, but in the dark, I don't want to risk laying it down and having it hit something and open, dousing me in its fuel. I know how to move a barrel. I do it all the time. But here, now, it seems different. Like the Carter boys as they tried to steal one last week, my movements are as jagged as theirs were.

Heat is pushing down from above, the sound of crashing and creaking along with it. I'm running out of time.

I get the barrel far enough into the middle of the room that I can squeeze my body into position to push on this new door, my hands at the top.

It doesn't move.

I try again, a harder push with both hands, my palms digging into the wood.

My left hand gives.

The panel is moving.

I keep pushing, using both hands on the left side as the panel swings from a hinge.

The breeze is stronger now, more darkness in front of me. I scramble into it and push the panel closed, leaving the brandy room behind me.

There's not enough room to stand, but the tunnel is wide, and I move as best I can in a crouched position, my hands out in case there's another wall or panel in front of me.

The tunnel doesn't end, but the farther I get, the cooler the air becomes, the fire now in the distance behind me. I don't know where this is leading, but I have to be a long way from the barn by now.

My hand hits metal first. At least I think it's metal, the surface circular and cold as my palm rests on it. I keep patting the area, hoping it's an exit. My hands touch the wood of a barrel, upright, without a top.

And then a ladder. I grasp each rung as I climb up, alternating my palms above my head to see where the top is. It's a small opening, and I push it, falling onto the rugged soil. I climb out and look down at what was below. The moonlight illuminates a large copper base with a funnel. The brandy still.

So this is where he kept it, here on the farm, creating the liquor he hid from all of us.

I'm on the far side of the vineyard, near the old winery building, or where it used to stand before we built the new one. I haven't been over here in years, the edge of the property where the grapes no longer grow after we shrank to only making sacramental wine.

The moon is bright, but the fire is brighter—large, angry flames from the barn flickering into the night air and extending into a plume of smoke. I don't see anyone in the light, but that doesn't mean that Raymond isn't still around.

Except the barn is not the only glow. The house is on fire, too.

And my mother is inside.

My legs move like the bicycle wheels a few neighbors ride around, my knees pumping so fast that my feet can barely keep up. I need to get to the house. Only to the house.

The front door is on fire, but I kick it in, the flames growing with every second, the smoke obstructing my view.

I hold my arm up to my face as I reach her bedroom door. It's open, and she's not in there.

"Mother!"

The fire has engulfed the front room now, blocking my exit, but at least I'm alone in here. She must have escaped already.

"Letty." She's standing in the kitchen, her face ashen, the green ledger in her hands.

"Come on." I race to the kitchen and grab her hand, but there's no way out for us. Nowhere to go.

"The cellar," she replies, her eyes staying on me as she moves deeper into the kitchen. I follow her to the door on the other side of the pantry that opens to stairs and a small room below.

"There's no way out down there."

Her eyes are emotionless, the light and heat of the fire growing around us. "There's no way out here, either." She moves down the stairs, and I close the door behind me, the cellar offering a respite from the fire's heat. But as we reach the dirt floor, I put my hands up, feeling the warmth above us. It won't be long now.

"Richard built this separation from the other half of the cellar. He wanted to store staples like flour down here." The darkness keeps me from seeing her gaze, though her voice is heavy with memories.

"He never did it," she continues, "though I think he might have had other ideas for it."

I nod, realizing what she's saying. And knowing how he built the other room, I think there might be an exit.

I feel along the walls, the wood solid and sturdy, a testament to my father's craftsmanship.

I hear a large boom followed by more crashes. The roof collapsing above us.

I push on a board, but unlike the others, it moves, the nails not quite holding it in place.

I try it again. It's weak. It will work.

I lift my foot and kick the wall as hard as I can. The wood only splinters, but it's enough for me to pull the board out. Now there's a hole, and I have more leverage for the next one. I repeat the process twice more, giving me enough room to get my arm, head, and torso through the space, the boards scraping against my legs as I do. I land on the dirt on the other side, the cellar cooler on this side, as its doors let in the night air.

"Come on," I say through the splintered gap.

My mother is still on the other side, sparks of fire raining from the ceiling.

"Now!" I yell.

She hands me the ledger, but I toss it aside. I don't want the book. I want her. She puts one hand out, but it's not enough. She motions for me to go.

"No. I'm not leaving you." I've lost one parent, and I'm not going to lose another. I reach through the hole, my head and half of my body on the other side. I grab her arms and pull. She moves, and her arms and head come through, but that's all. I pull harder, but she doesn't move.

My mother is trapped.

"Go," she says. "Go."

"Not without you." I dig my feet into the ground and pull as hard as I can, channeling everything that has happened in the last few days and everything that has changed. She comes through, along with the sound of tearing fabric, but both of us land on the cool dirt floor.

She looks at her dress. It's torn on the right side near her legs, but there's no blood, at least not any I can see right now.

The embers are crawling across the ceiling as the floor above us burns, the smoke growing thicker in the air. It will be raining fire, and house, here soon. We need to get out.

I run up to the doors my grandfather installed on the side of the house, the storm-cellar type that fold out to the sides. I push them open, the cold night air rushing into a battle with the smoke-filled basement.

I reach back to grab my mother's hand, but she's already running. We reach the vines, as if the roots planted decades ago are our best chance at safety, and both collapse on the dirt, coughing and sputtering as we try to take in the fresh air.

My lungs ache, and it's tough to breathe, but I'm alive. We're alive.

I push myself up, my palms numb to the rocks that dig into them.

The house is fully consumed by flames now—all of my grandfather's handiwork disappearing into the night sky. As well as the brandy in the barn. Our future livelihood. And the item I'm supposed to deliver tomorrow.

My mother is coughing next to me, the green ledger in her hands. "You brought it?"

She holds it close. "I'm not leaving it behind."

The sirens sound in the distance. A neighbor must have called, alerted by the glowing ball of light that the alcohol-fueled flames are creating.

We don't move, both of us watching as the fires eat away at everything we own.

The volunteer fire company pulls into the driveway, the wagon ready to salvage what I already know will be nothing.

A fireman notices us in the vines and runs over as his partners wheel out the hose, debating which of the two fires to try to extinguish first.

"Everyone OK?"

"Yes," replies my mother, her attention on the house.

"Is there anyone else inside either building?" He's around my age, and though he's never met me, his face is drawn with concern.

"No."

"OK." He glances back at the wagon, then returns his attention to us. "What happened?"

My mother looks at me.

"Not sure," I reply. "But we're safe; that's what matters."

"I'm glad to hear it." He runs back to his partners, who are spraying water onto the house, onto what little of the frame still stands.

I thought Raymond wouldn't come back to the winery after the raid, after he found so little. I thought we had a good system. But nothing is safe.

"What happens now?" My mother's attention is on the fire, but there are no tears. Not even a hint of sadness in her face, as if the flames are a campfire and not everything she owns.

"Now," I reply, "everything changes."

CHAPTER FORTY-NINE

FORMAN

Forman takes the same place she always does at morning meetings: the gap by the wall where she can lean if she wants to, but still in the circle with the rest of the officers.

Miller nods his head at Beaucamp. "Did you hear about the fire last night?"

"Quite a blaze," says Beaucamp. "Too bad it wasn't in your territory, Raymond."

"I went anyway." Raymond straightens his jacket. "Bootlegging."

"Anything left?"

"Of course not. You know how hot those stills can get."

Forman steps forward. "What's this?"

Raymond is standing next to Forman, but he doesn't respond, his lips tight and thin.

"A couple of bootleggers blew themselves up last night. I guess their still caught fire," says Beaucamp. "Out in the valley."

Forman freezes, her feet cemented to the floor. "Where in the valley?"

"What's it to you?" asks Beaucamp.

"Curiosity."

Raymond moves closer to her and adjusts his glasses. "Be careful with curiosity, Forman. It can be the death of you." He smiles, but his eyes are cold.

Forman doesn't flinch, and she doesn't look away from him.

"OK, OK," says Warrenson. "Let's get this started. We have some good news this morning. It's about time we had something to celebrate around here."

"Is this your promotion?" whispers Raymond.

"Not this time."

Raymond places his hand on her shoulder and squeezes. "You'll get the next one. I'll put in a good word for you."

"I'll put a good word in for myself," replies Forman.

He leans back and smiles. "Well, look who's become the cat's meow. This is a new side of you, sweetheart."

"Silence, gentlemen." Warrenson's eyes flick to Forman. "And women." He adjusts his shoulders and glances at the file in front of him. "There's been some good work done recently, and I want to call attention to it. Detective August Raymond, will you come up here?"

Raymond adjusts his glasses again and walks forward, his swagger more pronounced than ever.

"Detective Raymond here has been doing great things, and I'm proud to say he's captured two more bootleggers, who are now in our possession."

"Rumrunners, sir."

"Oh." Warrenson looks at his file. "Rumrunners. Like there's a difference." He laughs, and the men join in. "We should all strive to be like Detective Raymond, whose arrest record is climbing the charts. How many have you put away this year?"

"Let's just say a few," he says with a smirk on his face.

Warrenson slaps him on the back. "Always modest. Care to say a few words?"

Raymond looks around and shifts back on his heels. "I'm proud to represent the city of Los Angeles. As for the fire last night that many of you have heard about . . ."

Officer Jacobs raises a newspaper, the headline starting with the word *Fire*.

"Seems a few more bootleggers were caught in the middle of it," continues Raymond. "I'm sad that I couldn't save them in time and help them see the error of their ways."

"Am I late?" asks a blonde woman in her thirties as she enters the room, a white coat over her shoulders, a green dress beneath it. She carries a pie in her hands.

"Betty?" This is the first time that Forman has seen Raymond rattled. "What are you doing here?" he stammers.

"Welcome, welcome," says Warrenson. "Everyone, this is Betty Raymond." He laughs. "He had no idea."

Raymond is speechless, and he is never speechless.

Mrs. Raymond laughs, and her perfectly pinned blonde curls bounce up and down as she does. "Captain Warrenson called me yesterday to tell me." She's still holding the pie in her hands. "August, are you surprised? I hope you're surprised."

Raymond nods, but he still can't seem to find his words.

"I started baking as soon as you left." She holds up the pie. "It's cherry. Your favorite."

Raymond nods again. "Thank you," he manages, looking around the room now. "If anyone hasn't met Betty yet, this is my wife."

"I wore my best dress for the occasion." She looks at the officers in the station. "August never lets me see where he works. It's so nice to finally be here."

"We're glad to have you here. Let's take your coat." Warrenson removes the white coat from Betty's shoulders as the men gather round, the pie now on a desk in front of them, a stack of plates and forks already in Jacobs's hands.

Forman stays back. There's no need to rush forward with the crowd of officers tearing into the dessert like a pack of hungry coyotes.

"Come on, Forman, get some of this pie," says Beaucamp.

Jacobs glances up. "Nah, she doesn't want any."

"You're missing out," adds Warrenson.

Except Betty's eyes are locked on her. "Oh, a woman. Raymond said there were a few on the force and one that he worked with." Betty steps away from the group. "I'm so glad to finally meet you."

But now it's Forman who is speechless as Betty stands in front of her, a gloved hand outstretched. The sounds of the room, the clinking of the plates, of the knives and forks, recede as she registers what Raymond's wife is wearing.

Around her neck is a large diamond necklace with three emeralds in it.

CHAPTER FIFTY

LETTY

Southern Pacific's Central Station is bustling with people as we walk through the lobby, the large, arching windows highlighting our clothes, sooty from the ash and smoke, our faces drawn.

People turn to stare, nudging each other to look up from their benches as they wait for their trains. I don't blame them. I would stare, too, our appearances a stark contrast to the crowd gathered beneath the chandeliers and marble wainscoting. But I also know that anyone in this station could be a danger. A tiger ready to pounce the moment I lower my guard.

Hats obscure the faces as we walk past the waiting area, and I keep my cap pulled low, too, as we join the end of a ticket line, my eyes still searching for a menace I don't know and won't recognize. Anyone can report to Raymond, and he can't know we've survived.

The truck still works, untouched by the flames that destroyed the house and barn, but I didn't drive it downtown today. It's too recognizable. I also didn't want to take a Red Car. The trolleys take too much time, with too many people posing too great a risk of being seen.

Instead, I asked Father O'Leary to drive us, his words of prayer accompanying us the whole way into the city. How we're reborn from the ashes.

"Father, I have a favor. Please don't tell anyone that you brought us here," I said as I exited his car, the white stucco station a few feet behind us. "Anyone." I knew only too well that if Raymond thought we were still alive, he would travel miles to make sure he finished the job.

"My dear, I am a man of solemn words. It stays within the church. Within myself." His pale eyes shifted from me to my mother. "Be safe. When you want to come back, the church will help you."

My mother and I haven't said a word to each other since leaving his car, though our silence is not out of anger or irritation but rather out of weariness and exhaustion. We have nothing left, in more ways than one.

"Next," says a male voice impatiently. The ticket broker is waiting for us to move forward, but I had been too distracted by the crowds to notice the line was gone. Apparently, my mother had been, too.

"Two tickets to Salt Lake City." I take the money out of my pocket, the only bills that survived the fire, as they were still in the truck.

"The nine thirty-five leaves in fifteen minutes. Track eight."

I place the money on the counter, my other hand not leaving my mother's arm.

My father's words come into my mind: *Don't leave things unfinished. Ever. Finish everything you start.*

I look at the broker as he gathers the tickets behind the counter.

"No. Only one."

"Letty." My mother grips my arm.

He pushes one forward along with my change.

I gather the money and the lone ticket as we move out of line.

"Letty." Her eyes are glistening now, the tears about to fall.

"I'm going to take care of things here."

"No. He'll kill you." Her grasp tightens, her fingers digging into my arm, as if she can hold on to me forever.

She's right, of course, but I can't acknowledge that to her. "Your sister will be so happy to see you," I finally manage to say. "It's safer there. He won't find you."

Her head is moving back and forth, shaking gently, her eyes focused on mine. "I can't leave you here."

"Protecting us didn't work. I'm not going to run away from everything because one man thinks he can end us." I hold her hand, my right pinkie looping through hers. "I'm not leaving this unfinished."

"Then I'm staying with you," she says firmly.

"You can't. You need to be safe. You'll be safe in Salt Lake. Let me do this. I can do this."

She's still now, as if the severity of the situation is weighing heavily on her, stopping the movement. "I'm not going to be able to convince you, am I?"

I shake my head.

"I won't see you again."

"You will," I say, though everything inside me is telling me this is goodbye. "Stay in Salt Lake for two weeks, and then come back. Or, better yet, I'll come pick you up. In two weeks."

Her eyes are filled with the thoughts she can't say and I don't want to hear.

"I'm not going to leave you like he did. I never will," I promise.

She stays silent but directs her attention to the doors to the tracks.

We push through them, and I keep my hand on hers as we walk toward the train, but I can't help worrying who is around and who is getting on the train with her. I don't want to leave her side until she's safely in her seat.

We reach the track, the passengers climbing aboard, the engine ready to go.

"I'll see you in two weeks. It'll all be OK. I know it." The words sound hollow, even to me. It never feels good lying to my mother.

She wraps her arms around me, tighter than ever. Stronger than the time I fell off the fence when I was six and thought my arm was broken. Stronger than when she realized my father was never coming back. Stronger than after we watched the flames consume everything we owned.

She lets go, and I feel an immediate chill. She doesn't say another word and steps onto the train.

I scan the windows until I see her walking through the aisle. She takes a seat by the window, her expression blank. She holds up two fingers at me.

I smile, though I feel the tears coming. I hold up two back. "Two weeks," I mouth.

The train lurches forward.

"Be safe," I say.

"You, too," she mouths back. The train picks up speed.

Within seconds, she's gone.

At least now I only have to worry about myself.

And Raymond.

CHAPTER FIFTY-ONE

RAYMOND

Raymond is unsettled by Betty's visit, but she'll soon leave. Work and home-life should always be separate. Something Warrenson should have known.

"You're not having pie?" Beaucamp looks like he's on his second piece, his lips red from the cherry filling.

"I have another one at home. This is for you."

"Your wife should come around more often," says Jacobs, his elbow nudging Raymond in the arm.

Raymond doesn't reply. He needs to get back to work. This should be over. Warrenson doesn't like it when the morning meetings go too long. This one already has.

The pie plate is empty. It's time for her to go.

He looks around for his blonde-haired wife, eager to send her on her way. She's in the corner, talking with Forman. Women. They always stick together.

He navigates to where the girls stand, their hands moving in rhythm with their conversation.

"Oh, thank you." Betty touches her hand to her neck.

"What this?" asks Raymond.

"She was asking about my necklace. It was a gift from August. He's so sweet. Completely surprised me with it. Said it was to celebrate our wedding anniversary, even though it's next month. He's a good one. Always thinking ahead." She lifts up a plate with a small slice of pie, untouched, the cherry filling spilling out of the middle. "I don't think you had any. Would you like my slice?"

Forman shakes her head, her focus remaining on Betty. "Your husband has excellent taste. It's beautiful."

Raymond stares at Forman, her comment about the necklace causing an itch to crawl up his arm. But she continues to smile at Betty as if they are old friends.

"He does. Are you married?"

"No."

"Don't worry, dear. It will happen." Betty pats Forman's arm.

"And hopefully my husband will surprise me with gifts, too."

Both women laugh.

Raymond needs to get her out of here. "Betty . . ."

"I can't stop looking at it. It's stunning. Do you wear it often?" Forman's attention is focused on the necklace.

Betty puts the plate down on the desk. "Oh no. I only just got it. When was it, August?" She glances at him. "I think it was Friday, wasn't it?"

Raymond doesn't respond, doesn't move his head at all. He just stares at Forman, trying to read her thoughts. "A few weeks ago, at least."

"Don't be silly, August." She looks back at Forman. "It was Friday. He did a whole presentation." She taps her hand on Forman's shoulder. "You know how men can be."

"It's time for you to go home, Betty. We need to get to work." Raymond steps closer to her, crossing his arms as he does. The station is his kingdom.

He tilts his head forward as he stares at her. It's the same look he gives her when it's time for her to clean up the house. When it's time to get their daughter to bed. When it's time for her to perform her other wifely duties.

Betty meets his eyes, and it's clear she's understood the message. "Oh, yes, silly me. I'll get my coat and the pie plate."

He puts his hand on her shoulder to direct her to both of those belongings.

"Raymond," yells Beaucamp from across the station. "There's a call for you."

"Tell them I'm busy." He pushes harder on Betty's shoulder, but she's adjusting her gloves.

"They say it's important."

"Fine." Raymond begrudgingly leaves Betty's side, uneasy that she's still near Forman, and returns to his desk. He picks up the telephone, his eyes on Forman as she stands next to his wife. "Raymond here."

The line is silent.

"I said Raymond here."

Betty is once again in an animated conversation with Forman, like she has with her tea ladies, though her white coat has found its way around her shoulders.

"Eddie's dead. He killed him," the voice on the other end of the line says.

"Wait, what?" He readjusts the phone and turns away from the rest of the station, his chin down to his chest as he tries to focus on what Frankie is saying.

"All Eddie did was tell him that we lost two more, that two of his guys tried to make a delivery, and he shot him. Right there. In the warehouse."

"Frankie, you're going too fast. Why couldn't they make a delivery?"

"Because he's lost those two. Both places already had the booze when his men arrived. They didn't want to work with Blue anymore. They had someone else."

"What do you mean?"

"You messed up. That bootlegger, the one he told you to get rid of, she's still alive."

CHAPTER
FIFTY-TWO

FORMAN

Forman says goodbye to Betty Raymond, who smiles as she leaves, a final gloved wave to the department, her lipstick still intact, as she declined all offers of her own pie. If she has any idea she's married to a killer, she hides it.

But Forman knows who Betty's husband is and what he's done. And she's pretty sure Raymond knows she does, too. The way his face changed when she mentioned the necklace. How he kept trying to stop Betty from talking to her.

The station empties out now, the meeting over, the officers back to their normal routines, the desk sergeant processing a traffic violation. But Forman doesn't care about that. She's too busy watching Raymond, now on his third consecutive, and heated, call in as many minutes.

"No, I took care of it. I watched until the end. I said I took care of it," she hears him say into the receiver as he grabs his forehead in frustration and kicks at the desk. "How do you know? No. I've got it." He slams the phone down and glances out at the station. Forman looks down, head low as she focuses on a newspaper on the desk nearby.

She doesn't look up until she hears him on another call.

"Yes, it's me. No, I know. I need a favor."

It's followed by a long silence.

"Someone who knows. Thanks." Raymond throws the phone down and paces through the station, his hand continually rubbing his forehead as he does.

Forman avoids catching Raymond's eye. She's only seen him like this once before, when a suspect was accidentally released before trial. Raymond's suspect. One that he never caught again.

He had paced for hours that day before disappearing into the city, searching for the suspect, coming back long after his shift was over, empty handed.

The station phone rings again, and Raymond stops pacing. He waits.

"Raymond, you have a call."

His eyes are shifty, dancing over the room, briefly landing on Forman and then the other men. "I'll take it in the office over here." He storms into the office and slams the door, but it doesn't close all the way, the force making it bounce back slightly ajar. Enough to provide a funnel for the harsh whisper coming from Raymond.

"Yes, yes, we've met. Out in the valley." He pauses. "Yes, yes, I know."

He seems like he would start pacing again if the telephone cord didn't keep him tethered to the desk. Forman slips into a chair, pulls out her notebook, and writes *valley* and *favor* on it.

"Tonight? No, there's not. You know they won't come to the beach. Because I know. They don't go there."

Forman makes notes of everything she hears, her handwriting nearly illegible as she writes as fast as she can.

"You're late again." It's Warrenson. He's standing with his arms crossed, towering over her.

"Following up on some notes for the girls I see at the penny arcade," she says a little curtly, wanting to get back to Raymond and the conversation he is having.

He glances over at Raymond. "You should be more like him. He brings in arrests. What have you brought in lately?"

"I would if you gave me a chance."

"I did. Mrs. Michaels."

Forman stands, the pen still in her hand. "What if I can still solve that case? Would you change your mind about the promotion?"

Warrenson pulls out a pocket watch and holds it up to Forman. "Do you know what this is?"

Forman doesn't reply. She's not in the mood for these types of games.

"It means the time for that is gone. Now get on to your patrol."

"On it." She sits back down.

"Forman?"

She looks up at him. "Like any good officer, I need to take notes on a current situation. I'll be out the door in a minute. If you have a problem with my work ethic, then that's something we can talk about, but I'm working as hard as I can."

He moves back slightly, a nod to his head. "OK then." He takes his time, stepping away as if strolling down a lane and not through the station room of a police station.

Forman returns her attention to Raymond and his call.

"If you're lying . . ." He's standing again, moving around the desk, his normal long stride constricted by the small area. "OK. You're sure? Good." He laughs. "She thinks she can continue with me here? I don't think so."

Another pause. Forman keeps writing.

"She doesn't know their boats. No, she doesn't. She can't." Raymond looks through the glass, his eyes landing on Forman. He puts the receiver on the desk, reaches the door, and slams it shut.

CHAPTER
FIFTY-THREE

RAYMOND

The night air is cool as Raymond, standing next to his car, pulls a drag from his cigarette and exhales, the smoke carried by the breeze flowing off the ocean. Even with the vapor gone and the wind threatening to extinguish the ember, the release is still the same. The moment before the games begin. The thrill before the conquest. This conquest. The one that should have ended before but will end tonight. He's making sure of it.

It's been a long day of waiting, of arrangements, of phone calls and details, but the moment is finally here.

This beach is unfamiliar to him, a sloping sandy spot east of Topanga Canyon, not far from the shacks that people built to be close to the hills, which have become a weekend respite for Hollywood celebrities. Even with the sound of the ocean and the dampness on his skin, it feels wrong. He's used to the rumrunners reaching the piers at Long Beach, sometimes even the beaches near Palos Verdes. Not here, up past Santa Monica and the bright city lights.

And yet it makes sense. Closer to the county line. Less chance of a police encounter, especially since he took care of the last rumrunners he encountered when they no longer wanted to work with Blue, saying they could get better prices elsewhere. He didn't give them the full treatment, though. They're in jail, waiting for their trial. He was nice. He needed accolades. Not all of them can end up dead. But deceased or in jail, the result is often the same. They're no longer Blue's problem and therefore no longer his.

Raymond glances around. He's been here for at least thirty minutes already, if not more, his car parked in the dirt lot across the state highway. The highway is silent. Even the residents of the shacks up the road are tucked in bed by now.

And across the road, the beach awaits where the boats will arrive, bringing what? He has no idea. Most likely rum from Canada. Or tequila from Mexico. They'll race from Catalina Island to drop off their wares, pick up their money, and disappear back into the darkness.

Except it won't work that way tonight. The one to meet them won't be there when they arrive.

His eyes shift to Topanga, waiting for the headlights. A direct route from the valley. Easy access for her to meet her suppliers. Easy access for Raymond to meet her.

The waves crash on the nearby shore, the salt spray dampening the air, and he almost doesn't hear the click of the car door.

Raymond turns his head.

The passenger door of his car is open, and the gaunt boy is climbing out.

"Stay in the car," barks Raymond.

"But you're out here," whines Charles, his voice a mixture of frustration and nerves.

"Yes, and I'm police. You're not. Stay in the car."

Charles leans on the door. "But you're only here because of me."

Raymond pulls out his revolver with his right hand, the cigarette not moving from his left, and points it at Charles. "This is official police business. Let me remind you, Charles, you are not police. Your church rules don't apply here."

Charles hesitates, but he lowers his head in defeat and pulls the door closed.

Raymond grins as he puts the gun away and holds his cigarette near his lips. He can see Charles in the front seat, his thin arms now folded in his lap, a dejected look on his face from the scolding. He'll take care of him next. It's the church boy's own fault for insisting on joining him tonight, threatening to show up regardless, so he agreed to bring him along. And it will be the last journey that Charles makes. But first, the task at hand.

Raymond returns his attention to the road, the slope of the highway as it carries along the sand, a small embankment protecting it from the ocean waves during storms. That's the place, right near the large row of boulders, which have tumbled down from the Santa Monica Mountains over the years, creating a small beach hidden from the oncoming cars and out of sight of the residents up the road.

And this is where they will be. Where *she* will be, in that green truck, the one item he didn't burn at the winery. But that wasn't the mistake. The mistake was trying to make it look like an accident, not ensuring she was taken care of. There will be no accident tonight. He's not leaving until she's dead.

Raymond smiles. He should give Letty more credit. It's actually an ideal spot for rumrunners to pull ashore, their boats and dealings out of sight until they're already on their way back out to sea.

Except it wasn't her idea. She just took over for Shorty. His rumrunners.

He pulls a drag, the cigarette almost burned to its end, and takes out his pocket watch. It's 12:20 a.m.

Raymond leans down and glares at the timid fellow in the front seat. "You sure she's going to come? You sure you didn't bring me all the way out here in the middle of the night for nothing?"

Charles nods. "She said twenty-five past midnight."

"If I find out you're lying, you know what I'll do to you."

"She needs this delivery; she doesn't have anything else." Charles puts his hands together, his long fingers moving back and forth. "You're just going to arrest her, right?"

"Of course," replies Raymond with a smirk he doesn't bother hiding. "This is only to teach her a lesson."

"Good." Charles shifts again, continuing to rub his hands together, a longtime nervous habit. "You know I'm only looking out for her. It's what I've always done. Made sure she's OK. Made sure she does right. This isn't what she should be doing."

"And I thank you for that," replies Raymond. "You've done a good thing. A very good thing. A very Christian thing." He stands back up and refocuses on the road.

The cigarette no longer has enough left for him to smoke without kissing the heat, but Raymond doesn't throw it to the ground. That's not how this works. He holds it in his fingers, the final embers searing his skin as he waits for the lights. "She better be here soon."

"She will be," adds Charles. "She's never late to anything." He laughs a little at that, though, the sound almost girlish with glee. "I can't wait to see her face when I bail her out and save her. Then everything will be fine again."

"Sure, sure," says Raymond, but he's no longer listening to this verbal dribble, as a pair of highlights have appeared in the distance. One car, the dual beams illuminating a few feet in front as it navigates the curves of the canyon.

Raymond squats down next to the car. He has to be out of sight when she comes. If he's seen, it's over before it begins.

The truck passes the parking lot and pulls to the side of the road near the boulders, just as Charles said it would.

Raymond tosses the cigarette down, his fingers throbbing from the burn it left, and grinds the remnant into the asphalt, the windblown sand beneath his shoe making a scratching noise that now seems louder than the waves.

He taps the edge of his car, and Charles glances up.

"Well," says Raymond, "look who's finally arrived."

CHAPTER
FIFTY-FOUR

FORMAN

Forman crouches behind the large boulder where she's been for at least two hours, long enough for her fingertips to go numb with the cold. Even though she's well hidden here from the road, she gets down lower, the borrowed gun resting on her knee.

Borrowed. Sort of. She didn't ask her aunt if she could take the pistol, but she knew Caroline wouldn't mind. Forman will put it back after she's done. If she's still around to return it, that is.

The truck backs up alongside the road and then turns to face the ocean, its headlights beaming into the night air.

It's all happening just as Raymond said it would. He probably thought no one could hear with the door closed, and perhaps no one could at a distance, but Forman moved next to the office door as the call continued, stepping away the second he put the receiver down.

After the call was over and he had stormed out of the station, Forman slipped into the office and grabbed the notebook from his desk, taking it with her as she headed out to do her rounds in the city.

It was only minutes later, with the help of some charcoal, that she was able to read the impression left on the pad by Raymond's forceful and rushed hand: 12:25. Topanga.

After her shift, she stopped by her house and then took the Red Car as far west as she could before paying for a Yellow Cab with her savings to bring her here. For the first hour, she thought she'd chosen the wrong beach. Until the car showed up. The one across the street. It should be Raymond's sedan, but all she could see from here was the dark outline and the small orange glow of a cigarette. And now the truck's headlights are blinding her, everything else falling into darkness around it. The beams illuminate the beach all the way to the water, and she can see small crabs scurrying back into the sand after each wave.

Forman knows that two things can happen tonight. She can stop Raymond from getting away with murder and capture a large shipment of offshore rumrunning, earning her the respect of the station and even a promotion. Or he'll take another life tonight, like he did to Thomas, possibly even her own.

The waves continue to crash on the beach, but the two vehicles remain in place, as silent as they've been since the moment the engines died. It would be hard to hear the opening of a car door here, but as far as she can see, no one has exited the truck. As if they are waiting for something. But what? The occupant of the truck must be able to see Raymond's car. Do they know the danger at hand? Or are they in this with Raymond, to meet the shipment?

Forman glances at her watch, the mother-of-pearl background shining even in the low light. It's past time.

She takes a breath, her lungs shallow, her crouched position leaving her little room to breathe, but she knows that's not the only reason. Her experience with firing a gun is limited. If the department issued guns to women, she'd have more practice. She has fired one before—a family friend offering her target practice up in the hills of Pasadena—but it's been a while. She'd been suitable on the targets, but tonight she can't just be suitable. She needs to do better.

Forman wraps her fingers around the handle of the pistol, her finger on the trigger. Maybe she won't need it, but it's ready if need be. She stands, her back still pressed against the boulder that blocks her from the beach, the slope of the hill to her left further obstructing anyone's view of her. At least she hopes that's the case.

She's safe in her cove, though if gunfire erupts, it can go anywhere. But she has a plan. Intercept, hold them at gunpoint, and then arrest. She can do this.

A gentle hum sounds, one that's different from the wind blowing the sand and the waves crashing on the shore. It rings in the night air.

She takes her eyes off the vehicles and directs her attention to the ocean, the headlights still illuminating the water.

The sound grows deeper.

It's a motorboat, circling a ways out from the beach, the noise of the motor changing as it chops through the waves and circles again.

And then darkness. The truck headlights are out, extinguished like an outdoor candle in winter rain, and now the only light is from the stars in the night sky.

Forman shifts, the pistol raised by her shoulder. She tightens her grip on it and adjusts her position. If things go wrong, her whole career will be over. But she's not going to turn back.

Except now with the lights no longer blaring in her eyes, she can see the shape of the truck more clearly. It's the one she was in the other day. The bootlegger's truck.

Letty's truck.

The headlights flash, and Forman puts up her arm, blocking herself and her identity from the light. She retreats to the sandy boulder for protection. The headlights flash twice more, and then it's dark again.

The motorboat approaches the shore, the sound of the engine growing as it gets closer.

CHAPTER FIFTY-FIVE

RAYMOND

The headlights are the only sign Raymond needs. It's time.

He struts forward, his foot at the edge of the highway, his fingers itching to grab his gun, but the sound of the door opening behind stops him.

Raymond whips his head around. Charles is outside, his blue flannel jacket whipping in the wind as he rounds the back of the car.

"What did I say before?" Raymond narrows his eyes. "I said stay in the car."

"Why? I should be out there, too. She needs to know it was me."

"She doesn't need to know anything right now."

Raymond pulls his gun from his holster and aims it at Charles, the distance between them only a few feet. Earlier, he was kidding. Now he's not.

"You move one more inch closer, I'll shoot you. You don't get back in the car, I'll shoot you. You reopen that door again before I've dealt with the situation across the street, I'll shoot you. Do we have an understanding?"

Charles moves back slightly, but he's still not returning to the car. He pulls his flannel jacket closer to his body. "I don't want anything bad to happen. It's better if I just go up to her. This can all be over right now."

"Do I need to repeat myself?" Raymond steps toward him.

Charles exhales forcefully but doesn't move, as if he's debating whether Raymond is serious. This distraction is too much. The boat could already be close to shore. Raymond needs to be there before it arrives. He needs to see Letty first. To take care of Letty first.

"Do not try me, Charles." He takes another step. "You will lose."

Charles scampers back into the car and closes the door.

Raymond leans down to the window. "The offer stands until I come back. Are we clear?"

Charles nods.

Raymond focuses his attention back across the road. The headlights are out again, but the doors of the truck are shut. There's still time.

He moves across the highway, nearly giddy. He hasn't been this excited since Betty told him she was pregnant. A son to follow in his footsteps. Instead, they had a daughter. One like Betty, not like him.

He swallows the disappointment as he did last year and continues on, reaching the other side, the shoreline in front of him. A glance back at his car confirms that Charles is doing as he was told.

The motorboat is still circling out in the ocean.

Raymond doesn't even need it to come ashore. It would be better if it went away and Charles was the only one privy to what is about to happen. But he knows that after the signal Letty gave, the boat will land. They always land. They get the signal, and they come to shore. Raymond knows it all too well.

He needs to take care of this *now*.

The truck is about twenty feet off, a sizable distance, enough to keep Letty's attention away from him until he reaches her window. She should be focused on the boat anyway. He edges along the road, his shoes crunching on the sand-dusted dirt slope.

He feels a calmness mixed with excitement. He's been an officer for too long to be nervous. He knows he will win in these situations. He almost misses the early days, the uncertainty as he navigated the city. And then the traffic stop that resulted in a bullet in his arm. It was the last time he was hesitant to act. To fire first. The arm still aches now and again. A reminder.

Raymond's fingers are itchy, but he doesn't want to reveal the weapon until the last second, a surprise attack without the fear of the approach. They touch the handle of the gun, still in its holster, tapping it as he walks.

He prefers his other ways: a quick twist of the neck and a toss into the river, letting the flow of the water handle the rest. The fire didn't work, but tonight he's taking care of it, and he's not leaving. This time it will be different. This time he can watch the light dim in her eyes. This time he can be a hero. Any moment now.

He's close enough to see Letty. She's in the front seat, her hat pulled down to obscure her face, her attention on the water and the boat, no idea of the fate she's about to meet. It's perfect.

The motorboat continues to circle, its sound fading in and out, hesitant to land.

Letty flashes the headlights again. Two flashes. And then they remain on.

That has to be the full signal now. The boat will come ashore soon, Raymond's sure of it. But it doesn't matter.

He's only three feet away. He slides the revolver out of the holster and raises it up, holding it with both hands as he directs it to the driver's-side window.

He just needs her to look at him. He wants to see the fear in her eyes as she knows the game has come to an end.

"Raymond," says a voice, "I wouldn't do that. Not if I were you."

Except the voice isn't coming from the truck. It's coming from his left, below him.

Raymond keeps the gun aimed at the window but turns his head, tilting it as he does.

There's someone on the beach just outside the headlights' glare, the light revealing the silhouette of their body and a gun, pointed at him.

"Do what, exactly?" replies Raymond.

"Whatever it is you were about to do." The figure steps forward, the gun still aimed at him.

Though the light is weak, Raymond can see who it is.

It's Letty.

CHAPTER FIFTY-SIX

LETTY

My shoulders still ache from riding in the back of the truck, lying down and rolling out as soon as we stopped, even with Raymond's car across the street. People don't see what they're not looking for.

"Nice trick," says Raymond, his voice possessing the same level of calm as always, even with my revolver pointed at him. "Who's in the truck? A friend of yours?"

I almost want to smile at the surprise on his face. The face that doesn't ever react, doesn't show emotion. But now it does. "Forget her. I'm the one you're here for."

He moves his gun away from Margaret just slightly, and my breath releases.

Margaret isn't looking at him, her hat pulled down low, keeping the ruse going for as long as possible.

"Now how did someone like you get down there when I've been watching this area for a while?"

"I don't think that's the question you should be asking."

Raymond steps toward the embankment, his weapon now low and in front of him. Because he doesn't think I'm a threat. "What question should I be asking?"

I keep my gun aimed at him, the revolver Margaret helped me find after Raymond took away my rifle and burned nearly everything I owned. "The question is how will Letty kill me? How will I die?"

Raymond laughs, his gun falling to his side, his head back.

"You think I'm going to let you leave here unscathed?" I continue. "You tried to kill me. Now it's my turn."

Raymond chuckles again as he glances back at the truck. "Nice little trick you played there. I underestimated you."

"Clearly."

"So what are you going to do? Kill me, Hart? We both know you won't." He jumps down to the sand, no longer a danger to Margaret but still one to me. Even more so now.

I wave my left hand to give her the signal to leave.

The engine roars to life, and Raymond turns his head, raising his gun again at Margaret.

"She's not part of this, Raymond. This is between us."

He's still focused on the truck as it backs up, as I told Margaret to do when we went over the details for tonight. "Police! Turn off the engine," Raymond commands, moving up the embankment, his gun aimed at the truck as it pulls onto the highway.

"You fire that gun at her," I yell over the sound of the engine and the waves, "and you won't have time to assess the damage, because a bullet will already be in your head. Courtesy of me. There won't even be a moment to think about it."

He looks at me, his lips curving into a smile. "I know you can't do that." The truck speeds down the state highway toward Santa Monica. "But fear not. I'll take care of her later."

My revolver is still pointed at him. "Your issue is with me, not her."

He shakes his head. "I can't believe you had any success as a bootlegger. You don't follow any of the rules."

"On the contrary. My life is full of rules. They're just not yours."

He jumps back onto the beach from the embankment, his feet spraying sand as he does. The glow from the headlights is gone, but there's enough illumination from the moon and stars to see him approach. His gun is in his hand but not at the ready. He tried to kill me once, and he could do it again in a second, though I know he prefers strangulation. Or fire.

He's a car length away now. Close enough to get me, but I have my gun, bullets fully loaded and ready to fire.

"That's close enough."

He doesn't listen.

My finger twitches on the trigger.

"Don't fool me, Letty Hart. You can't. You're not strong enough." He pauses. "You've never been strong enough." He raises his gun.

"Wait!" A man is at the edge of the banks, where Raymond was only moments before. "Don't shoot her."

But I don't need more light to recognize the lanky body and the floppy hair blowing in the wind. Charles.

"Do you ever follow instructions?" yells Raymond, his eyes pinned on me. "Get back in the car."

I keep my revolver aimed at Raymond, who has stopped moving toward me for the moment, but my focus is on Charles, his hair tussled by the wind and his face marked with fear at the scene unfolding in front of him. "Go away, Charles."

He has one foot down on the embankment, but he stops, his expression transforming into confusion. "What do you mean, Letty? I'm here to help."

I return my focus to Raymond. "Help? Charles, you brought him here."

"This isn't supposed to happen," Charles says, panic growing in his voice. "He was only supposed to scare you. Teach you a lesson."

The wind is blowing harder now, and it's pushing my arm as I hold out the gun. "You need to leave, Charles. Raymond will kill you. After he tries to kill me."

"There'll be no trying," says Raymond, though I can hear frustration in his voice. "I will kill you."

"No!" Charles moves forward, his feet slipping on the dirt slope down to the sand.

"Stop, Charles." I keep looking at Raymond, though even he is rattled by the distraction on the slope, his head moving back and forth. "You need to go away. You shouldn't be here."

"I'm sorry, Letty. I had to. It was to save you. He's not supposed to do anything, only scare you back to the right side."

Raymond glances at me, a smirk on his face. "Yes, Letty. I'm here to scare you." He holds up his gun. "Are you scared?"

"No." My revolver is nearly the same as his, but I know he's not going to fire. It's all about the show. He'll strangle me first.

"Letty," cries Charles. "I'm sorry."

"If you don't leave right now, Charles, I'll shoot you myself." I keep my eyes on Raymond, who now laughs.

"Looks like you have no fans here, Charles," adds Raymond. "Even your friend doesn't want you around."

Charles moves back to the road. "I was only trying to help."

"I know," I reply, my voice cold, my tone steady. "It's what you've always done. You always had to try to save me from myself. But I never needed saving. Not ever." I glance at him now, his face strained with a horror I've never seen on him before. "It's what you've done my entire life. Tattled to try to save me. Letty broke the window," I say, repeating what Charles had said as he pointed at the farm window and then at the slingshot back when we were kids.

"But weren't you with her?" I remember my father saying.

"Yes, but it was only to look after her," said Charles.

My father stared at me. "Don't leave evidence, Letty."

"The slingshot," I say to Charles as the memories continue to play in my mind. "And then the fence. Remember? Letty fell off the fence, and she might have broken her arm. You should tell her not to do that again; it's not safe."

My father had looked at Charles instead of me. "Why didn't you tell her not to do it?"

"She didn't listen."

My father had shaken his head. "Keep your eyes on everything, Letty. Even the ground. Sometimes it's the only thing that will catch you."

The wind picks up, but I keep my gun aimed at Raymond while my focus darts back and forth between the two men. "Or when the barn was nearly complete. Mr. Hart, Letty didn't finish her side," I say, my voice carrying in the wind as Raymond smirks, clearly bemused. "You always had to stand on the right side of the law, Charles. You always had to tattle. It's what you do. It's what I knew you would do. Tonight."

"No," says Charles, moving back.

"Because it's who you are."

"No," repeats Charles. "It's to look after you."

"Even when it means disrupting my plans."

"It's to help you in the long run." His tone is nearly pleading now.

"But this time you did help, and not in the future. Right now. I knew you would betray me. To Raymond." I wait, but neither man reacts. "Go ahead, Charles. Tell Raymond how you knew about tonight."

Raymond tilts his head and looks at Charles, but Charles stays silent, the only movement his hair flopping in the wind.

"Because I told him. A little God is good for us, Charles. It's what you said every time you tattled." I glance up at him before turning my attention back to Raymond. "And you said it outside the barn. Right before you tried to kill me. I knew there was a connection, and all I had to do was plant the seed."

"Letty, he comes to the church," says Charles. "He's a good man."

"No, he's not. He wants me dead. Of course he would come tonight. How about that, Charles? You told the one person who wants to kill me exactly where I would be."

"Letty, I'm so sorry." Though it's too dark to tell, I'm certain there are tears running down his face.

"Don't be. It's exactly what I wanted to happen."

Raymond points his gun at Charles. "She's right. Get out of here."

"No."

"Start running." Raymond steps forward, and it's enough to frighten Charles.

He backs up down the road and scrambles out of sight. At least he's gone. Safe. I can focus on the situation now.

"What are we going to do about this, Letty Hart? Shall I fire first, or will you?" Raymond laughs. "Oh, wait, you won't. Because you can't." The words are still floating in the air as headlights pull up along the side of the road.

A car. An unplanned car.

I'm getting outnumbered, and I only have a few bullets. "A friend of yours?"

Raymond looks over his shoulder, and his frame weakens. "Not exactly."

The door slams, and a large man in a coat and a wide-brimmed hat walks toward us. "I knew it, Raymond. I knew you couldn't handle this."

"Blue, I'm handling it. I said I would take care of it, and I am."

It's Blue. The one Annabel first warned me about in the truck and then Margaret filled in the details on later.

"You've gotten careless," he says as he moves down the embankment, his hands empty, though I'm sure he has a gun. "I don't like careless. So I thought I better take care of it myself."

"I'm taking care of it right now." Raymond points his gun at me, but mine is aimed right back, ready to fire first.

"Forget it," says Blue. "I'm here to clean up your mess." He's still approaching, his shoes dragging lines in the sand.

I can fire at Raymond, but Blue might kill me immediately, drawing before I have a chance to shoot. I have to choose.

Blue moves past Raymond and stops, as if on a rope that has reached the end of its tether. "Letty?"

I swallow hard, my mouth dropping open as his face becomes clear. "Dad?"

CHAPTER FIFTY-SEVEN

RAYMOND

Raymond looks from Blue to Letty and back again, all energy he had prior to this moment draining from his fingertips.

"What are *you* doing here?" Blue's voice is different from the one Raymond has known for the past few years. The power has drained from it like a barrel releasing its plug, the strength of the wood no longer able to hold the contents inside.

"*Dad?*" repeats Letty, a waver to her voice, her head moving slightly back and forth.

Blue is motionless, his formerly rigid shoulders now sagging, his hands outstretched in front of him as if asking a question.

And Raymond knows it's real. This girl, this Letty, is Blue's child. His gun lowers.

"You have a daughter?" Raymond can't help himself, the question passing his lips before he can silence it. To think that Blue made threats toward Raymond's family when he had his own to protect and fear for.

"Silence," snaps Blue before returning his attention to Letty. "Why are you here?"

"I could ask you the same question." Letty's voice returns to the same steady tone Raymond has become used to in his encounters with her. He knows she's putting on a good show, because the news has surprised even Raymond.

"You're dead," she adds, the gun frozen in her right hand, still aimed at him, though there's a slight tremor in her wrist.

"Well, clearly, I'm not."

"John Corizano rises from the grave," says Raymond, the smile coming through in his tone.

"John?" Letty glances from Raymond to Blue and steps back. "That's not your name."

"It was. It is. These past few years. To protect you. To protect your mother."

Letty looks at Raymond as if waiting for him to say something, but he has nothing to say. His mind is racing now, trying to figure out how to keep control of the situation and make sure he completes the task he came to do.

She takes another step back. "Your name is Richard."

It clicks for Raymond. "Letty Hart. Richard Hart. Is that why you had me throw away pages in that guy's file, Blue? It was you. You're Richard Hart."

Blue doesn't reply, his attention only on his daughter. "Letty, why are you here?"

She motions with the gun toward Raymond. "He tried to kill me. He burned down the farm."

Blue turns and looks at him, his expression going from confusion to anger, then looks back to Letty. "You were the bootlegger? You're Marks?"

Letty stays silent as she stares at Blue. "I guess we're both good at hiding things," she says eventually.

Blue shakes his head. "All this time and you ended up just like me."

"No, I didn't." She pauses. "Because I would never leave my family."

Blue steps toward her, but Raymond raises his gun. This is his game. His rules. His ending.

"I have so much to say that I never could," continues Blue. "I never wanted this for you. I did everything I could to keep your mother and you out of this. Even leaving everything behind so there was no link. Finding a vagrant and putting him in the river with my clothes and my billfold. Letting Sal—"

"Identify him as you," says Letty.

"If you thought I was dead, it would keep everyone safe, and then I could take out the others. There would be no more danger. I did this for you."

"No," Letty scoffs, shaking her head. "You did nothing for me."

Blue is now halfway between them. He's going to kill Letty. Blue's going to finish the job that he told Raymond to do, and Raymond will be next.

"Step away, Blue. I told you I could handle this." Raymond moves closer to them, his gun aimed at Letty. "I told you I could do it. You didn't need to come here."

"This is still you?" says Letty. "You told him to kill me?"

"No," says Blue. "I didn't know it was you."

"Blue, move to the side. I'm going to finish the job."

Blue turns around and faces Raymond. "No," he replies, a tone in his voice that Raymond has never heard before.

"What do you mean no?" Raymond steps toward him. "You told me to take care of this. It was your wish. Your command. And I'm following your rules. Like you always wanted."

Blue moves in front of Letty, his arms outstretched like one of the dry chaparral bushes in the hills, barely concealing the area but reaching out wide anyway. "Not this time, Raymond. This is my daughter."

Raymond rolls his eyes and looks up at the sky as every order that Blue ever gave him goes through his mind. Two years of rules and trials. "I do everything you ask and you're still not happy. You would be nothing without me. I cleaned up this town for you. Because of you. And now you're telling me to stop? You're not that lucky, Blue."

"I'm the reason you even have a job." The strength in Blue's voice has returned, his moment of weakness vanished, and now it's back to business as usual.

Except it's not business as usual.

"You, Raymond, are nothing without me," says Blue.

"Not anymore." Raymond doesn't move his gun.

Letty is to the side of Blue now, still blocked by him, but her gun is pointed at Raymond, though she won't fire. He knows she won't.

Blue moves to cover her again. "Put down your gun, Raymond."

"Why? Or one of the twins will get me? Oh, wait, they can't. Eddie is dead." He glances over his shoulder to make sure Frankie isn't there, but there's no one coming. Blue came here alone. "Sorry, boss," he continues. "This isn't your game anymore. I'm the new king in town. You let your heart get in the way. Isn't that what you said to me once? I had too much of a heart. Not anymore."

"Gun down, Raymond. You don't tell me no." Blue's jacket is open now, the weapon on his side, but it remains in his waistband. "You don't tell me no."

"You're right," replies Raymond. "I don't tell you anything anymore. Our agreement is over."

"That's a joke. You can't survive without me."

"You think I don't know your suppliers? You think I don't know how this whole thing works?" Raymond laughs. "I'll do you the favor of fulfilling your last request, and then I'm on my own. Move to the side, Blue."

Blue stays in the same position, the crashing waves filling the silence between them.

"No," he replies. "Not this time."

Raymond's fingers are itchy again, the wound from the cigarette burn stinging in the salty air. "What do you care? You left them. Years ago."

Blue's hand moves to his hip, but he doesn't take out his gun. In the two years that Raymond has known him, Blue has always pulled his gun at the drop of a hat, the squeak of a door. Raymond's lost count of the number of times it's been waved in front of him over nothing. And he's seen it fired at people, at any poor soul who didn't do as Blue instructed, without a second thought. Until tonight. It remains on his hip. As if he doesn't think that Raymond will shoot. But he will.

"You wanted me to take care of this. Of her. And now I am." Raymond moves to the side to get a view of Letty, but Blue blocks his view again.

"I made a mistake. I didn't realize it was her. The order no longer stands."

"Too late, Blue. I always finish the job. Reveal the target."

"No."

Letty steps out from the side of him, but Blue continues to move with her, covering her every time she tries to get around him, the gun Raymond knows she won't fire still in her hand.

"Blue, I'm going to shoot if you're there or not."

He shakes his head. "No, you're not. You can make a choice, Raymond. We all make choices in this life. I've made some poor ones. But this one is right. I'm not moving. I'm not letting you kill my daughter."

Raymond tightens his hand, every muscle alive with energy, only his trigger finger still loose. "Is that your final decision?"

"It is."

"Your choice." Raymond squeezes the trigger.

CHAPTER FIFTY-EIGHT

LETTY

The sound of the bullet rings in my ears, the wind and waves failing to dampen the shock of the noise as it echoes off the rocks. I do a mental check of my limbs and my torso, but the bullet has missed me.

My father stumbles back but doesn't fall.

It's all an act.

An act to trick me. It's been years of his tricks. Of him leaving. Of him bootlegging. Of him dying.

I finally get around him, my gun aimed at Raymond and then back at my father. I don't trust either of them. They both have guns; this I know. And they're here to kill me.

My father is stumbling toward the rocks, his hand on his stomach. It's all an act.

Raymond is still holding the gun, but there's a different look to him, his strong facade finally cracked, as if he's in awe of something. In awe of his actions.

I look back at my father and then down to where he's holding his stomach. His hand is covered with blood.

He lowers himself to the sand, his palm failing to keep back the flow gushing from the wound. "Don't," he whispers as I turn to help him. "He'll kill you, too."

"Dad."

"No." His eyes move in the direction of Raymond. "Be careful."

I glance back, but Raymond's gun is by his side as he stands there with a blank look on his face, as if he can't believe what he's done.

"Dad." I place my hand on my father's arm, the muscle he had from the days at the winery now gone.

"No." He looks at me, his pale-green eyes tired. "I'm sorry. I never meant to—"

"Stop. We'll get you some help."

He shakes his head weakly. "Pay attention, Letty. You leave things out, it will only cause trouble."

"Dad." I shake his arm, but it flops to the side, the life draining out of him faster than the blood soaking into the sand. There's nothing I can do to help him.

"Always finish what you start," he whispers.

All of his rules and all of his scoldings when I got in trouble make sense now. They weren't to keep me prim and proper, to make me a girl who follows orders. They were to guide me in this world. His world. To keep me alive.

I came here to finish Raymond. To finish what I started. What Raymond started. I stand up and lock eyes with Raymond. The tears are threatening to fall, but I won't let them. I move forward, the revolver steady in my hand.

"You're weak," says Raymond, his gun still loose at his side. "And you'll be weak until the day you die. Which is today."

The emotions of the past few years well up in me like a hornet's nest struck down from its safe perch. My father leaving my mother and me alone. And not to be with another family, as I had been led to believe. "I can't live two lives anymore. It's not fair to you, and it's not fair to me." Those were his words as he left that day. His second life was this business. And the dangers went with him.

And now his sacrifice—his life to save mine.

It will only take one pull of the trigger to end Raymond. The man who tried to kill me. The man who killed my father. But my finger doesn't move.

Raymond lifts his gun. "Have any last words, Letty Hart? Now that you don't have your father to protect you?"

"I never did. I never needed him. I only needed myself."

"You're a sad little bootlegger, like your father." He laughs. "But a weak one. You can't survive in this world."

My teeth grind together as I steady my aim. Like shooting the birds when I was a kid, except I couldn't shoot them. They were too innocent. But Raymond isn't. He's a killer. He stands like a can on the fence, ready to be taken out with one bullet, and I'm the one who will do it.

Raymond laughs, the sound floating on the sea breeze.

My father rustles by the rocks. I don't dare take my attention off Raymond, but the motion continues. I flick my eyes to the left. Except it's not my father. His lifeless body remains still on the sand.

It's someone else.

And they have a gun.

Pointed right at me.

CHAPTER FIFTY-NINE

FORMAN

Forman is now out enough from behind the rocks that she can easily fire at either Raymond or Letty. She moves the pistol back and forth between the two of them, her feet kicking up sand as she maneuvers into a position so that both of them are within a quick shift of her aim. She should have been faster after the first bullet was fired, but she waited until the situation was static again. Waited until Blue was in front of her and no longer able to reach for his gun.

"Halt." Her voice is stern, unwavering.

"Who's there?" says Raymond, his gun aimed at her, Letty no longer a concern for him.

"Officer Annabel Forman of the Los Angeles Police Department."

"Forman," says Raymond, the relief in his voice puzzling to her. "It's you. I didn't know you were here."

Forman keeps her gun poised on him, but Raymond lowers his.

"I'm glad you're here. Actually, I never thought I would be so glad to see you. How long have you been here?"

Forman glances down at Blue, his chest still and the dark, wet sand around him confirming that she doesn't need to worry about him getting up again.

"You know, Forman, I don't think I gave you enough credit," continues Raymond. "You're here at exactly the right time."

But Forman sees that Letty still has her gun pointed at Raymond.

"Lower your weapon." Forman's voice is swallowed by the wind. "Lower your weapon," she says louder.

Raymond glances at Letty and back at Forman. "She's not listening to you. But don't worry, she won't fire. Listen, Forman, you can have this one. You womenfolk can stay together. Arrest her. She just killed that man."

Letty doesn't move, doesn't even look over at Forman, her body rigid as she aims at Raymond, the only movement her ponytail as it blows in the night air.

Forman shifts the gun back and forth between Raymond and Letty, the movement so slight she's certain neither of them knows which one she is aiming at as she moves.

"There's more we can add to her list," says Raymond. "Not that I'm trying to do your job for you, Forman. Just helping. But first off, murder. She killed him. Shot him. That guy right there."

"You mean Blue."

Raymond falters, tilting his head to the side as his eyebrows crease. "Exactly. She killed Blue."

"And you're going to tell me she's a bootlegger," continues Forman.

"Yes . . ." Raymond draws out the word. "But how do you know?"

"I know everything."

Raymond nods slowly, and Letty shifts her attention to Forman, her gun still aimed at him. Letty's face is unreadable. She's different than how she was in the truck that day. Her cheeks look sunken now, her eyes cold and unstirring. Forman glances back at Raymond, the pistol still aimed, both hands wrapped around the handle.

"What are you waiting for, Forman? Arrest this bootlegger for murder and violation of the Prohibition Act. Maybe this will even get you the promotion you want, though we'll see. I mean, I was here first. I was witness to it all. But maybe I'll split the credit with you. Don't worry, I'll still put in a good word for you."

"You'll be splitting nothing," says Letty, a slow step toward him. "Always finish what you start. You're not leaving here alive."

"I disagree." Raymond raises his gun to Letty. "Unwise, Letty Hart. Stay right there."

Forman readjusts her own gun. "Lower your weapons."

Letty doesn't. Neither does Raymond.

"I am Officer Forman of the Los Angeles Police Department," she repeats. "And you are under arrest."

"This doesn't involve you, Forman," says Letty, her attention still on Raymond. "You don't want to be here for this. Leave and protect yourself."

"Arrest her, Forman. End this circus," says Raymond. "I knew you weren't cut out for a detective. You can't even get this bootlegger, a woman, to drop her gun. A girl who's too afraid to ever fire one. This is the easiest arrest of your career. No wonder you didn't get the promotion. You can't do the simplest things. Arrest her, or I will."

"I'm not here for her," replies Forman. "I'm here for you."

Raymond tilts his head, a small smile on his face. "Excuse me?"

She steps forward. "Drop your weapon, Detective Raymond."

"You're making a big mistake here, Forman."

"Drop your weapon," repeats Forman, her palm sweaty as she grips the handle of her gun.

Raymond laughs. "And why should I do that? You think that I might shoot this suspect here and blame it on you? I wouldn't give you that credit."

"You've been killing them. All of them."

"I don't know what you're talking about."

"How long have you been doing this? Killing bootleggers. You're a police officer. We took an oath to serve and protect, not to steal and kill."

Raymond shakes his head, grinning.

"You made one big mistake," continues Forman. "You gave your wife the evidence."

Raymond laughs, the wind blowing the lapels of his coat open. "You're going to have to do better than that. No wonder you can't get promoted." But Raymond is bothered, she can tell. His left leg is moving back and forth on the sand, the same thing he does when he gets a call at the station, right before he starts pacing.

"The necklace," says Forman. "Mrs. Michaels told me that a deliveryman stole it from her. He also happened to be a bootlegger. Thomas 'Rudy' Rudinsky. You might remember him; he ended up in the LA River after you strangled him. But not before you took his belongings, which is how you got the necklace."

Raymond shifts his gun away from Letty to the space between the two of them. "You're mistaken, Forman. Must be that female intuition clouding your judgment. You lost your promotion, and now you're bitter. It's not a good look on you."

"I have the proof."

"You have nothing!" yells Raymond. "Now do what you're told. Arrest this woman, or I will, and then I'll make sure you're kicked off the force."

Forman keeps moving forward, Raymond only a few feet away now. "Put down your weapon. You are under arrest."

"I don't think so." He raises his gun, the barrel aimed at Forman. "You make this too easy."

A shot is fired.

Forman's hands clench to fire back at Raymond, but she doesn't pull the trigger, a momentary pause keeping her from sending a bullet through him. She can't feel anything. He's missed.

Except Raymond isn't firing again. He's looking down at his chest. The gray suit he's wearing has a dark mark on it near his heart, the circle growing as blood continues to seep from the wound. He touches the fabric and holds his hand up, the dark-red blood on his two fingers and thumb. He rubs them together, the movement small.

He looks up, his focus on Letty as his mouth falls open.

Forman looks at Letty, the gun in her hand pointed at Raymond for another round.

CHAPTER SIXTY

LETTY

The gun is still slightly shaking in my hand, but I'm ready to shoot again if need be. It didn't feel much different than firing at the cans on the fence. Except this time there was a rush of adrenaline, the power coursing through my body as I shot the man who confiscated my wine, destroyed my brandy, burned down my barn, incinerated my house, and tried to kill me and my mother. And murdered my father.

I've hit him in the chest, but he's still alive. And I have another bullet.

"Drop your weapon, Letty Hart," yells Officer Forman, but the words are meaningless. I have nothing left to lose. Raymond took everything from me. And now I'm taking everything from him.

Raymond steps wearily forward, the bloody fingers of his left hand outstretched to me, the gun in his right. He trips, his knees landing in the sand, his mouth agape and his eyes wide open in disbelief beneath his round glasses.

"You did it," he tries to say, but the words are slurred. "You actually shot me."

"I told you I would." I adjust my hold on the gun. "I know how to finish what I start. I know how to take care of myself."

"Drop your weapon," repeats Forman. She's closer to me now, her gun aimed in my direction. But I'm watching Raymond, ready if I need to fire again. He's still alive, the gun still in his hand. And I'm not done yet.

"You have fired on an officer of the law. You need to drop your weapon."

I lower my gun but only slightly, as I've adjusted to Raymond's position on the sand.

Raymond stares at the blood on his palm. "You fired. At me."

"Your only mistake was in thinking I wouldn't."

His face turns into a scowl. "I gave everything for your father. Everything. It was perfect until you came along. You don't deserve to be Blue's daughter. You don't deserve to exist." He lifts his gun.

I fire again, no delay this time, the bullet threading through his chest, right beneath his neckline. I could have chosen his head, but the thought of disfiguring his face, any face at all, was a step too far and made me drop my aim slightly lower.

He wavers for a moment, like a branch moving in the fall breeze, a gurgle as he gasps for air. "Unwise," he whispers, his voice light and strained.

He falls forward in the sand, his hat falling off as he hits the ground, the ocean wind blowing it toward the embankment.

"Letty Hart, put down your gun," repeats Forman. She can't be more than a few feet away now, but I don't meet her eyes. I'm focused on Raymond. I keep my aim, waiting for him to reach for his gun again.

"Check his first. I'm not a threat. He is." I keep my eyes on Raymond, his body seeming smaller than ever now. Forman moves into view, her gun still pointed at me, nearing Raymond. She kicks the gun out of his limp hand, the sand spraying up as she does. She kicks it again, the weapon now several feet out of his reach, and moves toward me, her stride strong and determined.

Raymond is motionless. He's either dead or dying, and his gun is gone. It's over. It's all over.

I let my hand fall to the side, my fingers still tight on the barrel, and look at Forman, my senses attuned to everything going on around me. The motorboat still circles out on the waves, the noise of the bullet still rings in my ears, and the perspiration that formed on my cheeks is cooled by the sea air.

It's the first time I'm seeing Forman clearly tonight. She's dressed in her police uniform, the fabric unwrinkled, her hair still tucked neatly under her cap. And I'm in my winery clothes, like the first time we met, except the wind is whipping the strands of hair that have fallen from my ponytail across my face.

We lock eyes.

Her pistol is pointed at me, just like Raymond's was only seconds ago. "Letty Hart, drop your weapon."

I shake my head. "You were going to arrest him. Are you like him?"

"You know I'm not."

"But how do I know for sure?"

"You don't. Now drop your weapon."

The boat sounds like it's coming closer, ready to land onshore, but I don't break my gaze from Forman.

She glances out at the ocean, her gun not moving from me. "Call them off."

"How can I?"

She shifts her stance, moving to the side so her aim includes the sandy location to my right, where the boat is sure to land.

"Do you kill them like he does?" I ask.

"No." She shakes her head. "What does Blue mean to you?"

Her words make more sense than ever. "Did you know? That he was my father?"

"I knew your father was a bootlegger. He was the first one to die a few years ago."

"Except he didn't."

She nods. "I didn't know your father was Blue."

I don't dare turn around, but I can tell by the growing sound of the boat engine that it's moments from landing onshore.

"Rumrunners?"

I shake my head. "They aren't coming tonight."

She moves again as the boat cuts through the waves, but still, I don't look. Because I know who it is.

It makes a thud as it skids onto the sand, the driver jumping out and pulling it ashore.

"Did it work?" asks Otto. "Was he fooled?"

"He was fooled." I'm still staring at Forman. "But stay back, Otto. You don't want any part of this."

"You under arrest, Letty?"

"Not yet."

Forman has her gun aimed at the two of us now, a slow movement back and forth. "Are you armed?"

Otto puts his hands up. "No."

"Leave, Otto. This is between me and her."

He hesitates, his arms lowering.

"Go on, Otto. She only needs one of us tonight." I toss my gun on the sand. Forman relaxes her aim.

Otto lifts his hand, as if waiting for a sign from me, but I shake my head. He nods and pushes the empty boat back into the water, the waves crashing up to his waist.

"Stop," says Forman.

"Let him go. This doesn't involve him."

The boat turns into the waves and heads back out to sea, the engine fading into the distance.

Forman moves toward me, her gun still aimed, mine now a foot in front of me. "Hands up."

I raise my hands but not all the way up. I can grab the gun from the sand if I move quickly. If I choose to do that. "That day in the car, you said you wanted to make sure no one else experienced the void you did," I say slowly.

Forman keeps moving.

"You wanted dignity. You wanted honor. What if that's what we both want?"

Forman stops. She's only three feet away from me, maybe even less. "You've been working with the girls. Ruthie. Dorothy. Taking care of them."

I nod, but I can see the slight change in her face. "You know," I say as I keep my focus on her, my hands lowering as I do, "this could work out for both of us. If you want it to."

CHAPTER
SIXTY-ONE

FORMAN

Forman smooths her skirt, the officers gathering in a circle for the morning meeting before the shifts begin. But today is different. Everything has changed.

"We're all disheartened to hear the additional details about the demise of Detective August Raymond," says Warrenson, his eyes moving around the group, briefly falling on Forman but moving on as quickly as they landed. "I'd like to say that he died a hero, but the information that's been revealed to me this last week does not reflect the high standards we expect of officers in this department."

Beaucamp nods, and Wallace's face appears more confused and uncomfortable than ever.

"But the department looks after its own, even if his methods weren't up to our standards. He was one of us. A fund has begun, thanks to Officer Forman, for Raymond's widow, Betty Raymond, and their daughter, Estelle. I believe a lot has already been raised. Correct, Forman?"

She nods. "But there's always room for more."

Forman knows the collection bucket will fill up again after this meeting, as it has every day the past week.

"Now," says Warrenson, "on to our next piece of business. Something a little lighter in tone. Days like this don't come along all the time." Warrenson glances around, his eyes avoiding Forman as he looks across the circle.

"I'm a man of my word, and it's also my duty, and my honor, to reward bravery. Those who go above and beyond, even when confronted with the evils of one of our own. To not back down but to hold the department and the code above all else." His hands open in front of him. "Well, there's something to be said for that." Warrenson's eyes finally meet Forman's. "Today, I want to commend Forman. Officer Annabel Forman."

The officers all clap lightly, but Forman doesn't smile. Her attention is fixated on Warrenson, waiting for him to say more.

"Her bravery in the face of danger is admirable, and you've all no doubt heard of her successful arrest of Franklin Fredman, a lackey who helped run one of the city's largest bootlegging operations. But that's not all. Not only did she solve the murders of several notable criminals in this city, but she also confronted the people responsible—Blue Corizano and his partner, August Raymond. She maintained a calm head during the gun battle that took both of their lives, neither of them surviving each other's bullets. While we will miss August Raymond, today is not about him. It's about Forman, a strong member of our force, who"—he pauses, his eyes shifting to the floor and back up to the group—"I'm proud to promote to detective."

The men surrounding her clap, the noise from their hands echoing throughout the room.

When the applause dies, he continues, "From solving the small crimes, like a missing necklace . . ."

Several of the officers laugh, but this time it's not a tease. It's a chuckle to themselves that Forman has heard before, when all the clues, and all the signs, were right in front of them but no one put them together.

"To the bigger crimes, like homicide," continues Warrenson. "With Forman on our force as a detective, and not assigned to crimes limited only to women, but to everything and anything that comes in here, we feel . . ." He pauses. "No, we know—I know—that Hollywood and Los Angeles are going to be safer for it."

Forman finally lets the smile she's been holding back beam.

"And because I'm a man of my word"—Warrenson holds up a finger and disappears into his office, then returns a moment later holding a white-frosted cake with a row of halved cherries down the middle—"I said my wife would bake a cake if you solved that case." He places it on the desk near him. "And here it is."

The officers break into applause again.

"Don't get used to it." Warrenson puts his hand up. "This won't happen with every case you solve, Forman. My wife makes a great cake, but I have a feeling that Forman is going to be solving a lot of cases." He grins and motions to Forman to stand next to him. "Would you like to say something?"

Forman steps forward and joins Warrenson. "Thank you. I'm proud to be a part of this department, and it's an honor to be a detective." She meets the eyes of every officer standing in the circle around her. "And my message to all of those lawbreakers out there, those bootleggers and criminals of all stripes, is that I'm coming for you."

The men in the station clap, and Forman allows herself a smile, but only a small one.

CHAPTER SIXTY-TWO

LETTY

Although it's dark, I can see that the beach holds no memory of what happened here just a week ago, the daily tides having erased all the evidence, having washed away everything that occurred. It now looks the same as the moment I first arrived that night, and yet, as the cool night air touches my face, it all feels different. Because it all is.

I stand against my truck, Otto and Margaret chatting inside, waiting for my signal.

This time there are no headlights. No motioning to the boats waiting out there. The only thing they want is time, and that's exactly what I have.

I pull out the long gold chain of my father's pocket watch, an engraving of an owl on the back of the metal. The hour hand is positioned at the one, the minute hand at the twelve. Shorty's ledger was precise: one o'clock in the morning on Topanga Beach every third Thursday.

The breeze is chilly, the ocean air heavy with mist and opportunity. I stare out at the water, the waves dark on this moonless night. I knew a boat would come last week. Because I had told Otto to bring it to help complete the ruse.

But tonight I have no say in who's coming. If they come at all.

I wait, my fingers moving over the engraving, tracing the lines.

The faint hum of a motor surfaces in the distance, the noise unsteady as it crosses through the crash of the waves. There it is.

I smile but don't move from my truck. I stay leaning against the metal side, my shirt a poor barrier from the cold on my back.

It's a small boat, similar to Otto's, but cuts through the water faster, circling once before pulling ashore, a man standing aft as he steers. He hops out as the boat hits the sand, his lean frame tugging the vessel onto the beach.

It's time.

I tap the truck twice to alert Otto and Margaret, but they know to wait until I give the official signal.

My boots slip down the dirt until I reach the beach, my efforts stirring the sand as I walk to the shallow point near the rocks where his boat is now resting.

He's already unloading a crate, and there's a soft thud as it hits the sand in front of him, the bottles of liquor clanging together. He looks up as he shifts the next one. "Hey—" He stops, his voice halting. "Where's Shorty?"

"He's not here. You're dealing with me now."

The man holds the crate, as if putting it on the sand near me would be too much. "But you're not Shorty."

"I'm better."

"I only work with Shorty." He glances around and tosses the crate onto the sand as he does. "Where is he? He's never late."

"Shorty's out of business."

He lifts his head, his brow furrowed. He's stopped now, his arms slack at his side, though nine or ten crates remain in the boat. "He doesn't show in the next minute, I'm out." He pats his hip. "I'm armed."

I pat my hip. "Me, too."

He stares, as if waiting for me to budge. "He doesn't come, I'm gone." He pushes his boat, edging it back toward the waves, as if to prove he's serious.

"That's going to be difficult. He's dead." I pull the newspaper from my back pocket, tucked there in the event of this exact situation. "In case you don't believe me." I toss it to him, the pages flapping like a seagull's wings as it lands near his feet.

His attention remains on me, but eventually he picks up the paper. I know it's too dark to see, but I'm hoping there's enough light for him to make out *Shorty* or *Quadling Garage*. It only ran once before the story disappeared, replaced by the next round of news. Just another day in the city.

He folds it again and throws it back to me. I catch it, unsure if he's seen what he needed to, but I place it back into my pocket.

"What happens now?" he says, his left leg against the hull, the waves lapping at the stern of the boat.

"We continue on as usual. I have the cash, and you have the supply."

He considers me, looks me up and down, a heavy train of thoughts running through his mind.

"Do we have a deal?" I say, not moving a muscle. I know how important this moment is. This man stands between me and the crates of whiskey and rum, and the promise of another day to rebuild my future, our future.

"You have the dough?"

I nod. "I said I did." Blue's liquor contacts needed a new outlet, and his customers needed a new supplier, and I was only too happy to fill the void.

"Then let's do this." He leans down and picks up a crate from the boat, tossing it onto the sand in front of him. "I leave them here. I don't carry them for anyone, not even Shorty." He heaves another one out of the boat, and it tumbles to the sand, the bottles clinking together.

I raise my right hand, and the truck doors open. Otto and Margaret are on their way.

The man grabs another crate and stops, his right hand moving as if trying to balance the load and still reach for his gun. "Who are they?"

"Don't worry. They work for me."

Margaret and Otto come down the slope and start lifting the product, their movements silent and rehearsed, as if they've been doing this for years. Otto secured the contract with Mr. Michaels for the speakeasy and the parties, and Margaret's given up on the dress shop, now working for me full-time out of my new house in Hollywood, with two of Blue's warehouses holding the liquor we bring in. But I'm still going to rebuild the winery. The plans are being drawn up right now in Salt Lake, my mother overseeing how it will be laid out, but this time with different tunnels underneath the property and much more security.

The last crate is out of the boat now. A few more trips to the truck taken between the three of us and it'll all be over, the tide soon erasing our footsteps on this beach. At least for another few weeks.

"Same shipment this time next month. You'll be here?" I ask.

"Yes." The boatman, the rumrunner, holds out his hand. I pull the wad of bills from my pocket and place it in his palm. He counts it as he eyes me.

"It's the right amount," I add. "I know it is. Same as Shorty."

He narrows his eyes. "What if the rate has changed?"

"That would be unwise." I put my hands on my hips.

He grins, amused by the answer, and pushes his boat into the water. He stops before he hops back into it, the waves cresting, splashing into the now empty hull. "You have a name?"

"Letty."

"What about a nickname?"

"Just Letty."

He jumps into the boat, the engine sputtering as he waits. "So, are you the new Shorty?"

I take a deep breath and look out at the dark water lapping around us as I think about the empire I'm building. "I'm the new everything."

AUTHOR'S NOTE

This is my first time writing in an era other than the present day, and while I loved diving deeper into the history of Los Angeles, Prohibition, and the 1920s (many of my days were delightful rabbit holes into this amazing time period), I truly tried to make sure every detail was correct. Please forgive any inaccuracies you might find in this story.

ACKNOWLEDGMENTS

I've long been fascinated by Prohibition, this time when everything was secret, hidden in special compartments, carried through tunnels, or brought ashore. Growing up in Los Angeles, I was always intrigued by the history of the city and how so many of the notable monuments I still see today were built in the 1920s (the Hollywood Sign, Grauman's Chinese Theatre, Biltmore Hotel, the Hollywood Roosevelt, Hollywood Bowl, Rose Bowl, LA Coliseum, Greystone Mansion, and much, much more).

Taking this key moment in time, just over one hundred years ago, and then adding my desire to tell a story of someone who was tired of hearing no, who wanted her own place in the world, and *The Bootlegger's Daughter* was born.

Publishing a novel takes a lot of luck, grit, and really wonderful people. This book was a journey over several years, so a very special thank-you to friends who took the time to read the manuscript and provide feedback, those who explored the lively historical details with me, and those who cheered me on simply by being by my side. By the time of publication, you will all have received bottles of wine or thank-you quiches.

Thank you to my agent, David Hale Smith, Naomi Eisenbeiss, Ingrid Emerick, and my editor, Chantelle Aimée Osman, whom I first met years ago during a discussion about wine and now here we are.

Thank you to my mom, my earliest supporter, my best litmus test for ideas, and my steadfast proofreader all these years. I've loved this journey with you so much.

And to Matthew, whose support has been invaluable, now and always. This book would not be here today if not for your love, your willingness to be a sounding board, and when I was stuck, the Post-it Notes and dry-erase markers that covered our windows.

About the Author

Photo © Matthew Semerau

Nadine Nettmann is a Certified Sommelier through the Court of Master Sommeliers and the author of the Agatha Award–nominated Sommelier Mystery series, which includes *Decanting a Murder*, *Uncorking a Lie*, and *Pairing a Deception*. Born in Los Angeles, she works full-time in the wine industry and enjoys discovering the history of the city she still calls home. For more information, visit www.nadinenettmann.com.